GIRL IN THE
WATER

GIRL IN THE
WATER

DANA MARTON

First Edition: 2016
ISBN-13: 9781940627199
ISBN-10: 1940627192
GIRL IN THE WATER - Copyright © 2016 by Dana Marton.

ACKNOWLEDGEMENTS

I cannot thank my fabulous team enough: Sarah, Diane, Linda, Toni, and Clarissa. Also, my deepest gratitude to Carmen Falcone, author extraordinaire, who was my consultant on Brazil and kindly gave me feedback on all things Brazilian. Despite all the help, I probably still made mistakes. All mistakes are my own.

PART
ONE

CHAPTER
ONE

Daniela

A dozen *jacundás* flopped in a palm frond basket next to the missionary, the small fish unappreciative of their role in the lesson on how Jesus called his disciples to be fishers of men. The basket rattled as the fish fought to return to the river—a hopeless dream. They would be sent to the smoking racks right after the lecture.

The schoolhouse sat on stilts, at least a hundred yards from the Içana, a small tributary of the great Rio Negro, deep in the Amazon rain forest. During the rainy season the river could swell a kilometer wide. The dark water stretched nearly as far now, after months of rain that never let up more than a few hours. Everyone went about in boats. They hadn't seen the ground in weeks.

The sound of water lapping at the stilts under the schoolhouse was as familiar to the children as their mothers' whisperings. They kept their eyes on the missionary up front who wore long black pants and a short-sleeved black shirt, and never anything else. He was twice as wide as the average villager, and nearly twice as tall. Among the brightly dressed children of the Amazonian jungle, he looked like a great vulture.

"When God brought the first Jesuits here, they carried the light of our Lord to the savages at a great cost," he intoned at the head of the one-room schoolhouse that had no walls, just a palm-thatch roof for protection from the worst of the rainy season. "Many of them were martyred. Thus have they earned their eternal place in heaven."

Daniela, in the first row, closed her eyes and pictured the village market and how she would be able to pick anything she wanted—not even just one thing, but one for *each hand*. She could not imagine anything more heavenly.

She liked when the missionary talked about heaven, but mostly, he talked about punishment, and how the wages of sin were death.

Someday, when Daniela became a teacher, she would only talk about heaven. She was not going to forever threaten the children with hell. She was going to be as respected as the missionary, but much kinder. The children wouldn't just sit around scared. She would let them smile and sing and even play.

She'd spent the past month working up the nerve to tell her mother about her teaching dreams. *Today. After school.* She would do it.

As the rain pattered on the roof, Senhor Wintermann sent his heavy gaze around. "Now who can tell me what it means to be *martyred?*"

Most of the children tucked their heads into their shoulders like turtles on the riverbank. They tried not to make eye contact.

Daniela's hand shot in the air, but when the missionary called on her, instead of the response she knew very well, something else burst out. "Grandmother Pula said that her grandmother told her that when a priest led the first Portuguese soldiers into the forest, they killed half the Baniwa and carried off the other half to be slaves."

Warm rain dripped from the sky, and if the humidity became any thicker, it could be woven into a floor mat. Yet a cold wind seemed to blow from the missionary's flaring nostrils.

He reached into the basket next to him, grabbed on to the largest jacundá without looking, and—*slap!*—smacked Daniela across the face so hard, her ears rang.

He held on to the stunned fish as he bent forward, until the sharpness of his spearing eyes and the dark caves of his nostrils were all Daniela could see. "Does your cheek burn?"

"*Sim, senhor.*" She tucked in her head like the others, wishing she had a turtle shell to hide her.

The missionary bared his precisely straight teeth. "Now imagine a burning a thousand times worse, the fires of hell, melting your heathen flesh off your bones." He tilted another few centimeters closer, until the air soured with his breath. Then he added in a grave tone, "And no water."

Daniela could not imagine no water. The idea squeezed her chest like an anaconda's embrace. She'd grown up by a river, in the middle of the rain forest. Water was like air, all around, all the time.

She didn't say another word for the rest of the lesson.

The missionary kept his heavy gaze on her anyway.

Daniela loved school learning, but she suspected she would love it more without the missionary.

Someday, she was going to travel far away, become a teacher, then return to her village. She would teach the Bible, but she would also teach the jungle. She loved going into the jungle with her mother, Ana, and learning about the plants and the animals.

She daydreamed a little about that, until the missionary said at long last, "Class dismissed. Go with God's blessing." And as the two dozen children clambered into their boats and canoes, he called after them, "And don't forget, if you take off your clothes, God will strike you dead."

He forever fought to keep everyone covered, especially during the rainy season. Wet clothes chafed the skin, so most of the children preferred to go around naked in the rain. A habit of the devil.

Daniela paddled her small dugout canoe home, dropping off two younger children on the way. The hut she shared with her mother stood on tall stilts at the edge of the jungle—the last hut before the path disappeared in the thick of the rain forest—but now the water nearly reached the threshold. If the Içana rose any higher, they'd have to hang their belongings in bags from the rafters.

Her mother's canoe, and no other, bobbed tied to the hut. As Daniela ducked inside, Ana glanced up from cooking rice and beans on the small woodstove in the corner, her long legs, toned from tree climbing, folded gracefully under her.

"Homework?" Her voice dripped with love and sounded to Daniela as sweet as dark jungle honey.

Daniela nodded.

"Best do it, then." Her mother pushed her heavy braid of hair off her shoulders and gave Daniela a big spoonful of food, a third of what they had.

Later, when the rice was fully cooked, they'd split the rest. Ana always made sure most of the food went to Daniela, always had a few extra bites for her when she came home from school, unless all their pots sat empty.

Daniela chewed the half-crunchy rice to make it last longer, but eventually had to swallow. She drew a deep breath. *Now.*

I want to be a teacher. Say it.

She opened her mouth. Then she looked at the thin layer of food at the bottom of the pot her mother stirred. Shame tightened her throat. They had no money for her to go away to learn. If she said something, she'd just make her mother sad.

So she tucked her dreams of higher learning away with dreams of a full belly. *Maybe someday. Maybe we'll have more money in the dry season.*

She climbed into her hammock with her books, which she was lucky to have, and sank into a story that matched none of Pula's tales about the Portuguese colonists.

Daniela's grandmother hadn't been a slave, but her great-grandmother, Ona, had been, on a rubber plantation.

Ona had told the tales to Pula. And Pula had told them all to Daniela. A few of the tales were happy. Other tales were dark. And some were downright gruesome, the kind of stories that scared her more than the night jungle.

"Bad things happen. Then good things happen," Pula once said, not long before fever took her. "They take turns like the rainy season and the dry season."

"What do we do?" Daniela had asked, hoping for a trick to escape the bad things. Pula had many tricks—usually jungle cures—to escape all kinds of unpleasantness, like a bad cough or a case of worms.

But that time, Pula said, "We endure."

Memories of her grandmother's toothless smile filled Daniela's head. The spicy scent of cooking food comforted her, and the sounds of the popping fire and the rain on the roof lulled her to sleep.

The sound of whispers woke her. For a moment, she blinked at the entwined couple in her mother's larger hammock—the missionary's broad frame on top. His white skin glowed in the dim light of the hut. As much as he preached about clothes and modesty, with Ana he didn't mind being naked.

Daniela silently turned the other way and let her thoughts drift.

Her earliest memories were quiet sighs, muffled grunts, and soft laughter from her mother's hammock. Men always seemed happy when they were shoving their sticker. And they were mellow afterwards. They often had a kind word for Daniela on their way out, sometimes even a piece of candy from their pockets.

For as long as Daniela could remember, men visited the bamboo hut she shared with her mother.

In the dry season, when someone came, Daniela skipped down to the Içana to look for coconuts that sometimes floated down from the jungle. She wished she could do that now, even if sometimes one of the bigger boys took what she found. Of course, at other times, those same boys might give her a fish they caught by hand.

On lazy days when she had nothing else to do, she could sit by the river for hours and watch the boys fish. If they were in a good mood, they might even let her try for eel. Those were the best days, even if the big river eels were too powerful, and she could rarely wrest them from the water.

But this was not the season for eels. Yet when she still couldn't sleep, she quietly slipped from the hut anyway.

She paddled through the flooded village, each hut a little island. She headed for the largest.

Many people had stands at the market in the dry season and sold straight from their boats in the rainy season, but only Pedro had a store. He also had the biggest boat in the village. And he had the largest hut, larger than the schoolhouse. He had nine children and three grandchildren, and even the missionary said that Pedro had been blessed.

Pula used to say Pedro could sell dry land to fish.

As soon as Daniela scrambled out of her canoe, Pedro popped his head out the open door. "The store needs sweeping."

So she swept. And then she arranged all the fruit on the shelves in a pretty pattern as Pedro liked, making sure to put hard fruit on the bottom, soft fruit on top.

When she finished, Pedro said, "I need you to fix a hole in the roof in the back. Come stand on my shoulders."

They went back to where rain dripped down on tin cans of cooking oil. She climbed Pedro's back, braced her bare feet on his shoulders, and with her small fingers wove the palm fronds back into place as fast as a bird weaving a nest.

When she slipped back down, Pedro caught a closer look at her. "Why is your cheek red?"

Daniela hung her head, glad that in the dimmer light of their hut, her mother hadn't noticed the mark. She didn't want to add to Ana's troubles.

Pedro huffed. "The missionary?"

Daniela bobbed her head.

Pedro said no more, but he paid her in sugarcane—a chunk almost as big as the missionary's fish!

Daniela smiled all the way home. Unhappiness was impossible when someone had sugarcane.

She was grateful to have Pedro as her friend. When the missionary talked about the saints on Sundays, Daniela often wondered if Pedro was one of them, but she never dared ask. Nobody ever asked anything during the hillside sermons. When the heavenly father talked, you listened. No back talk, *não senhor*.

That night, as a heavy storm cracked lightning, Daniela's mother let her wiggle into the big hammock. She put her arms around Daniela and kissed her head. She told Daniela some of Pula's tales about their people, the Baniwa, the people of the forest.

Higher up the river, the villages had more native Baniwa, but Daniela's village had been built by *soldados da borracha* brought from Ceará to a nearby rubber plantation by the government in her grandmother's time. Most were killed by the jungle. When the plantation shut down, some of the survivors went home. Others stayed and built a tiny village on stilts on the bank of the Içana. The village was a mix of all kinds of people.

Ana was half Baniwa. She spoke Baniwa almost as well as Pula had. She knew the sacred name of things: *u:ni* for river and water, *kepizeni* for bird, *a:pi* for snake, *haiku* for tree, *dzawi* for jaguar, and a great many others.

Daniela loved rolling the words off her tongue.

She loved the rain, loved the flood that washed everything clean. But when a particularly loud thunderclap boomed above, she jumped.

Her mother took her hand. "The storms will be over soon. Then the nights will be quiet."

She spoke truth. The following week, the water began receding. And then the week after that, at the start of June, the rainy season ended and the dry season began. Loggers came up the river to go deep into the jungle.

They didn't come out again until the beginning of the next rainy season in December. They floated down the Içana with their overburdened barges, hurrying to the city of Manaus, where they'd get their pay, then could drink their *cachaça* and enjoy the women at the countless *puteiros*. They rarely stopped at Daniela's tiny village.

But that December, a young logger did saunter up the path to Daniela's hut. She was home alone, cleaning cassava in front of the hut for Pedro, who promised to give her some as payment. She meant to pass half her share to Tereza, the oldest woman in the village, who, without any teeth, liked eating the roots cooked and mashed.

The logger meandered up to Daniela. "Ana?"

She brushed the dirt from her hands and scrambled to her feet. "I'll go find her. She's not here."

"I don't mind," the man said.

He was rangy—just bone and muscle, like most loggers—his dark eyes hungry as he looked her over. He pushed her down, then pushed himself between her legs.

It hurt very much, but it was over very fast.

Her mother came just as the man stood and fastened his pants, stepping around Daniela, who sat with her arms hugging her pulled-up knees.

Ana made the man pay. And when he left, she crouched next to Daniela and put her arms around her. They sat there like that for a long time before her mouth said, "Now you're a woman." And her eyes said, *We endure.*

She took Daniela to the market. She let Daniela pick two things, one for each hand, but for some reason, it didn't feel like heaven.

They went into the jungle next, and Ana pointed out the plants to pick for the tea that would make sure Daniela wouldn't have a child of her own.

After that, the men sometimes came for her mother, and sometimes they came for Daniela. She didn't like it, but it no longer hurt. Most of them managed quickly enough. And even the ones who didn't weren't as bad as gnawing hunger.

A whole year passed like that. But at the end of the rainy season of the second year, at the end of May, the Içana rose higher than ever, the village flooded in the middle of the night, and Daniela's mother drowned in the churning water.

Like an anaconda with a tapir, grief swallowed Daniela whole, trapped her and squeezed her in its bottomless dark belly.

"You can't bury her in the hillside cemetery, not in hallowed ground." The missionary's tone was hard and unforgiving. "Ana was a sinner."

He looked very black and very grim, more like a vulture than ever, the villagers in all their colors pulling back from him like scared macaws.

Daniela stood in front of him, anger bubbling inside her, rising like floodwater. Her body could not contain it all. So she looked the missionary right in the eye like she'd never dared before. "To slap you with a fish, senhor, would be an insult to the fish!"

Then she turned on her heels and marched away while the man shouted behind her.

Pedro helped Daniela bury her mother in the middle of the night, the old way. They hollowed out a log stuck in the mud of the riverbank, placed the body inside, covered it with palm fronds, then pushed the log back into the river, and watched it float away into the darkness.

After that, the missionary said she was too old for school. And he sat her in the very back in church.

Daniela had no one to hold her when lightning cracked overhead, and sometimes she cried at night, alone in the big hammock, missing her mother.

Pedro visited from time to time. She didn't feel so alone then.

One day, after Pedro rolled off her, breathing hard, he said. "You're wasted here, Daniela. Tomorrow, I'm going to take you downriver, to a great big house. You'll like it there."

But Pedro had lied about that.

* * *

Ian

All Ian Slaney wanted was a moment of oblivion.

He leaned against the cold brick wall in the alley behind Shanahan's, one of the seediest bars in DC, with a hand on top of the woman's head as she knelt in front of him.

Christ, she was like a fricking vacuum cleaner. On turbo setting. No finesse.

She'd come into his bar with three girlfriends: office girls, wanting a night on the wrong side of the tracks to finish off their year, clearly looking for trouble, and too dumb to know they were out of their depth.

The first time the blonde had sidled up to Ian, he'd ignored her. He'd already built a close relationship with half the bottle of whiskey on the bar in front of him. All he wanted was some private time with the other half.

"I'm Victoria." The blonde flashed an expectant smile, as if she'd just given him a gift and was waiting for his thanks.

She wiggled closer, in the how-do-you-like-my-tits dance.

"I bet my girlfriends that I could get you to buy me a drink," she said in a rich-girl whiny voice that probably got her boyfriend to buy her the expensive-looking shoes and matching purse that came from an alligator who, frankly, should have fought harder.

When Ian stayed silent, she said, "So do you work in construction or something?"

He couldn't blame her for that. They *were* in a blue-collar neighborhood. And he clearly didn't look like a stockbroker. "Used to be military."

She perked up. "Navy SEAL?"

"Army."

She only flagged a little. "Still, you probably killed like a ton of people, right?"

He kept his voice flat as he said, "Not at Shanahan's."

She had no response to that. After a few awkward seconds, she slinked back to her friends, and they ordered more drinks, watching him and whispering.

Ian's bottle went down to the last quarter.

"She'll be back," Dean Shanahan predicted from behind the bar, then gave him a mock once-over. "Thirty, six feet even, two hundred pounds of mostly muscle. Face it, boyo, you look like a good lay."

Ian stared into his drink. "Wish she'd realize I'm a hell of a bad bet."

Even as Dean moved on with a nod, the woman was prancing over again.

In the same you-should-be-grateful tone she'd used before, she said, "Hey, so, wanna go out back?"

And Ian was in a dark enough mood to nod, still without fully looking at her. "Yeah. Sure."

He knocked back his drink and gestured to Dean behind the bar not to put away the bottle.

He slid off his barstool and checked out the woman more thoroughly at last: overdressed for these parts in a black skirt and red silk blouse, flawless makeup, slick hair, fancy Christmas-themed manicure with snowflakes. She probably spent more on maintenance than Ian did on his apartment.

He led the way to the back door. He'd been to the alley before. For a quick retch, a quick fight, a quick fuck. The alley didn't encourage lingering. At least now, with the cold, the stench was a little more bearable than in summer.

As soon as the metal door banged closed behind them, she moved in for a kiss.

He put a hand on her head and pushed her down, her hair sticky with some spray stuff, and she glanced up as if ready to protest.

He paused. Waited her out. If she balked, they were done. He was happy either way.

But as soon as he took his hand off her hair, she undid his belt and tugged down his zipper, then she latched on to him with a suction that could give Dyson a run for their money.

He liked a little more technique, but she did the trick. Soon he was close, but one of her back teeth had a sharp edge on the inside, and it kept rubbing against him.

He pulled her up by her shoulders.

She licked her lips with a haughty little snicker. "I bet you didn't get *that* in the army."

He wasn't here to talk. He pushed her against the wall and yanked her skirt up. Except the damn skirt was too tight, so he grabbed harder and ripped the stupid thing.

"Hey! Do you have any idea how much that cost?"

But by that time, he had a rubber on his dick, and he shoved into her.

He gave it to her rough, didn't care if the bricks scraped her ass. Coming into a bar like this, walking up to a guy like him, she'd been looking for rough. Rough and dangerous, something to give the sex an edge.

She proved him right when she moaned, her eyes rolling back in her head. "Oh. Oh yes."

He banged her harder to keep her quiet.

Christ. She squealed loud enough to be heard on Mars.

Fuck that. He let it go. Came.

She didn't.

When he pulled out, she turned eagerly to face the wall, bent forward and braced herself with her hands, pushed out her ass. She thought they were just switching positions.

What she thought was her problem.

Ian tossed the rubber into the open Dumpster, belted his pants, then walked away.

"Hey," she called after him. "What the hell? Hey!"

He kept on walking and didn't look back.

The night was cold, but he didn't mind. He'd seen colder in the Afghan mountains.

He stepped back into the bar through the front, grabbed his bottle, and left enough money to cover it, plus tip.

"See you tomorrow, boyo," Dean said without a note of judgment.

Dean Shanahan was an Irishman who didn't drink, didn't play the ponies, and didn't fight. No joke, a bleedin' Buddhist. If Shanahan's patrons could overlook him turning into the Dalai Lama, he stood prepared to overlook just about anything from them. Which was why Ian liked the place.

He grunted his good-bye, then booked the hell out of there.

He walked the six blocks to his apartment building, saw Sharon on the street again—bony and jumpy-eyed.

He looked at her. She looked at him.

He'd known her long enough not to need conversation. Her new man had left her, the kids needed to eat.

Ian dug into his pocket and passed her what money he had. He didn't tell her to take the night off and go home to the kids—she'd do that anyway. And she didn't offer to earn the money from him—he would turn her down as he had every time in the past.

To any onlooker, the exchange would have looked strange—a man passing by a prostitute, giving her money, then the two of them walking off in opposite directions.

Ian went inside, climbed up to his studio apartment on the top floor of the four-story walk-up. He dropped onto his couch that'd been old back when that meteor wiped out the dinosaurs. He drank straight from the bottle and didn't bother turning on the TV.

From the corner of his eye, he caught the light blinking on the answering machine on the side table. He swung the bottle in the general direction of the Play button.

"Hey, it's Finch," a familiar voice shouted over traffic noise in the background. "I'm in Rio. I'm in trouble, man. Gonna clear out for a while. When things settle down, I wanna come up and see you."

Ian took another swig. He and Finch had saved each other's lives a couple of times in the army. Finch was as close to a younger brother as Ian had. Impulsive as hell, but heart in the right place. Most of the time. *What kind of trouble has the idiot gotten into now?*

As if anticipating that question, Finch said, "Can't tell you more on the phone. But just don't take off. I had a helluva time tracking you down. I'll be there in a month or two. I'll bring a present. I have a sweet little package for you. And don't you worry about me. I got my lucky belt." He laughed.

As the message ended, Ian glanced at the machine. The displayed showed: UNKNOWN NUMBER.

Dumb and Dumber all in one. If Finch told him where the hell he was going or who he was running from, Ian could go down and help him. He hadn't even known that Finch was in South America. Last they'd talked, the idiot had been in Seattle.

He'd probably gone down for some job or other—a shady one, judging by the message. Still, he was a tough kid. He should be able to handle it. And if not, maybe he'd learn from the experience.

Ian finished the bottle, then lay back on the couch, hoping he'd drunk enough for oblivion. Not much scared him, but sleep…Just the thought of dreaming burned his stomach with acid.

He always dreamed the same thing: Linda in the car with the twins, Connor and Colin screaming for him as they were drowning. Drowning because their father was half a world away.

He'd been in Afghanistan when the van had gone into the Potomac. The neighborhood cops had ruled it an accident.

Was it?

Or had they been trying to spare him? Because they knew him, because he was a decorated war hero. They didn't want to add to his grief.

Just two weeks before, when he'd been home on leave, Linda had begged him not to go back. She had postpartum depression, her mother said when Ian had called her to see if she could come and stay with Linda and the kids for a while.

Maureen *had* come.

But Linda still…

Ian shoved himself upright with a curse.

Hell, fuck. Now that he'd started thinking about all *that*, he'd never fall asleep. He shuffled out to the kitchen and searched through the cupboards for another bottle, and tried hard not to think how his wife and baby sons had ended up in the river.

According to the police report he'd managed to sneak a peek at, there had been no skid marks on the road, no sign that Linda had used the brakes.

CHAPTER
TWO

Daniela

For one moment, Daniela was free.

Then caught, beaten, and dragged back.

"A girl who runs away makes me look like I can't handle my own house," Senhora Rosa said. "So the next time you run away, I'm going to feed you to the piranhas in the cove."

The big red house down the river where Pedro had taken Daniela had a floor of boards instead of bamboo, glass windows, and a bathroom. The electricity came from wires, not from generators. About twenty girls like Daniela lived here, at least half of them peeking around doorways at the moment to watch the new girl's fate.

Daniela hung her head, her heart frantically flopping inside her chest like a river dolphin stranded in mud.

Piranhas didn't like the fast currents of the river, but at the cove at the edge of town where the water stood nearly still, piranhas hunted. Daniela had heard gruesome tales from the men who visited Senhora Rosa's establishment.

"Do you understand me, *garota?*" Senhora Rosa snapped.

"Sim, senhora," Daniela mumbled.

"Then off you go, and thank these nice policemen for bringing you back."

Daniela led the two men to her room, her back and arms aching from the beating they'd given her.

The aches wouldn't hurt long, not beyond a day or two. Senhora Rosa beat her too. And sometimes so did the paying customers.

Not all of them. A lot of men liked her, *but*, because of that, the other girls didn't. Which, at the moment, was the least of Daniela's worries.

The snake-eyed policeman shed his rumpled clothes in seconds, but the fat one huffed and puffed and struggled with his belt. He caught Daniela looking. "Too old for this, aren't you?"

She thought he meant Rosa's house, since the other girls were even younger.

But he said, "Too old for still not knowing your place. Are you wrong in the head? You better learn quick, girl."

He yanked off his belt at last.

Her blood rushed loudly *wroom, wroom, wroom* in her ears, like the distant sound of chain saws in the forest, the sound of loggers.

"Look lively, girl. Nobody likes a sulking whore."

She plastered a smile on her face.

At the beginning, she had cried and wished she could return to her village, but Pedro never came back to see what had become of her. So Daniela stopped crying. She stopped missing her mother. She stopped missing the village. She stopped feeling altogether.

She no longer thought about going far away to become a teacher. She understood that dream had been washed away forever. The dark water had carried her dead hopes down the river like it'd carried her mother's log coffin.

The fat policeman pushed down his pants.

She thought about how long it might take for the piranhas to kill her, and how much it might hurt. She must never give Rosa a reason to take her to the cove.

The snake-eyed policeman closed the door with a *thud*, a tree falling in the forest.

And in Daniela's head, her grandmother softly whispered, *We endure.*

✳ ✳ ✳

Carmen

Through the hazy morning, Carmen Barbosa looked across the Içana River at the red house that hung out over the water, raised on stilts, a flat blob like a well-fed caiman—the Amazon's version of an alligator. She tapped her foot. Chewed her lip. She could see people move behind the lit windows at night, but she couldn't see enough of what went on inside.

She was waiting for the girls to come out for a swim as they usually did, but time seemed to stretch endlessly like the rain forest itself. The humidity was already oppressively thick in the air, pushing down on her, making her tired.

Even as she watched—eyes forward, attention focused—every cell of her body was aware of the man behind her in the small kitchen.

Tap, tap, tap. Phil Heyerdahl was typing away on his laptop at the table.

She glanced back. "Sounds like it's going well."

Phil looked up from his laptop, rolled his neck, his shoulder muscles shifting under his tanned skin. His short blond hair stood up in spikes from running his fingers through it as he worked. He looked hot and handsome in a geeky kind of way.

He was writing a book on the *soldados da borracha*, rubber soldiers.

During the World War II rubber boom, the Brazilian government had forced tens of thousands of people to the region to harvest white gold, aka rubber. They were promised they'd be treated as war heroes, returned home after the war, and given housing. But the government reneged. The jungle killed most of the rubber workers. Some of the survivors made new lives for themselves in nearby towns and villages. Only six thousand found their way home at the end.

"Did you know the US government paid a hundred bucks for every worker the Brazilian government dragged here to supply latex to US factories?" Phil went back to typing. "We needed rubber for the war."

Carmen and Phil were both twenty-three, one year out of college—Carmen from Penn State, daughter of Brazilian immigrants, Phil from Stanford, son of two professors. They'd met in Africa the year before, working for a charity that installed wells in remote villages.

They'd both planned on doing a year of volunteer work between college and entering the workforce in the US. But by the end of the year, they were in love—with each other *and* with volunteer work. So here they were, in Brazil, in the Amazon rain forest, hundreds of miles from the nearest hospital, helping to build a clinic while Phil wrote his book on the side, inspired by a nearly hundred-year-old local priest who'd ministered to the *soldados da borracha* back in the day. Father Angelo had personally administered last rites to well over a thousand, and he had a little notebook with the names of his dead carefully recorded.

Phil was obsessed with the story. He was happy here. They both were. Although, they would be happy anywhere as long as they were together.

Carmen looked back across the black river, at the girls who spilled through the back door at last and jumped from the deck into the river, a short six-foot drop. *Splash. Splash. Splash.* A bamboo ladder tied to the deck would help them climb back.

Rain dripped from the sky, stopped, then dripped again, as if the weather couldn't make up its mind. At least they were in the dry season. In the rainy season, a good downpour could last for days, and the river would rise, probably all the way to the red house's deck. The girls wouldn't need the ladder then.

Carmen rubbed her aching arm. "I want to do something to help those girls."

"It's a private school for orphans."

He'd actually gone over one morning the week before, knocked on the door, and inquired—to set Carmen's mind at ease. An older woman had responded and told him that she ran the school, explained what they were.

"What else was she going to say?" Carmen tapped her foot again, watching the girls splash in the water. "You were wearing your clinic volunteer shirt. She was probably afraid that you were the kind of foreign do-gooder who would try to interfere."

Sometimes she worried about Phil. He was more of a geek than a warrior. A writer at heart. Was he strong enough for this kind of work?

She watched the girls swim.

Once again, they were rough on the skinniest one, who was also the prettiest, tall compared to the others. She was the newcomer and had the saddest eyes. For some reason, Carmen kept seeing herself in the girl. Maybe because Carmen had been as skinny at that age. From chemo and radiation.

"It can't be a brothel," Phil said. "The girls are way too young. You haven't seen them close-up. I have."

Carmen *had* seen them. Every time she had to go across the river for something, she made a point to walk by the place. The property was fenced in the front, but she could see through the gaps in the bamboo fence.

She loved Phil's gentle heart for thinking the girls were too young, but she knew there were men with darker hearts who wouldn't think so, not for a minute.

She chewed her bottom lip. "How about the men who visit?"

"Mrs. Rosa said they were the school's patrons, local businessmen." Some doubt crept into Phil's voice at last. But then he said, "I've seen the police over there. If something bad was going on in that house, they would have dealt with it."

Carmen could only shake her head. "The police are customers, like the others."

When she'd met Phil in Africa, they'd both been naïve and innocent in the ways of the world. What she'd seen there had changed that.

Africa was a vast continent, with amazingly prosperous countries like Botswana, South Africa, Morocco, Tunisia, and others, cities as modern as London and Paris, but aid workers went to areas that hadn't caught up yet. The parts Carmen had seen were where young girls were walking miles to school and being raped on the way, but took the risk and went anyway, because they wanted to learn so badly.

She'd seen girls in puberty dying of infections from female circumcision. Preteens being married off, then dying in labor because their bodies weren't developed enough yet for pregnancy, and because there was no doctor for many miles.

Carmen had lost her innocence in Africa. She'd spent most of her time in homes, talking to women, helping them, while Phil had been with the well equipment, surrounded by men, explaining how things worked, and how to take care of everything once the volunteers left. Phil hadn't seen as much real life as she had.

Even here in Brazil, with his head in the book he was writing, he missed things. While Carmen...

Carmen watched the swimming girls in the river. The strongest-looking jumped on the newcomer, and for a moment, it looked as if she was holding the poor girl under water. *Too long.* Alarm shot through Carmen, but before she could say something, the skinny girl came up, sputtering.

Had they just been playing? They were too far away to tell.

Carmen shuddered. "There's something sinister about all this black water."

"The water is dark from the decomposing organic matter in the swamps. Think of it as dark compost tea. Same reason why the Rio Negro is black," Phil said with patience.

"I want to talk to one of the girls."

"How?"

"When they come out tomorrow morning, I'll swim over."

She was a strong swimmer, and the Içana wasn't that fast or wide, just a small tributary of the Rio Negro. She could more than handle the current.

Phil closed the laptop and came to stand behind her, then enfolded her in his arms. "You want to help everyone you meet. You have a beautiful heart, you know that?"

He turned her in his arms and kissed her. And she kissed him back. He had a beautiful heart too. She loved him so much, more than she'd ever thought it was possible to love another person.

She didn't resist when he tugged her toward the bed, tugged the rubber band from her hair so the dark waves spilled onto her shoulders, or when he laid her down, or when he unwrapped her sarong-style skirt.

They were young and healthy, full of hormones and full of love, so within a minute, they were naked, their limbs entangled. Phil could make her body sing as quickly as he could make her heart sigh.

"I love you," she whispered as she floated off into pure bliss, her body contracting around his.

"I love you too," he said, rolling them so she was lying on top of him. He ran a gentle hand down her back.

They kissed, then soon they were making love again.

They didn't use protection. When she'd been a teenager, she had bone cancer and received chemotherapy, which resulted in infertility.

Phil didn't know. She couldn't tell him. Phil wanted a bushel of children. But she wouldn't be the woman to have them. Eventually, she would have to let him go.

She *would* let him go.

But not yet. *Not yet.*

Later, when she lay in his arms, glowing and spent, she said, "I want to do more than talk to those girls. I want to save them."

And he said what she knew he would say. "I'll help."

She couldn't stand thinking about the girls in misery just across the river, when here she was, happier than she'd ever been. The girls' fate seemed incredibly unfair and, more than that, tragic.

Carmen kissed Phil's cheek and sat up in the bed next to him. "I want to talk to the girl the fat man brought down the river two months ago. I see her standing in her window sometimes, looking upriver. There's something in the way she stands, in the set of her shoulders, that's just heartbreaking."

The skinny, tall girl was definitely the most vulnerable of the bunch.

Phil sat up against the headboard and took Carmen's hands. "All right. You talk to her. If she says that she's there against her will, we'll bring her across the river and hide her. I can take her down to Manaus, find her shelter and maybe a small job at one of the international charities."

Carmen squeezed his fingers.

They knew another American in Manaus, an older woman, Mrs. Frieseke, who worked for See-Love-Aid. They'd met her at the airport in Rio when they'd arrived in Brazil, had a good chat while they'd all waited for their connecting flight.

"How about the others?" Carmen asked.

She wanted children, desperately, but since she couldn't have any, she at least wanted to help the needy children of the world. She couldn't stand seeing a child harmed.

Phil drew her into his arms. "First things first. One saved is better than none saved."

She nodded against his chest. She was the more impulsive one, the more emotional one, in the relationship. He tended to be the voice of reason. They complemented each other well. They made a strong couple. Under different circumstances, they might have had a strong marriage.

"I'm going to swim over tomorrow morning. And if the girl says she needs help, I'm going to bring her over with me right then."

If the old witch, Mrs. Rosa, saw Carmen talking with the girls, she might not let them out again. Carmen had to be prepared to act at first contact.

She said a silent prayer for the skinny girl with the sad eyes. And then she said firmly, "Tomorrow morning."

* * *

Daniela

Daniela woke at dawn to Senhora Rosa's bony hand shaking her shoulder. The old woman's fingernails were so sharp, they felt as if they'd cut through Daniela's skin.

"Up," Rosa snapped, her voice gravelly this early in the morning. She sounded like a gurgling caiman.

The house slept around them, the other girls still resting, each in her own tiny room that held little more than a bed.

The old woman dragged Daniela out of the house, then shoved her into a boat tied off the dock. For a startled, fearful moment, Daniela thought Rosa would take her to the cove with the piranhas, but instead, the old woman maneuvered the boat into the middle of the water, where the current ran fastest, and they went downriver.

They floated farther down the Içana than Daniela had ever been, past villages, past where the Içana poured into the much larger Rio Negro, far, far away from home, until they reached a sprawling town and Rosa angled the boat toward shore once again.

A sign in the harbor said they were welcome in Santana.

Daniela had never seen so many dwellings before, or buildings so large. In the giant harbor sat a ship so big, it could never go up the Içana to her village, not even in the middle where the river was the deepest.

Rosa led her to a house near the water, nearly as large as the one they'd come from, but instead of many girls, only a foreign man lived there, an American.

"This is Senhor Finch," Rosa said.

Senhor Finch was almost as pale as the missionary but younger, and as tall but not nearly as round. He looked as strong as the loggers. He had boots and pants like the soldiers Daniela had once seen come up the river with the naval patrol. Except for his yellow hair, everything about him was drab, including his tan T-shirt. He had a big smile, and he had all his teeth, as white as cane sugar.

Rosa let go of Daniela's arm. She pulled a plastic bag of little white pills from her pocket that she had every girl take to make sure they didn't end up pregnant. She handed the bag to Daniela. "You will cook for him, clean for him, and do whatever he says. You will stay with him until he sends you back."

Then Rosa took a large handful of money from the man and left.

The water rushed behind the house, almost as loud as the street noises. The smell of fish blew from the Rio Negro, nearly overpowered by the smell of sewer mixing with the smell of engine exhaust that drifted from the town. For a moment, the new, strange mixture made Daniela dizzy.

She tried to stand very straight as she waited to be told what to do, even while her stomach cramped with hunger.

Her missed breakfast was the least of her worries.

But Senhor Finch didn't reach for her clothes, or for his own.

Daniela didn't know what to make of him.

"Are you hungry?" he asked in a funny accent that sounded like the missionary's. Then he showed her into the kitchen where he had piles of food: fruit, vegetables, rice *and* flour, even a gutted fish.

Her stomach growled. She wasn't sure what she was allowed to touch. Rosa had said she was to cook. So she cautiously picked up a coconut.

The man smiled again.

Buoyed by relief, Daniela smiled back.

The house had a stove with a propane tank next to it like at Rosa's, only bigger and newer. *What luck that I know how to use it*, Daniela thought. If she didn't, the man would probably beat her.

She cooked quickly—fish with *mandioca frita*—then put the food on the table and went to sit on the floor in the corner. But the man told her to sit at the table with him. And he put food on two plates, giving her one, filling it completely.

She remembered the missionary's sermons in her village and thought, *maybe* this *man is a saint.*

After the meal, Senhor Finch showed her a small bedroom off his larger one. He had a big bed. She had a hammock. But they both had mosquito nets, which was the most important thing.

"Good?" he asked. "*Bom?*"

"Very good, senhor. *Obrigada.*"

A pleased smile showed off his perfect white teeth again. "You settle in. I need to go out for a while, but I'll be back."

He didn't lock the door when he left.

Daniela hurried to the front window and peeked out from behind the curtain. This had to be a trap. He was probably waiting outside, so if she tried to leave, he would catch her and beat her. Rosa had done that.

But Senhor Finch was walking down the street, going and going until he disappeared in a swarm of other people.

Daniela's heart beat fast, then faster as she walked to the door and opened it a crack. Nothing happened.

A soft, warm rain drizzled outside.

She eased down the steps, holding her breath.

Nobody paid her any attention.

Still no sign of Senhor Finch rushing back.

Daniela moved forward. Before she knew, she was standing in the middle of the street, her heart racing. *Shouldn't have left the house.* Now she'd be caught, and she'd have to go to sleep with her whole body aching from the beating she'd get.

But since she'd come this far…Her legs trembling, she began walking down the street.

The crowd was large and loud. People brushed against her. *Too many people.* After her small village, then the confines of Rosa's house, Daniela felt as if she was drowning.

One tentative step at a time, she walked all the way to the end of the street before she stopped. She didn't know where to go from there. The street opened into a large square with a church, shops, and stalls right on the sidewalk, and even more people.

She couldn't see Senhor Finch anywhere.

* * *

Ian

The latest pop hit pulsed through Orpen, an upscale nightclub in Washington DC, flashes of an overhead laser show illuminating the crowded dance floor. Everyone was focused either on their next drink or on their next lay. Except Ian Slaney, who headed across the room, keeping an eye on the party. He didn't drink at work, and he didn't mix with the women here either. *You don't shit where you eat* had always been his policy.

He was one of the bouncers. Didn't mind the hours. He couldn't sleep anyway.

A young guy at the entrance caught his eyes. Six foot even, hair buzz cut, nothing but spikes of gold. For a moment, Ian thought, *Finch.* Then the lights flashed brighter, and for a second a beam fully illuminated the guy's face. A stranger.

Too damn bad.

Finch hadn't called again. The thought that the kid had met with more trouble in Rio than he could handle had been like a sharp tack under the sheets, digging into Ian at night, making sleep even less likely.

He'd finally gotten his passport renewed and a visa to Brazil, intending to go to Rio, although he hadn't made definite plans yet.

The guy at the door moved forward, deeper into the crowd, stepping around the small party that was leaving, a young woman escorted by two men.

The woman was around twenty, one asshole on each side of her, tugging her toward the exit to Constitution Ave, toward the dark night outside.

On the surface, they looked all right, but instinct pushed Ian forward, and as he reached within a few feet, he could hear the woman say, "I have to get up early for work. I'll just call a cab," to one of the men.

But he overruled her with "We'll just pop up to my place for five minutes. You don't want Joey to think you don't like him, do you?"

He was too smooth, his dark hair had more gunk in it than hers, the kind of guy who was probably manscaped under his slick suit. His buddy was the same, their fancy suits nearly identical. The girl had on a modest little black dress. She wasn't dressed to seduce, but to impress.

Ian had a fair feeling for what was going on. Jerk took his new girl out, told her she was going to meet his best friend. Now he was pressuring her to go home with them, where they wanted to share her. She was smart enough to have caught the vibe, but between the two of them, they would railroad her into their car before anyone noticed something was up.

He stepped up to the threesome as they reached the door. "Everything okay, miss?"

"She had a little too much to drink." The boyfriend flashed a half-embarrassed, what-can-you-do smile. "We'll help her get home safely."

Ian pulled his phone from his pocket. "Why don't I just call her a cab?"

The boyfriend leaned closer to him and slipped him a twenty. "I wined her, I dined her, I'm entitled to a little fun. Don't be a cock blocker, man."

The guy wasn't lying about the wine-and-dine part. The dance club had a pricey restaurant upstairs. Ian had seen the three of them come down earlier. But he didn't think the two dickless idiots had a right to the woman's body for the price of the garden salad she'd likely had.

They pushed for the exit, and he walked out with them, shoving the twenty into his pocket as the summer heat hit him.

"Would you like me to call you a cab, or would you like to go home with your friends, miss?" he addressed the woman directly.

She moved toward him, but the boyfriend hung on to her elbow, so she didn't get far. She looked between them, hesitating only a second before she said, "Could you, please?"

"No problem." Ian pushed the cabbie on the speed dial, didn't say anything. Hung up. Afiz would see the call and come. That was their deal.

"Listen, jerk." The boyfriend shoved the girl behind him and stepped forward, no longer smiling. "How about you mind your own business?"

"The safety of our customers *is* my business, sir." Ian kept his tone polite.

The man glared at him for a second, then backed away, dragging the girl. "Come on, Madison. Screw this guy."

"Madison will be staying," Ian said, still very civilized. "Her cab is on the way."

And then the two guys turned and *really* looked at him.

They weren't built like gym rats, but weren't wimps either—the kind of preppy guys who might have been on the rowing team at college.

From the way they exchanged a glance, Ian knew the exact moment they realized they weren't going to get Madison without a fight. Then he knew the exact moment when they decided that, hey, what the hell, between the two of them, they could take Ian. They thought of him as nothing but a dumbass bouncer, their inferior in every way. And older. Like Madison, they were in their early twenties. Close to thirty, Ian probably seemed halfway to ancient to them.

Boyfriend shoved Madison aside. And then the punches started flying.

Ian let them get in a few, let them get going. He didn't mind the pain; it woke him up. Made him feel.

When he let loose on them at last, the release of his deep, endless anger felt like physical pleasure. He knocked them back, knocked them down, until they were a single bloody heap on the ground, the girl screaming.

A horn blared. Ian pulled back, barely breathing hard. Hey, the cab was here. *Too damn fast.* But he put the whimpering girl in the backseat.

She couldn't get away from him fast enough.

He filled his lungs. Hadn't meant to scare her. "Stay safe. All right?"

He gave the twenty to Afiz, then went back inside, let the dickwads crawl off at their leisure. He washed off his bloody, throbbing knuckles in the bathroom, straightened his tie, then returned to work.

When the bar closed at two a.m., he checked around outside to see if the pricks had waited for him. Not that he wanted another round, but hey, free entertainment. If he was tired enough, sometimes he could actually sleep when he went to bed.

But no more fights tonight.

The walk home was quiet.

Sharon wasn't on the corner.

Ian was content not to run into anyone, but his new neighbor, a redhead with impossibly pillowy breasts, waited for him with a bottle of Jameson in the hallway outside his apartment. Skimpy tank top. Short skirt.

The whiskey had potential.

"Hey, Ian." She flashed a smile that said the bottle was his, along with anything else, for the asking.

"Hey…" He tried to remember her name. She'd introduced herself twice already this past week.

"Nicole," she said. "Wanna have a drink?"

She was maybe a year or two younger than Ian. She was a big girl. Safe to assume she knew what she was doing. He unlocked his door and opened it for her.

She sashayed into the kitchen like she lived there, and grabbed two glasses from the counter, rinsed them in the sink, all very domestic.

His eyes strayed to her breasts. "You came to do dishes?"

"I came to come." She winked, smiling from ear to ear.

"Gotta appreciate a straight-talking woman." He walked up behind her and caught her around the waist, pressed himself against her round ass, rubbed a little while his hands snuck around for the girls.

She giggled and poured them each a glass.

He let her go long enough to knock the whiskey back. Then he knocked back another. Then a third. A comfortable buzz began to build in his brain. *About time.* He'd been dry all night.

She walked her fingers up his chest, her voice breathy as she said, "Hey, handsome."

He lifted her onto the Formica counter. Her short skirt was flouncy enough to slide up without trouble when the time came. She'd been thinking ahead. He had a feeling they were going to make great neighbors.

"You got a boyfriend?" He hadn't seen one around. Didn't care either, just wanted to know if he should keep an eye out for a pissed-off dude kicking the door open behind him.

"Shithead ran off." Her mouth tightened, but only for a second, then her smile came back. "I'm hoping you'll help me take revenge."

He put his hands on her knees and parted them. "I try to step up to the plate for others if I'm in a position to help."

And he was in position. Between her legs.

He ran a hand up her skirt. No underwear. "My kind of woman," he murmured.

"Yeah?" She tugged his shirt out of his pants.

"Yeah." He grabbed his wallet out of his back pocket, then he unbuckled his pants and shoved them down to his knees, along with his underwear. The next second, the wallet was on the counter, he had a condom in hand, and the second after that, he was protected.

"You need a little warm-up…Nicole?"

She flashed a look that began shy and ended up anything but. "I warmed up a little while I waited."

"I think we're going to be friends," he said as he pushed into her.

And then she moved on him, like she'd taken lessons. *Damn.*

He pulled down her tank top, no bra either, and sucked a raspberry-size nipple into his mouth as they rode off into the sunrise together.

When they finished, they reconvened to the couch and polished off the bottle. A damn good night, all things considered.

Unfortunately, the good vibes didn't last long. As soon as Ian got to work the next day, the boss called him into the office.

Chandler, the club manager, was short, pudgy, and bald, which he tried to balance out with a beard. A garden gnome in Gucci loafers.

Two beat cops, both black, waited with him: one man, one woman. Ian knew the mostly Irish cops in his own neighborhood, but not these two, not here on the better side of the tracks.

*   *   *

Daniela

Daniela stood at the edge of the square and swayed at the sight of the swirling crowd, more people than she'd ever seen in one place. A whirlpool of tourists and locals.

The Içana had whirlpools just above her village. Sometimes those swirling funnels of water swallowed even strong swimmers. Daniela shivered despite the heat.

She'd followed Senhor Finch this far, but now her feet wouldn't move. She could go no farther.

And even if she could, where would she run?

Senhor Finch had given her food. He hadn't beaten her. Yet.

She wrapped her arms tightly around herself and turned around. Breathed. She felt better with the crowd behind her.

She walked back toward the house on the river.

Senhor Finch kept his door open. If he turned out to be a bad man, she could always run away later. So Daniela went back into the house.

The man didn't have much. A few cargo pants and shirts hung on pegs on the wall. The bamboo furniture was worn, had probably come with the house.

Why did he come here? How long would he stay? How long would he keep her? What would he want with her?

The house gave no answers.

Daniela aired out Senhor Finch's pillow and sheets. Swept the floor and washed the boards. Scrubbed the kitchen until it sparkled.

The girls at Rosa's house took turn with the chores, so Daniela knew how to do a good cleaning in a fancy house like this. They'd all learned, if only to avoid Rosa's bony hands.

The sky had turned dark by the time Senhor Finch came back. He flipped on the lights. Looked around. "Very good," he said, and smiled.

He definitely hadn't seen her leave the house and come back. Daniela relaxed a little.

She didn't even mind the sudden swarm of bugs the light drew in through the holes in the window screen.

He swatted madly at them while Daniela cooked again.

After dinner, Senhor Finch went for a swim in the river, and then he went to bed.

Daniela cleaned the dishes, and after that, she washed herself in the barrel of rainwater she'd seen out back. She didn't like the night river since it had taken her mother.

Without bothering to put her clothes back on, she slipped into the bed next to Senhor Finch.

"Whoa," he said.

She could see enough in the moonlight to tell that his eyes were wide open, watching her with surprise. But when she slipped her hands between his legs, he didn't push her away.

"You don't have to," he told her.

And she said what Rosa had taught her to say to all the men, "I want to, senhor."

Daniela wanted to make the foreigner happy. He gave her food, he didn't lock the door, and he didn't beat her. He was just one man. She didn't want him to send her back to Rosa's. So Daniela did with him what men liked her to do with them.

***

Ian

As the cops looked Ian over, his boss, Chandler, said, in a tone of restrained pissed, "We had a complaint."

Ian had a fair idea what about. "Listen, two guys tried to take a young lady out against her will last night. I had to step in. It'll all be on the security recording."

The boss queued the video footage right then and there, turned his laptop toward the cops. They all watched as the dickheads went for Ian. He clearly had not initiated the altercation.

"I'm going to need a copy," the male cop said, the suspicion not exactly gone from his eyes, but he had another look now too, as if he was impressed, at least a little.

The lady cop looked at Ian as if she knew where the girl had been headed last night. She said nothing. Gave him no grief. Ian supposed she'd seen a thing or two on the job. He liked her.

After the cops walked out, Ian stayed, since Chandler's pointed stare said the man wasn't done with him yet.

The manager leaned back in his seat, his mouth still in a pissed, hard line. Eyes still full of unhappy. "You're a good bouncer. But if the cops have to come here one more time because of you, you're fired. Just so we understand each other."

"Understood, sir."

Chandler watched him. Shook his head with a slow intake of breath that sounded suspiciously like a sigh. As the irritation leaked out of him, his shoulders deflated. "You have to stop punishing yourself."

Ian pressed his lips together. He hadn't discussed his past with Chandler. *Freaking Dean.*

Dean Shanahan knew Chandler, had gotten Ian this job.

"I'm not—" Ian bit off the rest.

To his credit, Chandler didn't point out that this was Ian's third fight this month, always outnumbered, always letting the jackasses beat him up first.

Instead of saying any of that, the boss nodded. "Forget about it."

Ian did just that for two mind-numbing, uneventful weeks until, one morning, just before dawn, he woke to the crash of his door being kicked in. The next second, four men were on him with baseball bats.

Christ, for a second, he didn't even know where he was, with Linda or in Afghanistan... *What the hell?*

Then someone flipped on the lamp, probably so the four attackers wouldn't accidentally hit each other.

Ian blinked in the bright light, still fuzzy around the edges, but his body knew what to do without his brain having to be engaged. His military training kicked in.

He grabbed for a bat, ripping it from the man who held it, knocked him back. *Oh, hello.* Recognition flashed. One of the jerkwads who'd tried to force that girl into going home from the club with them.

At one point they must have followed him home to figure out where he lived.

The idiot's buddy was here too, and slammed his baseball bat into Ian's knee. Ian dipped but didn't go down. Teeth grinding, he forced himself back up.

Shit. He was too old for this.

He smacked his bat into the face of the little bastard like he meant it. Blood spurted as the guy went down with a scream.

His buddies fought harder. So did Ian. He kicked one back so hard, the guy skidded halfway across the room on his back. But, to his credit, he came back up. Hell, Ian hadn't wanted to kill him. He didn't want to have to talk to the damn police again.

Another idiot flew at him. Gently, Ian tapped him back with a right hook, but not before he got his ribs bruised first. Because he was holding back. *All right. This needs to end.*

Most of the time he didn't mind a good fight, but they'd woken him up when he'd finally been sleeping. That made him grumpy. He wanted them out before he got grumpier and did something he'd live to regret in a jail cell.

Only two of the jerkwads had a personal stake in the fight. Ian just needed to show those two that they'd made a mistake when they came for a visit. One was already down. Ian sideswiped the other with his bat, and that one dropped too, blinking hard and bleeding harder. And as he felt that blood run down his temple, he panicked, scrambled back.

As the two injured men crawled for the door, the other two ran too, dragging their buddies with them, yelling back from the threshold, when they thought they were safe. "Don't think this is finished, asshole. We'll be back."

"I'll be here." Ian was breathing hard but buzzing nicely with adrenaline. "Bring a few more friends. We'll make it a proper party."

He limped to the door and slammed it shut behind them, then limped back to the living room.

The adrenaline ebbed. His knee was throbbing. And his ribs. And his head.

He limped to the window anyway, saw the douche bags pour out the front door of the building. One had to be carried. At least Ian's kneecap was only cracked, if that. A bottle of whiskey, a bag of ice, and he'd be good as new by morning.

He watched them pile into a BMW.

Rich douche bags. Figured.

Ian rubbed his knee.

If Finch had been here...But Finch hadn't called again after the message he'd left back in December. Summer had arrived since. Finch hadn't showed like he'd promised, which was unlike him. At the very least, the Finch that Ian knew would have called to say something about the change of plans.

Ian looked around his destroyed apartment and swore at the broken side table in particular.

Where the hell was he going to put his whiskey glass?

And what the hell was the sense in him getting jumped here in DC and Finch getting jumped wherever the hell he was? They used to fight together, back to back.

Ian kicked the broken table leg across the room. The douche bags were lucky they were gone, because he was full-on pissed now. Anyone he knocked out now wouldn't get up in a hurry.

He limped out into the kitchen and went through the cupboards for a bottle, but all the bottles were empty. The fridge had nothing in it either. Not even ice for his kneecap. He slammed the door so hard, it bounced open again.

The place was shit. The job was shit. The pay was certainly shit.

Fuck it.

He grabbed his phone from the counter, glad to see it in one piece. He bought a one-way ticket to Rio and went to pack his bag.

On the way to the airport, he called his mother in Connecticut, told her he'd be out of town for a while, maybe out of cell phone reach, not to worry about him.

Whatever he found down in Rio, couldn't be much worse than what he had up here in DC, could it?

***

Daniela

The only thing Daniela feared was having to go back to Rosa's.

She cooked for Senhor Finch, she cleaned, and at night, she went to bed with him. He was very little trouble. He didn't spend a lot of time in the house. He didn't tell her where he went during the day, and she wouldn't dream of asking.

She prayed that whatever was troubling him would go away. He smiled a lot, joked a lot, but he also watched the street. He kept a gun on the top of the fridge, and when he went out, the gun went with him.

Sometimes, he took her to the market and let her pick whatever she wanted, even clothes, even a new pair of rubber flip-flops that fit her feet exactly. But he kept looking over his shoulder.

If it rained very hard, he might stay home. On those days, he taught Daniela English. She already knew several words from the missionary in her village, so the learning progressed quickly.

Senhor Finch seemed happy with her willingness to learn, so she tried hard, eager to please him, although he never beat her and never threatened to send her back to Rosa. But Daniela didn't want to take the chance.

Senhor Finch liked her looking happy. "Smile," he would say in English.

So she would smile for him. She tried to remember to put a smile on her face when he was at home. It cost her nothing.

One month passed, then another. During the day, she relaxed. But at night, after he'd gone to sleep, she would hear Rosa's words echo in her head. *You stay here until he sends you back.*

Daniela wanted to ask Senhor Finch how long she had, when he would send her back up the river, but she didn't dare question him. Maybe he'd forgotten. Maybe, if she didn't remind him, Senhor Finch would keep her with him forever.

She never left the house without him. She didn't like the crowds. Especially when she remembered that one of the girls she'd been with at the red house on the Içana said that she'd been stolen from the street, from a big town, then sold to Rosa. Daniela didn't want to be stolen.

Senhor Finch probably sensed her reluctance, because he never sent her anywhere on her own.

Nobody came to visit them.

Nobody really paid them any attention.

So when a man showed up one afternoon across the road and stared at their house, Daniela, home alone, wasn't sure what he wanted.

He looked Brazilian—dark hair, dark eyes, but definitely not from the Amazon tribes, bigger, part Portuguese, part something else. He had a little beard on the top of his chin. He wore a white linen suit with a white hat, a city man, maybe even a government man.

Senhor Finch never asked her to lie down for any others. If this one came in and asked, she wasn't sure if she should or she shouldn't. She didn't want to. She didn't want to so bad, she held her breath until her lungs ached.

Then the man left. When Senhor Finch came home, Daniela didn't tell him about the strange visitor. She was afraid that Senhor Finch might say that next time, she had to invite the man in.

The stranger returned the following day. This time, he came to the door, knocked.

When Daniela opened up, he looked her up and down. From this close, she could see the scar on his nose. He tossed her a coin. "Tell me who lives here."

Her heart raced. "Senhor Finch."

She held her breath again. But he didn't ask to come in. He went away.

That night, Senhor Finch came home late. Daniela told him everything.

He had no smiles then, nothing but grim determination on his face. He slammed his fist into the table.

She ducked her head, but he said, "I'm not angry at you, Daniela. Listen…" He rubbed his stubble-covered chin. "Maybe it'd be best if you went back to that old woman for a couple of days. Take your clothes, whatever you need."

He reached into his pocket and gave her a handful of money, more than she'd ever seen. More than he'd given to Rosa when Rosa had brought her.

Her stomach clenched. She felt tossed around, as if a whirlpool on the river had caught her. She felt as if the dark waters were trying to pull her under. She wished Senhor Finch would take the money back. Just take it back and keep her instead.

"Have you eaten?" he asked, walking to the window, looking out at the street.

"Sim, senhor." She hadn't, but for once, she didn't feel like eating.

"I don't want anything." Exhaustion weighed down his voice. He turned from the window. "Let's just go to bed."

For the first time, he locked the door. And, for the first time, he brought his gun into the bedroom from the top of the fridge and tucked it under his mattress, within easy reach.

After he fell asleep, Daniela lay staring at the ceiling for the rest of the night, understanding that whatever the man in the white suit wanted would be something very bad. Whatever trouble Senhor Finch had been waiting for had arrived with the stranger.

She must have fallen asleep toward morning, because when she opened her eyes, the sun shone outside, and the house was empty, save for herself. She dressed. She didn't want to leave, but would Mr. Finch be angry if she was still here when he came back? He *had* sent her away.

She picked her favorite dresses, in case Rosa didn't let her come back here. She rolled them up, tucked them under her arm. The money she had now would buy her a trip up the river in a boat, with plenty left over.

She glanced at her bundle of clothes and held it tighter. What if getting in and out of the boat tore one of her dresses?

Senhor Finch had a large green backpack under his bed. She didn't dare touch that. But he had an old canvas bag under the sink he kept cassava and yams in. The bag was missing one of its handles. He *had* said for her to take what she needed. And she didn't think he'd miss the ruined bag. So she dumped out the cassava and yam, shook the dirt out of the bag outside, then neatly folded her dresses in there. And then she left.

She didn't think of running away. That had been a stupid dream. If she ran away, Senhora Rosa would find out, and then she would send the policemen after her again. Then they would beat her. She hadn't been beaten so long, she wanted very much not to be beaten again. She wasn't sure she could endure now what she'd been able to endure back at the red house. She'd gotten out of practice.

Daniela couldn't think of anyplace she could hide from the policemen, not even in her village. The police were always boating up and down the river. And Pedro had taken her to Rosa in the first place. He would just take her back.

She went all the way to the edge of the Santana harbor and looked at the boats going upriver. For money, any of them would take her. If only she waved and shouted to them.

She held her bag of clothes tightly under her arm. *In a minute. Just another minute.*

She waited for her heart to stop clamoring. It wouldn't. She even reconsidered running away. She couldn't hide in her own village, but maybe she could hide in another. She could have her own little hut, and…

She'd missed her mother's hut over the past months, but now she wanted something different. After living in the house with Senhor Finch, she didn't want a little hut and the men who'd show up day after day. She wanted to finish learning English. She wanted to be something different from what she had been.

The sudden hope that Senhor Finch might let her—might even let her keep studying and become a teacher—hit her so hard, she swayed and almost fell from the dock into the black river. She jerked back and was bit in the back of the arm at the same time. She whacked at the insect.

The night bugs were coming out to feast. She'd waited all day. She hadn't left. And now that the old dream was reborn in her heart, she couldn't.

So she left the docks and snuck back to Senhor Finch's house to beg him not to send her away, to promise him that she'd never open the door again to any strange man. It was the only thing she'd done differently, so she was certain that was why Senhor Finch was mad at her. Even if he'd said he wasn't mad at her. At Rosa's, if a man got mad, it was always the girl's fault, *always*. Rosa had beaten that into them.

Daniela quietly crept into the house, stopped right inside the door. *Oh. What's that?*

She squinted to see better. The furniture had been thrown around and now lay scattered on the floor, broken. Her heart had been pounding already, but now it pounded harder.

Senhor Finch was even angrier than she'd thought. She hesitated. But then she put her bag down and softly padded toward the bedroom, ready to suffer even a hard beating—she *would* stand it if she had to—just as long as she could stay.

She didn't make it halfway when, as she passed the table, she saw Senhor Finch in the kitchen.

He lay on the floor, a dark pool under him, his eyes staring at the ceiling. One of his ears had been cut off, resting now down by his knee on the floor. And his hands looked…Someone had shoved slivers of bamboo under his fingernails.

Daniela's stomach roiled.

Senhor Finch was dead.

CHAPTER
THREE

Ian

Ian hated Rio with a hot, burning passion. Cheerful little fuckers. All tourists and dancing and partying in skimpy clothes, sparkling skyscrapers, fancy cars, then the barely there bikinis on the beaches, Ipanema and Copacabana, the playgrounds of the rich and famous. He preferred the Zona Norte, so he rented a room on the edge, among normal, working people.

Finding the first trace of Finch ate up two whole weeks. He had a job in security for a while, it seemed, for some big international company, Lavras Sugar and Ethanol, according to the old man the kid had rented from, but then Finch had quit work and left the apartment. Nobody knew what for.

Another two weeks went by before Ian found a faint trail, indicating that Finch might have gone up to the Amazon. *Fucking Amazon. What the hell?*

Ian tracked him to Manaus, then up the Rio Negro, deeper and deeper into the jungle. The farther he got from the beaten path, the easier the tracking got—fewer foreigners. Blond as a love child of a Viking and a honeybee, Finch had stood out, had been noticed.

Ian tracked him all the way to Santana, a small municipality in the state of Amapá.

When he finally found the house Finch was supposedly living in, Ian settled in to watch the place. Small house, bamboo walls, steel roof, two bedrooms at the most, a decrepit piece of shit.

He cursed it, and the legion of bugs, as he waited. Before he barged in, he wanted to make sure he had the right place. He wanted to make sure nobody else was watching it. Finch *had* said in that call that he was in trouble.

So Ian did a little general reconnaissance. A soldier who rushed into a situation was a dead soldier.

He arrived in the morning. Watched the house for two hours. No movement. Nobody went in or came out through the front.

Time to go a little closer, check out the back.

The back of the house stood maybe thirty feet from the river, but high up a tall bank that'd protect it from flooding. An empty dock reached into the water. No movement there either.

A couple of boats had been dragged up on the flat of the riverbank. Nobody around. Ian sat in the shade of the largest boat and pretended to be watching the barges and tugboats going past him.

He stole a glance at the house, hoping to spot Finch. Nothing there, but something rising out of the water maybe thirty feet from him caught his attention.

At first, he thought it might be a caiman. Caimans were native to the area, although he had no idea if they lived in this part of this particular river.

But instead, out of the river, rose a young woman.

She seemed to be struggling with…an anaconda?

When the shiny, black, long body wrapped around hers, Ian moved, ready to dive into the water to help her, but she had the upper hand and dragged the wriggling beast toward shore with a triumphant smile. He could see that she had a giant eel.

He couldn't take his eyes off the thing. The eel stretched as long as the woman was tall, over five feet. They wrestled in the shallow water, the scene stunningly primal and elemental.

She had a piece of rag tied around her small breasts, and another around her slim waist, covering only the private parts of her body. She was the most stunning sight he'd ever seen, long dark hair streaming down in wet rivulets. A goddess risen.

A goddess in mortal struggle.

His Western sensibilities pushed him to run and help, but the woman and the eel and their battle seemed somehow the spirit of the Amazon itself, and he felt like an interloper. He felt that he couldn't take the woman's triumph away from her.

And she did win, dragging the eel to shore, grabbing a rock the next second and smashing the eel's head. The eel was still squirming when, with the same, sharp-edged rock, she gutted the thing, dumping the insides back into the river. She was not a peaceful goddess.

She washed the eel efficiently, then picked up the carcass and carried it, staggering under the weight, up the tall, steep bank, and in through the back door of the house Ian had been watching.

Ian's chin might have dropped a little. Or a lot. In fact, he felt as if his chin just hit his lap.

Who on earth was *she*?

Did he have the wrong house, after all that travel?

He stole back around, back across the street, and watched her leave the house a few minutes later with a beat-up canvas bag, wearing a simple green dress now, the heavy bag over her shoulder, hefting what looked like most of the damned eel.

She took her catch to the market and sold it to an old woman with a fish stand. She bought rice and fruit with some of the money, saved the rest, didn't buy any sweets or trinkets.

When she returned home, Ian followed her once again, and stayed just a little up the street for the rest of the day, watching the house.

No sign of Finch.

The idiot had probably moved on. The young woman was probably the next tenant. Finch was running from people, so it made sense that he wouldn't stay long in any one place.

He'd been traveling upriver until now. Most likely, he would keep going in that direction. Ian eyed the boats roaring up the Rio Negro. Maybe he needed to hire one to take him up that way. But he decided to check out the house from a little closer first—the very next time its new occupant left the place.

Unfortunately, she stayed in for the rest of the day.

Ian spent the night on the street. He had enough bulk and a mean enough face when he chose so that nobody bothered him. And at least, miraculously, it only drizzled a little. The bugs ate him alive, pretty much, but there was no helping that.

Finch never showed.

The girl came out in the morning. She wore the same green dress as the day before, with one very significant difference. The dress was cinched with Finch's lucky belt.

Ian's hands fisted. He relaxed them with effort.

Finch had worn that belt every single day he wasn't in uniform. Won the buckle in a rodeo in his home state of Texas. He wouldn't have traded it for a thousand acres.

The only way Finch had let that belt go was if he was dead.

Ian watched the girl and swore under his breath. He waited until she disappeared in the throng of people, then he hurried into the house at long last.

A pair of combat boots waited just inside the door. Probably Finch's, but Ian couldn't tell for sure. Combat boots all looked the same.

Shirts and cargo pants in the bedroom. Could have been Finch's. Could have been any other man's. Roughly Finch's size, though, so that was something. He was a pretty big guy. Around here, the locals were smaller.

Ian searched under the mattress, found a Glock G43—the gun Finch liked to carry concealed, less bulky than the SIG Sauer P938, Finch had always claimed. Fully loaded, and one in the chamber. Ian tucked the weapon in the back of his waistband.

When the bedroom didn't turn up anything more interesting, he checked the smaller room where the girl kept her things: a few dresses, a few trinkets.

Why would she be living with Finch?

Ian backed out, checked the main room and the kitchen. Nothing and nothing. Except, in the kitchen, the bamboo floor had some brown stains he'd missed when he'd come through earlier. Someone had scrubbed those boards regularly, he could tell, but in the grooves, that rusty brown had set in.

He stilled. He knew what stained like that.

And then he knew more than he wanted. A large blood stain on the floor. The young woman wearing Finch's belt. Finch nowhere to be seen—even leaving his weapon behind.

Acid bubbled up in Ian's stomach.

He was very likely standing on the spot where his friend had been killed.

***

Daniela

Daniela bought soap at the market, paying with her own money. The eel had been a lucky catch. They didn't usually come this far down the river.

She had long ago run out of the money Senhor Finch had given her. She felt guilty for staying in his house. She should have gone back to Rosa like he'd told her.

But every day, she convinced herself to stay just one day longer.

She walked back slowly with the soap. She had stopped by the soap maker's cart yesterday, but he had asked her where Senhor Finch was, and the crowd had overwhelmed her and made her heart beat too fast, so she'd run home without buying soap from the old man.

She was proud of herself for doing better today.

And she had food, *and* she had some money left. She still could barely believe that she'd caught that eel.

She walked through the door of the house, as happy as she'd ever been.

But in the middle of the house stood the largest, scariest man she'd ever seen. Senhor Finch had been sunshine, but this foreigner was a night storm. He seemed to fill the house like a dark cloud. He was too big, too strong, his gaze too sharp on her. As she turned to flee, he thundered, "Stop!"

And the next second, the man had her arm in his grip.

***

Carmen

Carmen Barbosa watched the red house over the dark waters of the Içana, her back and arms aching from working at the clinic all day. Her right arm hurt the most, had been hurting since last week. Too much hammering. They'd been installing doors on the examination rooms, a big improvement over curtains.

The day's work had been satisfying, yet contentment eluded her.

"What do you think happened to that girl?"

"Maybe she escaped on her own." Phil sat at the kitchen table, writing a letter to his parents back home. No Internet this deep in the rain forest.

He was an only child. His mother and father worried about him. Sometimes he joked about wishing for at least one brother—a war correspondent or a policeman—so the parental worry would get spread around a little. "Maybe a relative came and got her."

"Maybe," Carmen echoed, but she didn't believe it.

After they'd decided to save the girl, they'd never seen her again. The girl hadn't gone into the river the next morning with the rest. Carmen had swum over anyway and approached the others, but none of them talked to her. They scampered up the ladder to the red house's deck and hid inside, as if they were scared of her.

Going to the police station to inquire about the house hadn't helped either. She'd been told to mind her own business. A police officer with disaffected, reptilian eyes had told her that people around here didn't like foreigners who caused trouble. He suggested that she'd be more comfortable in Rio or one of the other big cities.

No way would she leave the clinic before the work was finished. And since she knew the police *could* make her leave, she stopped going to the police.

But she hadn't stopped investigating.

"I put out the word to the foreign volunteer networks, with as good a description of the girl as I could give. Somebody will see her." She rolled her right shoulder. Maybe she'd ask the doc at the clinic for some cream for her sore muscles.

"Marry me." The words, soft but sure, floated to her on the evening breeze. Her heart lurched.

Now? Oh God. Don't ask me.

She turned to look into Phil's eyes that sparkled with love and hope. She couldn't speak. She could barely breathe. The air was thick with moisture and the tiny shards of her broken hopes and dreams.

"Please, say yes." Phil rose to his feet and padded over to wrap her in his arms. "I want you to be Mrs. Heyerdahl. I want you to belong to me. I want us to belong to each other."

Everything inside her thrilled and at the same time panicked. *Oh God.*

He kissed her neck. "I want to tell my parents to get ready for grandchildren. The book is almost done. We can go home. The time is right."

Grandchildren. At least Carmen had a brother and a sister, so her parents had two other chances. *But Phil. God, Phil...*

He acknowledged her hesitation with a nod. "I know it's sudden. But you're everything I want. Just think about it."

I'm not everything you want. Her heart dropped to her stomach, then through and out of her to fall clattering on the floor at her feet.

Heart-achingly handsome and heartbreakingly out of her reach, he nuzzled her face. "I want us to get married, and have kids, and live happily ever after together."

She pictured children who would look like him, a little blonde girl with Phil's sparkling blue eyes. She hadn't known the meaning of longing until that moment.

She stepped out of his arms, because even letting him hold her seemed a lie. Why hadn't she told him before? She had been selfish, and now she would hurt him.

She backed away, drew a long breath, and prepared for her world to collapse. "I need to tell you something…"

* * *

Ian

Ian spoke English, because he sure as shit didn't speak Portuguese. He hoped the young woman could understand him.

"Who are you?" He put himself between her and the door. Now she would have to get by him to escape. Which was not going to happen.

Did she have anything to do with Finch's death?

Finch wouldn't have gone down easily. He'd either met overwhelming force, or the danger had come from somewhere he'd least expected. Such as the young woman. And she'd done a fearsome job on that eel. She certainly knew how to bash somebody's head in with a rock.

"Who else lives in this house?" Ian's gaze flashed to the faded bloodstain on the kitchen floor, then back to her.

That he'd arrived too late to save Finch about killed him. He was never there when he was needed, dammit. Not with Linda and the twins, not with Finch. But this time…This time, at least he had an enemy to focus on. Whoever had killed Finch was going to answer to Ian.

"I'm Daniela," the girl said, wide-eyed and pulling away from him to cower in the corner, her hands half up to cover herself from the blows she clearly expected.

Someone had beaten her in the past. Not Finch, but somebody. Beaten her enough so that cowering and covering had become a reflex. The thought disgusted Ian, but he didn't back down with the questioning. He was here for answers.

"What are you doing here? Did you live here with Finch?"

Her tan face paled. Her large eyes—a million flecks of different shades of green—filled with tears, but she held them from spilling. "Senhor Finch. He was good man."

Ah, hell.

Was. Was! Dammit.

Finch was gone. *And* she knew.

Ian had been half hoping she'd come after Finch had been dead, was squatting here, stealing his things. If she'd lived here with Finch…What the hell was Finch doing with her, for fuck's sake? Not that it was unusual around here, but she was too damn young. Too damn scared. Too damn—

"How old are you?" he asked, then wished he hadn't, because he didn't want to think any worse of his dead friend than he already did just now.

She just looked at him and shook her head.

Great. She didn't even know how old she was. Fricking perfect.

"How long have you lived with Finch?"

"Since the middle of the dry season," she said.

So for a couple of months. *Christ, Finch, you freaking asshole.* Was it possible to hate a guy you loved like a brother? "How did you meet him?"

"Rosa brought me." The way she shrunk said Rosa was a frightful bastard, probably the one who used to beat her.

Ian watched her—small, defenseless, scared.

He sank onto the floor across the room from her and leaned his back against the door, his anger draining away as if someone pulled a plug. "I'm Ian Slaney. I'm Finch's friend."

He struggled to see the full picture.

Finch, on the run from some bad guys, hiding here, sure. If God had ever made a place for disappearing, it was the Amazon, with its swamps and barely accessible tributaries.

But Finch buying a girl from some pimp? Ian clenched his jaw. He didn't want to even think about shit like that.

"Do you go to school?" He was hoping to hear her say that she'd graduated already. She looked about that age. Okay, not really. She looked damn young, except he had a feeling she hadn't grown up with sufficient nutrition, so she was on the thin side. But her eyes weren't the eyes of a child. "Did you finish school?"

She shook her head.

His heart sank.

"Senhor Finch teaching me English," she volunteered.

And what else, Ian wanted to say but didn't.

"When did he die?" he asked, instead of when was he killed.

For the moment, Ian was willing to pretend that Finch had fainted and hit his head on the corner of the stove, if that gained him any cooperation from Daniela. If he scared her any more, she might not answer at all.

She pulled into as tight a ball as possible. "Senhor Finch went away. He will come back."

Right. She was wearing his lucky belt. Ian had Finch's Glock in the back of his waistband. No way had Finch gone anywhere.

"He died on this kitchen floor." Ian gestured in the general direction with his head. "You and I both know it. Let's cut the bullshit. When did Finch die?"

Silent seconds ticked by.

"A month ago." Her voice was barely audible.

Ian's throat burned. A month ago, he'd been halfway between here and Rio.

He swore, then when Daniela flinched, he said, "I'm not going to hurt you."

But, fuck, he wanted to hit someone. And he wanted a drink. He'd been on the road for months. He hadn't had a drink since he'd blown into Santana the day before.

And while searching through the house earlier, he hadn't found a single bottle of hard liquor, for which he blamed Finch. The bastard was a beer drinker, and not much of one at that.

Ian cursed him silently. For getting into trouble, for dying without waiting for Ian to get here, for not having a fricking bottle of rotgut tequila in the house, goddammit.

"How did he die?" he asked.

Daniela folded in on herself even tighter. Any more of that and she might disappear. The goddess of the river was gone. She didn't belong here. She belonged to the Amazon. Her staying at the house with Ian was wrong, as it'd been wrong with Finch. Somehow the setup stripped her of all her power.

"I don't know." She tucked in her chin, obviously not believing that Ian wouldn't hit her.

He was so damned tired, only his grief and anger kept him awake. "How did he die?" he asked again.

"I wasn't here," she said.

And he believed her.

She'd been fierce with the eel, but she was scared to death of him. Probably all men. If she'd been sold to Finch…Ian didn't even want to think about what her life might have been beforehand.

Now that he'd spent a little time with her…He didn't think she would have attacked Finch. And if she'd been here when someone else had, they wouldn't have left her alive as a witness.

"All right." He pushed to standing, beat as shit. He'd been up all night watching for Finch, and months of endless tracking before that. "We're going to get some sleep."

She immediately rose and walked into the bedroom, got on the bed. Her shoulders looked tight, her jungle-green eyes filled with apprehension, but as Ian watched her, he knew with a sick feeling in his stomach that she'd do anything he told her.

"Fuck you, Finch," he said under his breath.

He took off his belt, sat on top of the covers, put his feet up on the bed, then grabbed her ankle and pulled her over. She didn't protest. The resigned look in her eyes said she wouldn't protest anything.

He fastened her left leg to his right one with the belt. "I'm going to tie us together, so you don't run off while I sleep. I have more questions, but I'm tired."

She could undo the belt, but her efforts would wake him up. The last thing he wanted was her in his bed, but it was the best idea he had at the moment.

He put Finch's gun under the mattress on his side, exactly where he'd found it, then lay back down.

She lay down next to him. Then she scooted closer and reached her hand toward him.

"No," he snapped, and ground his teeth, because what the hell else was he supposed to do in this damned situation?

She pulled her hand back, her gaze filling with worry and confusion.

He closed his eyes. "Tomorrow, after you answer all my questions, I'll let you go."

She was so quiet, he wasn't sure if she didn't stop breathing. But he didn't open his eyes to check.

CHAPTER
FOUR

Daniela

The Rio Negro rushed on outside, the sounds of the water filling the night, along with the sounds of the bugs in the trees. In Senhor Finch's giant bed, Daniela held her breath as she folded her body until her fingertips could reach the belt buckle.

She had to escape.

She'd waited too long. She should have run away right after Senhor Finch had been killed.

She hadn't, because here at least she had a roof over her head without having to entertain men. Living in Senhor Finch's house, people assumed she belonged to Senhor Finch, and nobody tried to take control of her, tried to sell her again. They didn't know Senhor Finch was dead.

But now, Senhor Slaney knew.

He had eyes like a jaguar, like he was lord of life and death, eyes that pinned her and saw even her thoughts. He'd looked at her, and she told him everything. She didn't think he was a bad man. But he was the most dangerous man she'd ever known.

Senhor Slaney was going to send her back to Rosa tomorrow.

"I'll let you go," he'd said, meaning Daniela was done here. Time to go back.

He hadn't meant he was setting her free. He would have to buy her from Rosa for that, and why would he do such a thing? Paying good money, then letting Daniela go would be the same as just throwing his money in the river. What would he benefit? Nothing.

In the morning, Senhor Slaney might give her to a fisherman going upriver and ask Daniela to be delivered to Rosa. Or simply give her to a policeman. Rosa knew all the police.

Daniela had to run and trust fate that she wouldn't be caught. She had to run now. In the morning, it would be too late. So with trembling fingers, she tried to loosen the belt without waking the man next to her.

A beam of moonlight, softened by the mosquito net, fell over his face.

He had hair and eyelashes almost as dark as hers. He was the most physically powerful man she'd ever met, and he moved like the jungle hunter. Like a jaguar.

She'd seen a jaguar once.

They rarely came out of the forest as far as her village, but Daniela had seen one the night her mother had drowned, the night of the flood. All the village had run uphill, into the jungle, looking for high ground. When Daniela had realized that her mother wasn't there, she had run back, and met the jaguar on the path.

The roar of the river and the people in the forest had probably disturbed the beast's night hunt; he'd come to check out the clamor.

As Daniela had rushed around a bend in the path, a dark shadow separated from all the other dark shadows in front of her. She froze. Precious little moonlight filtered through the double canopy, but that dim light glinted off sleek black fur.

Daniela held her breath.

The jaguar sniffed.

Keen tension stretched in the air, strings of tension so taut they could have been played as a musical instrument. Her heart *thump, thump, thumped* in her chest, louder than it'd ever beaten, and still not as loud as the blood rushing madly in her ears.

Then a goat cried in the distance, maybe caught in high water.

And in a blink, the jaguar had disappeared.

Daniela had fallen down, dropped like a monkey shot out of a tree. She gasped for air. All that time, she hadn't breathed.

When she recovered, she was too scared to continue on toward the village, so she ran back to the people huddled together in the jungle. She hadn't found her mother until morning, tangled in tree roots at the edge of the flooding river.

Ana's long hair streamed out around her face, the locks half-covered with mud, as if reaching into the earth, as if she was growing roots herself and would now simply transform into another form of being, but still very much part of the rain forest.

That image often returned in Daniela's dreams. But not tonight. Tonight, she wouldn't sleep.

She shifted on Senhor Finch's bed. Senhor Slaney's bed now.

The jaguar was here for her again. And again, he would let her go. Yet she'd still be trapped. Just as she hadn't been truly safe in the village after her mother's death. The jaguar had let her go, but then Daniela ended up in Senhora Rosa's clutches.

Not this time.

Not again.

She worked silently and carefully, her fingers like the delicate legs of the water bugs as they ran across the shallow ponds without disturbing the surface. She nearly worked the belt free when a large hand closed around her wrist.

Slowly, she turned to face the man who captured her. His dark gaze burned into hers in the dim moonlight.

"If you run, I will find you. Do you understand?"

Her heart beat in her throat. "Sim, senhor."

The jaguar would let her go. But only when he was ready.

***

Ian

Ian dreamt of Linda and the twins under water, Connor and Colin screaming, "Daddy!"

He startled awake drenched in sweat, and for a moment, he didn't know where he was. The bamboo walls, palm thatch ceiling, and oppressive humidity brought him to Brazilian reality.

Connor and Colin couldn't have screamed, he told himself. They had been too young to speak. And too young to know who was at fault for not protecting them, letting them go into that river. The father who hadn't come when he was needed.

The air and the room around Ian felt like a wet, dark weight, like it could drown him—not like a river, but a slow sinking in thick swamp water. His head pounded.

Next to him, Daniela was still sleeping.

He took in the small, curled-up heap she made in the bed. With tear streaks all over her face, she looked about sixteen. He felt like a dick.

He untied himself from her and fastened her to the bamboo footboard. He tucked the gun into his waistband, then hurried off to piss, hurried back, half expecting to find the bed empty, but she was still there, now sitting.

He leaned against the doorjamb, didn't step any closer.

"You can unbuckle that now." He nodded toward his belt.

And then what?

He needed a shot of something. Jameson's would be good—a couple of shots, actually. He shoved his shaky hands into his pockets. Hell, he'd settle for some rotgut tequila, if Finch had only stocked some.

"I'm not going to hurt you," he told Daniela again, because judging by the tight set of her slim shoulders, it bore repeating.

She nodded but didn't relax.

"Why don't you use the bathroom, then we'll see about breakfast."

The promise of food seemed to galvanize her, and she sprang into action, confirming his suspicions that she'd gone without food in the past. *Better and better.*

He padded to the kitchen barefoot, found eggs in the ancient fridge and some coconut oil, used the pan on the stove to make scrambled eggs. When he heard her behind him, he turned.

She was staring as if he had a tap-dancing monkey on his head.

He had no idea what was wrong now, so he pointed at the table. "Sit."

He put the eggs on the table. Half a dozen forks sat in a cup on the counter. He grabbed two. He didn't feel like hunting around for plates. He grabbed a lone flatbread from a plastic bag, then carried everything over.

He hadn't had breakfast with someone at a kitchen table in two years. Hell, this was probably the first time he'd have breakfast in the past two years that hadn't come from a bottle.

For a second, he thought of Linda and the twins, the last breakfast they'd had together before he'd shipped out. Linda had been crying, begging him to stay.

"You'll be fine," he'd said. "I'll be back before you know it."

But it hadn't been fine. What happened after he'd left was so far from fine, he didn't have a word for it.

His head pounded harder. He had to squeeze his eyes shut as he stood, because movement made the pain worse. There had to be a place somewhere in the neighborhood that sold liquor. Tequila was the same word in every language, right? Somebody would point him in the right direction.

But as he cautiously opened his eyes so he could leave, his gaze fell on Daniela. She was squirming on her seat, chewing her bottom lip.

"What's wrong?" He spoke quietly, but each word was like a cannon shot in his head anyway.

She immediately stilled. "Nothing, Senhor Slaney."

She could control her actions but couldn't hide the worry in her large green eyes. Worry tinged with fear.

He silently cursed, sat back down, then handed her one of the forks. "Just Ian. Dig in."

He waited until she hesitantly did go for the food, because he had a fair idea that otherwise, she'd hold out for leftovers. He hated that she expected him to treat her like a dog. *Had Finch?* Dammit, he didn't want to think that about his friend.

He wanted to ask her about the day Finch died, but he didn't want to scare her out of her wits by starting with murder, so he asked, "So, you always lived around here?"

And was glad he did, because her shoulders did relax a little as she told him about her mother, Ana, and her village, then the trip with Pedro down the river.

Of course, then, the more she said, the more Ian wished he hadn't asked.

Pedro. A fucking bastard who'd sold her to some whorehouse, apparently. Ian hoped he might run into the man while he was here. He seriously wanted to punch something, and Pedro's face would be as satisfying a choice as he could imagine.

Then Daniela told him about Rosa bringing her to Santana and giving her to Finch, and by that time, Ian's stomach was flooded with acid, so he gave up on breakfast.

If Finch was alive, Ian might have strangled his friend himself, even if Daniela had nothing but praise for him, and told Ian how happy she'd been, how Finch had never even beaten her and fed her every day.

Because Ian couldn't handle the praise, he said, "Tell me how he was killed."

And then they were suddenly at murder.

Daniela paled. "I don't know, Senhor Ian. I came home, and he was dead."

She'd told him as much yesterday. He needed more. "You didn't see anybody?"

"A man came to the door the day before. And he watched the house the day before that."

"Did you tell Finch?"

"Sim, Senhor Ian."

"What did Finch say?"

"He said I should go away for a few days." She hung her head. "But I came back in the night," she muttered, tucking in her neck as if expecting to be punished for the disobedience. "Senhor Finch was dead."

Ian pushed for details and got more than he bargained for when she gave him a full description. Slivers of bamboo under the fingernails. And a cut-off ear.

Tortured. Christ. Finch had been twenty-seven. Too damn young to die, and even with all the stupid things he'd done in his life, he hadn't deserved to die like that.

Dark fury choked Ian. The desperate need for a drink pounded in his head, using it for a punching bag. Left hook, right hook, uppercut. He squinted against the sunlight pouring in the windows. "What did the man who came to the door look like?"

"He was a goat man," she said, touching her chin.

"He had a goatee?"

"Yes, like a goat's, dark. And big ears that held up his hat."

Not much to go on.

"Anything else? Scar on his face? Limp? Anything I could find him by?"

"A scar on his nose." She drew a line straight across the bridge with her finger.

"What did he wear? Poor clothes, rich clothes, a uniform?" A uniform would be helpful. A uniform would be an actual lead.

"Rich clothes, senhor," Daniela said. "A white suit with a white hat." And then she added, "Once, a man in a white suit came to visit one of the girls at Senhora Rosa's house. Senhora Rosa said he was an important man. He worked for the police."

But not a cop, if he didn't have a uniform. Maybe he'd been a detective. Or higher. The police commissioner. Ian considered that for a few seconds before he asked, "What happened to Finch's body?"

She shrank again.

Ian made a point to relax his body language. He leaned back in his chair, stretched his legs in front of him, and gentled his voice. "I'm not going to be angry."

Still, several seconds ticked by before she said with reluctance, "I buried Senhor Finch, like my mother. I just…" She swallowed hard, wouldn't look at him. "I couldn't find a log to carve out."

Ian stared. He pictured her struggling to drag Finch down to the river on a sheet, then rolling him into the black water.

Damned if Ian knew how to feel about that.

Not mad at her, though. She did what she had to for survival, and Ian was glad that she'd done it. If she'd gone to the police, they would have either locked her up for the murder or taken her back to Rosa. He was glad that she'd had this past month here, without anyone to abuse her.

He kept asking questions, repeated some he'd already asked, but she didn't have much new information to add.

The best Ian could figure was that whoever had been after Finch in Rio had found him here in Santana and killed him.

Daniela finished her food and immediately jumped up to clean the table.

Ian stood too. The food had knocked his headache back a little.

All right, what's next?

Maybe he could talk to the neighbors. Maybe someone had seen more, seen the man come into the house the night of the murder. Or more than one man. Hard to see how one guy could have taken down Finch.

Before he could think more about that, Daniela was in front of him, her hands tightly clasped together, her eyes downcast. The table was already clean. "Please don't send me back to Rosa, Senhor Ian."

The quiet desperation in her voice made acid claw at his stomach lining. He needed a shot of whiskey, the sooner the better.

"You go back to Rosa over my dead body," he said through gritted teeth.

But she only stood still with her head down, nothing but hopelessness and misery in the set of her slim shoulders. Maybe she didn't believe him.

Why the hell would she believe him? When the hell had anyone done right by her before, dammit?

He worked to tamp down his rising fury so it wouldn't come through his voice. "Where would you like to go?"

"Please let me stay with you." She folded herself smaller. "I won't be any trouble. You won't even notice me."

Christ, he couldn't stand to see anyone like this.

"All right. If you want to stay, you can stay."

She was the only one who could positively identify Goat Man, anyway. "But I don't want you begging in front of me, or anyone else. Do you understand? This is where it ends, Daniela. You're starting over."

Her head snapped up, an equal measure of confusion and relief on her beautiful face. "I can stay with you?"

"You can. In your room," he added.

Relief won, and the next second, she was kissing his hand, grabbing it so tightly, he could barely get away from her.

"None of that either."

She dropped his hand immediately. "Yes, Senhor Ian."

"Call me just Ian."

She flashed a cautious smile, the first he'd seen on her. "Yes, Senhor Ian."

He sighed. What the hell, they could work on that.

"We're going to take a walk around town, see if you can spot this Goat Man," he said.

"I will." She couldn't promise fast enough.

The top of her head didn't quite reach his shoulder. Her straight black hair hung down to her waist. She had large eyes and a small nose, a mouth that someday might grow into generous. Small hips, small breasts.

"Before we go…" He cleared his throat. "Can you do something to make yourself look older? Put your hair in a bun or something."

She looked puzzled. "Like Rosa?"

He nodded.

And while she disappeared into her room, he searched the cupboard for tequila again, just in case he'd missed something the day before, all the while wondering what in hell he was doing here. Anyone seeing the two of them together would think she was his fricking concubine or some such shit.

But the only alternative to keeping her with him was sending her back to Rosa, or setting her loose so some other fucker could take control of her. So when she came out in a longer dress and her hair in a bun, still not looking a day over seventeen, he bit back a curse and decided he didn't care.

But shit, he couldn't even remember being this young. At thirty, he felt ancient next to her.

He moved toward the door, but then something popped into his head, and he looked back at her again.

In the army, he'd known recruits as young as eighteen, some almost as petite as her. They'd fought fine. So why not Daniela?

He cleared his throat. "We're going to look for this Goat Man. Then we'll come back here and eat lunch. And then I'm going to teach you how to fight."

And when she learned that, he was going to teach her how to shoot a gun. She was done being anybody's victim.

Daniela looked at him, bewildered. But she said, "Yes, Senhor Ian."

He stifled a groan. They were also going to work on that *senhor* bit. But first, he wanted to find the man in white and see what the guy had to do with Finch's death.

* * *

From the shadows between the two houses across the road, the very spot where Ian had spent the night before last, a boy watched as the newly arrived foreigner and the girl left the house.

The boy grinned. Good thing he'd come today. The man who paid him for watching had given him the job a month back, but after the first week, when nobody showed up, the boy didn't watch all day, every day.

Luckily, he did today, which meant he would get the promised bonus.

He followed the foreigner and the girl from a safe distance. They walked around Santana, sat outside a café across the road from the police station and drank coffee, watched the policemen come and go for hours. Then they walked around some more. Nothing interesting.

The boy kept track of them until they returned to the house. Then he ran off to find someone with a phone he could borrow to call in the news. He had the number on a piece of paper in his pocket.

CHAPTER
FIVE

Eduardo

Eduardo Morais listened to the kid over the phone as he looked out his living room window from his tenth-floor apartment at the rushing city traffic of Rio de Janeiro below him. Only two bedrooms, and five whole blocks from the beach, his home was nothing like his father's mansion. But Eduardo was on his way back up in the world. He envisioned a penthouse apartment overlooking Sugarloaf Mountain and Guanabara Bay in the very near future.

On the other end of the line, the kid jabbered on about how hard he'd worked, watching the house day and night, never sleeping. Eduardo hung up on him. The little maggot would get his bonus; no need to squeal about it.

Eduardo turned from the window, the kid already forgotten. The news was what mattered.

Another foreigner had come.

Meu Deus, that had been a long shot.

Eduardo walked through the air-conditioned flat and into the kitchen, and, as he grabbed a bottle of cachaça and poured a glass, he silently congratulated himself for leaving the little whore alone. He'd made a strategic decision at the time, and he didn't regret it.

The men he'd sent to make Finch talk had panicked when Finch had fought back harder than they'd expected. One of the idiots shot the American. Eduardo had decided not to interrogate the girl living with the bastard. If Finch could keep a secret so well that he didn't reveal it under torture, he wouldn't have blabbed it out to his whore.

So Eduardo had left the girl in place and waited. Finch had made a call to an unlisted number in the USA the night he left Rio. He had a buddy. And

Eduardo had bet big on the buddy showing up sooner or later to find out what had happened to Finch.

The American would come if he was a close friend. And if he was a close friend, Finch might have told *him* where he'd put what he'd stolen. And if the friend knew, he'd definitely come down to grab the package.

Looked like the friend was finally here.

And this time, Eduardo wasn't going to settle for some stupid local muscle. This time, he would take his own best men with him.

He drank his celebratory drink. Then picked up his phone from the counter, ready to call and reserve a seat on the first flight from Rio to Manaus, the city of his birth, but his phone rang before he could dial.

As he looked at the display, he rubbed his thumb across the patch of beard on the top of his chin and smiled. *Marcos.* And, at long last, Eduardo had good news for his older brother. This time, Eduardo was riding to the rescue. This time, Eduardo had the answers. This time, Eduardo would be the hero of the story.

He answered the call with "I think I finally—"

"Doesn't matter," Marcos snapped on the other end. "The old hyena had a stroke. He might be dead by morning. Get over here. We're going to contest the will."

* * *

Ian

A light rain fell outside, which meant no evening bugs, thank God. The lack of flying and biting insects was the only thing going well. Technicolor pain pounded through Ian's brain as he sat on the couch. The headache was back in full force and then some. Nausea swirled in his stomach.

As the rain pitter-pattered on the metal roof, he felt as if each drop was pinging off his brain. He regretted not buying booze while they'd been out earlier. But with things as they were, he couldn't afford to get plastered. He couldn't afford the oblivion he craved.

He needed to find the man in the white suit. And then he needed to beat the life out of the bastard. After the man answered some questions. Like who was he, and why did he kill Finch. What had the bastard been after?

Finch had been tortured before he'd been killed. To give up something. Which he didn't give up, because, according to Daniela, the house had been tossed.

Two possibilities existed: either the killers had found what they were looking for, or they hadn't.

Ian was betting on the latter.

When he'd headed out earlier with Daniela, he noticed a boy—about ten years old—following them around. He'd seen the same boy across the road when he'd looked out the window that morning.

The boy was gone now. If he came back, Ian planned on walking across the road and having a talk with him.

"Food is ready, Senhor Ian," came from the kitchen.

Daniela was fast and competent. They hadn't been home ten minutes. She wanted to prove her worth to him.

And he needed to show approval so she could stop worrying that he'd send her back to Rosa, but dinner was the last thing he wanted. Just thinking about eating hurt.

Even so, he got up, closing his eyes for a second as his head threatened to blow. She had cooked for him. The least he could do was try, so he shuffled over to the table.

The sight of the food didn't fill him with confidence. The two plates held nothing but razor-thin slices of fresh, raw fish wrapped around chunks of fruit.

She looked at him with hopeful expectation.

"It's the most appallingly healthy meal I've ever seen," he muttered as he sat.

And she smiled at him across the table with relief, obviously having no idea what *appalling* meant in English.

She picked up a piece with her fingers and shoved it into her mouth.

He did the same. What the hell.

His stomach didn't roil. Actually, it settled. Food gave the acid something to do.

He ate in silence. Maybe she sensed that he needed that, because she didn't say a word either as Ian cleared off his plate piece by slimy piece.

And he was glad he did, because the empty plate seemed to fill Daniela with joy and satisfaction. She smiled from ear to ear as she cleared off the table.

Next, she brought him some bitter-smelling tea from the stove. "You drink this, Senhor Ian."

The brew had the color and consistency of swamp water and smelled like an overused outhouse at high noon in hundred-degree weather.

Maybe she *had* killed Finch, and now she wanted to kill Ian.

Ian backed up. "No way."

Undeterred, she pointed at his temple. "Jungle tea for the head pain."

The food had helped a little, but his brain was still pounding so hard, just talking with her hurt. Either he went back out for some hard liquor or drank this swamp water. Since he didn't want to be impaired tonight, he drank the brew.

Jesus, Mary, and Joseph!

His stomach rolled.

He held still as if that could hold back an eruption.

And maybe it did, because as seconds passed, the nausea settled. And then, little by little, his headache began to fade.

"I think I'm keeping you forever," he said on a sigh, without thought, focused on the bliss of dimming pain.

She stood frozen to the spot, eyes glistening, and she blinked hard. The amount of innocent hope on her face was truly heartbreaking. And the admiration completely undeserved.

Ian pushed back his chair and stood. "You'll never go back to the Rosa bitch. I meant that." He filled his lungs with air that smelled of fish and rain, then cleared his throat. "We'll see about the rest. Now, let's get to work."

He sounded gruff, even to his own ears.

She sprang into action, happy as a stray at the offer of leftovers. "I'll clean, Senhor Ian."

"Forget that for now. We'll clean up together later. Right now, you're going to learn how to defend yourself." He moved to the living room, pushing the furniture out of the way.

Every piece was made of bamboo, except the couch pillows. He could see where things had been broken when the house had been ransacked, saw how she'd fixed things with rope and glue. She was industrious, he had to give her that.

He stood in the middle of the room and turned to her. "Attack me."

She paled. Stepped back. "Oh no, Senhor Ian."

He sighed. "Just Ian."

"Yes, Senhor Ian."

He shook his head. "You said if I let you stay, you'd do anything I tell you."

Her gaze dropped to his crotch. She hung her head, her enthusiasm leaking away. Her voice dropped to a whisper. "Yes, Senhor Ian."

Not that!

"Attack me," he snapped.

She looked up, her gaze unsure.

"We are *never* going to have sex." He was embarrassed just having to say that. And when was the last time he'd felt embarrassed, for fuck's sake? "We're not even going to see each other naked. Ever."

She was watching him, uncertain, disbelieving.

"Attack me," he ordered again.

No was written all over her. But here she had a dilemma, because she also wanted to please and obey him. After a moment of struggle, she carefully stepped up to him and kicked him gently in the shin with the tip of her toes.

Christ, they had a long evening ahead of them.

* * *

Daniela

Senhor Ian was a scary man. He was also a nice man. He confused Daniela to frustration.

He spent the evening ordering her to beat him up, until she had no choice but to fight him, as honestly as she'd fought the boys back in her village when they'd taken her coconuts. She hit him, hard. And he didn't hit her back. He patiently showed her how he was deflecting each punch.

Then he sent her to bed. In her own room. He did not tie her up again.

He'd told her they would not have sex. He'd also told her that he wouldn't send her back to Rosa.

So what did he want with her, then? He bought her food, let her stay at the house, and didn't want anything from her. She didn't understand him.

He must want something. But what is it? She had trouble falling asleep, trying half the night to answer that question.

She didn't consider running away. Where would she run? To do what? Even if she slept in the streets, she'd need money to eat. And if she slept in the streets, she'd be at the mercy of everyone who was stronger than she.

With what Senhor Ian had taught her, she could maybe fight off the village boys back home, but if a couple of loggers grabbed her, she wouldn't stand a chance.

She wished she could stay here, in this house, with Senhor Ian forever.

Not only did he not make her do things she didn't want to do, but he had said he would protect her. With Senhor Finch, she'd lived in the constant fear that Senhora Rosa would come for her. After Senhor Finch, the first man who realized that she was on her own could have taken control of her.

But now…Was she safe? The idea took time getting used to. She hadn't felt safe since she'd been a small child. She tried to relax into the thought, into the night, little by little. She couldn't.

Her thoughts kept returning to Senhor Ian.

He had pain deep in his eyes that had nothing to do with the pain of his headaches. Hidden pain. The pain of things he tried not to think about. Daniela recognized the look from the mirror.

Senhor Ian…

Senhor Ian acted friendly toward her, but Pedro too had been her friend once, then he'd given her to Senhora Rosa.

So maybe Senhor Ian was telling the truth about wanting to help her, and maybe he wasn't. But if he was…

Even if he was, he would leave someday. He'd only come to find his friend. And only stayed to find his friend's killers. When he did, he'd leave.

Daniela thought about that, and whether it'd be best not to help him.

***

Ian

Ian hated the bugs and the humidity and the heat, and the way Daniela would shrink from him if he spoke too loudly or moved too fast, as if she expected him to start beating on her any second. He wanted to find out who killed Finch and why, have his reckoning with the bastard, then go the hell home. After he made some sort of safe arrangements for Daniela.

He spent his second full day in Santana going around town asking about Finch. Other than Daniela, nobody knew that Finch had been killed, so Ian was playing it as if his best friend had simply disappeared, and Ian had come to find him.

That might bring the bad guys out.

His head hurt like a sonuvabitch. His insides felt jiggly. His hands trembled. He wanted a drink more than he wanted the rain to halt, the bugs to quit biting, and pickpockets to stop targeting him. Only Daniela's jungle tea, when they finally returned to the house that night, made life bearable. Without the nasty brew, he was pretty sure he would have caved.

But the next day, he went back out and kept asking his questions. Then the next day, and the day after that.

Wherever he went, he took Daniela with him. He didn't want to leave her behind alone, not when he wasn't sure what the boy he'd seen watching the house was about.

Ian kept an eye out for the kid. If someone had paid the kid to watch the house and report, maybe Ian could pay more and the kid would talk to him, tell him where he'd gone to give his report. Unfortunately, the boy disappeared.

A full week passed like that, nothing but an exercise in futility. Sunday night, after spending hours in town yet again, spreading the word about who he was and what he wanted, Ian finally returned home with Daniela just as empty-handed as he'd begun the week.

She cooked, something coconuty this time, and the meal went down nice and easy. Sure beat the fast-food burgers he would have had back home. After a week of her cooking, he barely even had acid.

She also made more jungle tea, for which he didn't know whether to bless her or curse her.

He watched her as he sipped his tea, trying to hold his nose. She was drying dishes. She kept the house in meticulous order. He usually fried some eggs for breakfast, and they grabbed lunch from a street vendor while they were out, but she cooked dinner every single day.

Falling into a domestic routine with her was oddly comforting and at the same time disturbing. After two years of being alone, did he like it a little too much? He knew one thing, he didn't want to get used to it.

He'd find Finch's killers, make them regret the day they were born, then he'd go home, back to his lonely bastard self.

He finished his tea. As always, it did knock his headache back a notch. Enough to move around without feeling as if his head would explode any second.

He pushed his chair back and stood. "Let's train."

She put away the last dry dish, then followed him to the living room without protest, maybe even some eagerness.

"Today, I'll *pretend* to attack you," he said. "Just pretend. I'm not going to hit you. I want you to do the moves I showed you before."

He stepped forward and moved to grab her slim shoulder. She immediately cringed. But even as she did, she turned to slip away from his grasp.

"Good. You're a quick learner." And she had good instincts.

He was beginning to understand that it wasn't that she couldn't defend herself, but that she'd been forbidden to. Whatever anyone told her to do, she'd been trained to do it. Rosa had probably instructed her not to resist, no matter what men wanted to do with her or to her.

"You don't ever have to do anything you don't want to," Ian told her now, emphasizing every word. "Do you understand? Not even if I tell you to do something. You just say, 'I don't want to do that, Ian.'"

Her large eyes dominated her slim face. Sometimes she had the most cartoonish, comical expressions, as if he was some rare foreign idiot the likes of which she'd never seen. At the moment, she was staring at him as if he'd lost his mind.

Maybe he had.

But he kept on with her training anyway.

She was scrawny but tough, had a certain wiry strength to her. And this wasn't about strength, in any case. Whoever might come after them would certainly outmuscle her. But they wouldn't expect her to have US military hand-to-hand combat training.

She would have the element of surprise. And that was all she needed to get away, in case for some reason Ian wasn't around to protect her.

He swung a punch.

She deflected like he'd shown her earlier in the week.

She got nearly everything on the first try. Her brain was as quick as her limbs.

"That's good," he said when she nearly swept his feet out from under him. "Let's try that again. Give it everything you got."

And she did.

They practiced until even he grew winded. Then they cleaned up and went to bed in their separate rooms. The next morning, they did everything all over again.

They settled into an easy rhythm.

By the end of the month, Daniela grew pretty good at self-defense and could speak English even better. She picked up everything insanely fast.

The boy who'd watched the house before still hadn't come back. Ian kept asking around town, but he couldn't find a single lead on Finch. He should have gone back home, but he didn't want to leave Daniela alone in Santana, not until he was sure she could fully take care of herself.

He stopped detoxing. His head no longer hurt; his hands no longer shook from lack of alcohol. He felt better all the way around, maybe because of the food she made from fresh ingredients every day. He hadn't felt this healthy and clearheaded since his army days. Staying was easy.

Another month went by.

He called his mother every other week, reassured her that he was doing well and was safe. And he promised, upon his return to the States, a quick visit to Connecticut.

"A long visit," she negotiated, then said, "I know you're down there on serious business, but try to live a little."

"I'm living."

"I can still hear the sadness in your voice. I'm never going to forgive Linda. I'm sorry, but I can't."

Ian stayed silent. He didn't want to talk about Linda. Linda and his mother had never gotten along. They were too different: Linda high-strung and a perfectionist, assistant director of accounting at one of DC's top firms; his mother as laid-back as they came, living on an organic farm in Farmington in a trailer she named Robert Redford, so she could tell everyone at the farm shop at the end of the day that she was going home to Robert.

She'd had a couple of good boyfriends over the years, but she'd never married. Ian's father hadn't stuck around past Ian's birth. Ian knew nothing about the man beyond his name.

"I want to talk to Daniela," his mother said. She knew about Finch's death too. She'd known and liked Finch.

Ian handed the phone to Daniela, and she chatted on with his mother, mostly about cooking and the weather. Daniela ended the call after ten or fifteen minutes, with a grin.

"Iris said I shouldn't let you boss me around. And if you do, you'll answer to her." Her eyes danced. "She said next time she's going to tell me some embarrassing stories about you."

He knew what his mother was doing, making friends with Daniela so she'd have one more chick to care about besides Ian, and she was mothering Daniela because she knew Daniela had lost her own mother.

Ian reached for the phone. Daniela didn't flinch.

She no longer cringed if he stepped too fast in her direction. She stopped expecting him to beat her if she as much as dropped a spoon. And, thank God, she started to believe that he wasn't going to expect sex from her. Ever.

If he had needs, he worked off the extra energy. He swam in the river. He got used to the heat and humidity. He even got used to the bug bites. Damn if the town wasn't growing on him.

The fishing was great, and he found walking in the jungle with Daniela oddly relaxing. When they hiked through the jungle, he couldn't think about anything else, not Linda and the twins, not the van in the river. His mind had to be on his surroundings one hundred percent. He had to watch out for poisonous spiders, snakes, plants, drug runners, and poachers. He couldn't afford to get distracted by the losses of his past or worries about the future. He had to be in the present.

In the jungle, Daniela was a revelation. She walked differently, talked differently—with more confidence—could literally run circles around him. The roots he tripped over, she seemed to be able to avoid without even looking.

She spotted flowers and animals that completely escaped him. One time, she found an orphaned baby monkey that had fallen from a tree.

Her face lit with joy as she picked up the small animal. "Can we take her home, senhor?"

And it hit Ian all over how young she was, how, of course, she'd want to play. All he did all day was go about his business, grumbling along, then force her into hours of self-defense training in the evenings. She spent her free time cooking and cleaning. She needed a playmate.

He considered the monkey. Cute little bugger. "You think you can train her into a pet?"

Daniela blinked at him. "Oh no, senhor. To eat. I could cook her so good, it'd be the best thing you ever ate."

He politely declined the offer.

Daniela was a ferocious eater. Once she figured out that he put no restriction on food, she ate whatever wasn't nailed down. But she moved around so much, she didn't seem to gain an ounce. While he studied the rain forest, wanting to learn this new environment, she spent their jungle trips foraging.

Ian didn't mind. Not even when she filled her pockets with grubs, then when hers were full, she asked to fill his.

The incredible variety of sounds and colors around him—playful monkeys, noisy parrots, stunning displays of orchids—seemed like the very dance of creation and filled him with a new kind of energy.

It was that energy that drew him down to the Rio Negro before dinner to watch the barges, tugboats, and the tourist boats that carried sunburned and bug-bitten foreigners with their too-large backpacks on the river.

A hundred or so feet from him on the dock, two fishermen were fighting, fists flying, the men shouting in Portuguese too rapid for Ian to understand.

Drunks and fights were pretty common in town. Yet Ian hadn't exchanged blows with anyone since he'd arrived here.

He could have gotten rough with a couple of pickpockets. He hadn't.

Maybe his boss in DC had been right. He'd fought as a punishment—punishment and distraction—to numb the pain. He picked up women for the same reason. He'd probably followed Finch to Brazil for the same reason too. And he'd stayed with Daniela because she distracted him.

Because if he didn't distract himself, then what?

Would he go into the river after Linda and Connor and Colin?

There'd been a time when he'd wanted to. But as he stood on the bank of the dark waters of the Rio Negro, it was just a river, not a solution.

He considered his current situation.

His only clue in Finch's murder was a guy who wore a white suit and had a scar on his nose. He could be anywhere in Brazil by now. Anywhere in the world.

Maybe the boy Ian had caught watching the house at the beginning hadn't meant anything. Certainly nothing had come of it. Nobody came.

And Ian couldn't stay in Brazil forever. For one, his visa would be expiring soon.

But before he left, he needed to fix Daniela up with an honest job that would support her. He decided to buy the house for her as a gift. A steady home would be good for her. Ian had looked into it, and Finch had been paying month by month, was currently past due.

Real estate was dirt cheap here. Ian had combat pay tucked away. He wanted to make sure Daniela wouldn't be anybody's victim again. She should have a bright future. She'd gone through an incredible change already. As she learned to defend herself, she gained self-confidence. She smiled more often, and not just because she thought it was expected of her.

So, Ian went back to the house, and, over dinner, he said, "I'll need to go home at one point. What do you think you'd like to do after I leave?"

She paled and shrank back as if he'd slapped her.

"You'll be safe," he promised. "I'm going to get you this house and see you settled. I'll help you find a job. I'll teach you how to shoot. I'll leave Finch's gun here with you. You'll be all right. You can make a good life here."

"I don't want to, Ian."

He stopped moving, his fork halfway to his mouth. She said *no* to him for the first time. *And* called him Ian instead of Senhor Ian.

He was so damn proud of her, but at the same time, he couldn't understand why she chose this moment to disagree with him. His plans for her future made sense. She'd be as safe as possible under the circumstances.

He set his fork down. "You'll be fine. You're strong, and you're smart. And I'll always be just a phone call away." Shit, even to his own ears, that sounded lame.

He'd be *thousands* of miles away.

Hurt filled her eyes.

Christ.

"You are not going back to Rosa," he emphasized.

She lifted her chin. "Rosa couldn't make me."

He didn't bother hiding his smile. "Damn right. You'd ice the old hag."

Daniela's voice gained confidence as she said, "I don't want to live in this house alone."

"What would you like to do?" If he could, he'd help.

She held his gaze, her clear green eyes steady. "I want to go with you, Ian."

And then the front window exploded.

CHAPTER
SIX

Eduardo

"Get the girl too," Eduardo Morais shouted the order as he sent his men into the house.

He'd seen Finch's friend. That guy wasn't going to respond to torture any better than Finch had. But the man seemed to have grown fond of the little whore. Maybe if they tortured the whore in front of him…

Eduardo wasn't going to fail his brother, Marcos, this time.

He stayed outside, at a safe distance, listening to the sounds of fighting, furniture crashing. A gun popped. Then another.

Few people were out on the street after dark, and those who were weren't bothered by the sounds of violence. They weren't much interested either. They took a look at Eduardo, dressed as an important man, in a suit, the silver of his gun glinting in his hand, and they hurried by.

The crashing and yelling continued inside.

Eduardo had brought six men from Rio. If he lost one or two…He was a businessman who understood the cost of doing business. And there was no way Finch's friend would fight off all six.

As if to underscore that thought, the house fell silent. No more crashes, no shouting, no gunfire. Just the sweet silence of success.

Now that's how you take care of business. Eduardo smirked to himself as he strode in. Then…*Meu Deus.* For a moment, he faltered.

Bloodied men covered the floor.

Six.

All his.

Fernando, the bald one, was shaking his head, coming to, his nose broken and bleeding. His shoulder stuck out at the wrong angle, dislocated.

Merda.

Fury burned through Eduardo. "What the hell happened?"

"They went out the back." Fernando gasped out the words in a nasal tone. "The whore can fight like a freaking ninja."

"What the hell are you talking about, you useless piece of shit?" Eduardo kicked him. "Get up. Get after them."

He finally had to help the guy up—carefully, so his suit wouldn't get bloody. Then the two of them, with guns drawn, hurried out back into the darkness together. Or, more correctly, Eduardo hurried, and the idiot Fernando limped behind him.

Something in the river caught Eduardo's eye as soon as they were down the backstairs. A white fishing boat chugged across the black water.

Monte de merda.

He ran to the end of the dock and knocked the sole fisherman coming home from the night into the water, jumped into the man's ancient motorboat, waited for Fernando, then headed after the people he was chasing.

Nothing but jungle waited on the opposite side of the river. The foreigner and the girl weren't going to escape him there.

* * *

Ian

Ian looked up from under the tarp that covered Daniela and him as they lay pressed together on the bottom of a small canoe stuck in the mud on the riverbank.

They were a tight fit lying down like that, but lack of room was the least of his worries. He was more concerned about poisonous snakes or spiders that might have bedded down for the night in the canoe. He hadn't had time to check.

"We'll go upriver." He whispered because water carried sound a little too well.

They climbed out and pushed the canoe into the water. He did look for other occupants in the moonlight then, but they lucked out. Nothing too scary save a few bugs here and there.

Daniela smashed the biggest one with her rubber flip-flop without missing a beat. "The bite makes you hear things that are not there," she whispered.

He gave her an appreciative nod. Tonight would be a bad night to start hallucinating.

They climbed in, then paddled hard, keeping to the river's edge where the current was much slower and more easily overpowered than in the middle. And here, near the bank, the shadows of overhanging trees would soon hide them.

Moving upriver in a canoe required hard work, but between the two of them, they managed.

Once the bastards who'd attacked them realized that the fishing boat Ian had sent across the river for twenty US dollars held only a lone, local fisherman, they would search for Ian and Daniela downriver. People fleeing nearly always went downriver. Easier. Just like on dry ground, people fleeing went downhill, nine times out of ten.

When you ran from someone, instinct said to get as far away from your pursuers as quickly as possible, so you picked the fastest path. Of course, most professional trackers knew that. Doing the opposite was a basic evasion tactic Ian had learned in the army.

He paddled hard, and the canoe made decent progress. They both put muscle into it, as much as they each had.

Daniela didn't burst into tears, didn't freak out, didn't go into shock.

He hadn't been sure she wouldn't. Being tough while training was wholly different from reacting to a live, armed attack where bullets flew at your head.

He respected the hell out of her for the way she'd responded. But at the same time, he hated that an armed ambush wasn't even the worst thing that had happened to her in her life. Being attacked by killers was something she could take in stride, and it hadn't been only because of the training he'd given her.

They passed two sleeping villages, each no more than a smattering of huts. Hours passed before they reached the next town, smaller than Santana. A brightly lit-up house sat at the edge of the water, sounds of music floating from inside.

"That's Rosa's house," Daniela whispered.

Ian's blood boiled. His paddle stilled in the water. He would have liked to have a few words with Rosa, or, say, set the damn place on fire. But now was not the time to cause that kind of disturbance. He began paddling again.

He wanted to know what Daniela was thinking, but she didn't say anything, and he couldn't see her face.

"How far is it to your village?"

"Another hour, I think."

She sounded winded. So was he. But he was willing to get more winded to get her to safety.

"We'll go there."

If the men behind them did search for them up this way, they'd search the first town they came across. They wouldn't think anyone would want to go farther, against the current, on the night river.

He didn't like doing it either. A floating log could easily capsize them. But Daniela sat in the front, and she had excellent night vision. He trusted her. He ignored his aching muscles and kept working against the current.

They reached Daniela's village in a little under an hour and a half. Fewer than a hundred huts scattered on a hillside, nothing but shadows in the scant moonlight. The village slept.

Ian and Daniela pulled up the canoe and got out. They didn't stop to rest.

Daniela took his hand and drew him forward. "I'll show you my home. We can spend the rest of the night in the hut."

Had that been excitement in her tone? She walked fast, clearly happy to be here. He followed her, ruled by entirely different emotions: anger and protectiveness.

He wanted to go from hut to hut and shake people. Why in hell had nobody protected her?

A couple of dogs ran up to them, but they were friendly—small jungle dogs to keep houses free of snakes and rats. They sniffed the visitors, then licked their hands, tails wiggling in greeting.

Goats bleated in their pens.

Daniela led the way up an overgrown path to a small hut that was leaning off its stilts, the roof in tatters.

The spring went right out of her step. She came to a lurching halt and stared at the ruin. And in the moonlight, Ian saw tears roll down her face for the first time ever. He'd seen her with tears in her eyes, seen her with tear streaks that one morning. But she had never once cried in front of him.

She cried silently now, her slim arms wrapped around her.

First he thought, *What the hell is here to cry over?* But then, in another minute or two, he began to understand. This had been her home. The hut symbolized her mother and what little childhood she'd had. This was where she'd come from, and it was just about erased, would be erased in another year. The jungle would claim the hut; the vines and weeds would simply overgrow the small ruin.

She'd had a hard upbringing, and yet...

Her past was a part of her, as Ian's past was part of him. Neither of them could divorce themselves from the things that had happened to them. And if they couldn't erase the past...

We will have to make peace, the thought came to him. *But can we?*

As he watched her, something in his chest began to ache—the first time in years that he felt he might still have a heart.

He didn't care for the feeling.

He liked his chest numb. Hell, he'd drunk barrels of whiskey to make sure his feelings were good and drowned and nothing could make them surface again.

Daniela wiped her eyes. Sniffed.

Ian wanted to give her a reassuring hug. He didn't. He'd put a distance between them for a reason, and he meant to keep it. But that didn't mean that he wasn't going to help her.

He moved over to the nearest tree, kicked the ground clean, and sat, leaning against the trunk. "If you want to leave the country, if you want to come with me, you're going to need some kind of papers."

He'd never seen anything at the house in Santana.

She walked over to him, stopping in front of him and looking down. "What kind of papers?"

"Passport?" He doubted she had that. "Birth certificate?"

She sighed. "I don't think so."

Looking at the village that could have come straight out of the Bronze Age, he believed her. "Did you ever see your mother with any papers?"

She sat down next to him, pulled up her knees, and wrapped her arms around them as she thought. For one minute. Two. Three. Then she jumped up.

"My mother kept a metal box buried in the ground at the back corner of the hut." She hurried over.

A metal box had potential.

"In the morning," Ian called after her, relaxing. He closed his eyes. "Let's sleep."

After a moment, she returned to the tree and sat back down. "Are you really going to take me with you?"

"We'll see."

She stayed silent for a while, but not for long. "You are not going back to Santana to take revenge for Senhor Finch?"

That was the question of the day, wasn't it?

He'd been a right idiot about that. He'd gone around town, asking about Finch. How in hell had he thought he was going to bait a bunch of killers and not have Daniela hurt in the process?

He could go off on his own, go after whoever killed Finch, figure out what in hell Finch had died for. But he'd have to leave Daniela here in the village alone, or send her off to some other place she'd never been.

Buying Finch's house for her to live in after Ian had gone back to the US wouldn't work. Ian cursed himself for being stupid enough to have ever thought of that as a solution. Finch's enemies knew the place.

Now that Ian thought about it, he hated the living shit out of the idea of sending her off alone into the great unknown. Which left one option: give up on taking out the bastards who'd killed his friend, and get her out of here.

Ian hated that option too.

But when it came right down to it, bottom line was, he wasn't prepared to sacrifice Daniela. For anything.

"We'll go someplace safe," he said. "To the United States if we can."

Then he could find her a safe place to live, set her up with a safe life. And *then* he could return to Brazil and take care of business.

In his pocket, he had a cell phone he'd picked up as they'd run from Finch's house. The phone had to have been dropped by one of the attackers in the fight. That cell phone would have numbers in its memory. And those numbers would lead him to names.

Daniela shifted next to him. She blended into the shadows of the tree, a part of the jungle.

Would it be a mistake to take her someplace else?

"If you could be anything, what would you be?"

She didn't have to think about it. "A teacher." Then she asked, "Did you always want to be a soldier?"

He'd told her that was how he'd met Finch.

Ian looked up into the starry sky. "When I was young, I wanted to be an astronaut. Someone who flies in a spaceship to the moon," he explained, in case she didn't know the word.

She thought about that for a moment. "But you didn't go."

"Turns out I have dyslexia. It's something in your brain that makes it hard to learn. Mine is not bad, just enough so I couldn't pass the test."

"I'm glad you didn't go to the moon," she said. "I think it's better that you came here."

He closed his eyes.

With jungle sounds all around him, he slept. And didn't dream about the van going into the Potomac. He rarely had that dream anymore. And thank God for that.

He woke up with Daniela's head on his shoulder. The sky was lightening over the village, some people already out and about. Even after two months in Santana, the village was something else, an alien landscape, the kind of place he'd only seen on TV before, on the National Geographic Channel.

He nudged her. "Wake up."

She blinked at him slowly, sleepily. It was the first time they'd slept together, since that first night he'd met her. A fine mist drizzled on and off, and the moisture had clumped her eyelashes together.

Ian pushed up and away from her, walked into the trees, then stepped behind a wide trunk to take a leak. Wished he could take a shower and have breakfast. He stayed there for a while, giving Daniela time to do whatever she needed to do this morning.

By the time he went back, she was digging at the corner of the hut with a bamboo stick.

He helped her and got himself good and muddy in the process. "Let's hope we'll find what we need."

In ten minutes, they had the box. It hadn't been buried deeply. Rope held it to one of the stilts, probably so the river wouldn't steal it if the floods reached all the way here and washed away some of the dirt.

They crouched behind the ruins of the hut, and he pried the cookie tin open. Its lid decorated with a picture of the Manaus Opera House, the box was a little rusted, but whole—it hadn't let in water.

Inside was a copper ring, and a medal carved from some kind of bone, hanging from a string. Next to the medal, they found a small wooden cross. And under it all, one piece of folded paper in a plastic bag: Daniela's birth certificate, stained but readable.

Ian released the breath he'd been holding.

He still didn't know much Portuguese, but he didn't need to know much to read the date.

"You're eighteen years old." Surprise pushed the words from him. "Your birthday was a month ago." He grinned. "Hey, happy birthday."

Daniela's eyes lit up, as if he'd given her a gift.

He glanced back at the paper and found another line that needed no interpretation. "This says your father is William Wintermann. Do you know who that is?"

He handed her the rumpled birth certificate and thought about how little the last name Wintermann fit her. Even Ian's last name fit her better. Slaney was a large river in the southeast of Ireland and the name of a Celtic goddess.

Daniela read through the sheet of paper, then, as fat raindrops began to splash all around them, she carefully put the paper back into the plastic bag and into the safety of the metal box.

She dropped the box on her lap, then blinked at him, rubbing her thumb over the tan skin on the back of her hand, as if trying to uncover another layer. "He's the village missionary."

The man who wouldn't let Daniela's mother be buried in the cemetery?

Daniela had told Ian the story. He wanted to choke the Wintermann bastard.

Before he could decide if they had time for that, and before Daniela could recover from discovering the identity of her father, a man plodded up the path, drawing their attention. He walked with the ambling gait of a water buffalo. And he looked like one too.

"Pedro," Daniela whispered.

Talk about people Ian wanted to strangle…

The man was watching the path in front of his feet and hadn't seen them yet. He was about two decades older than Ian, in his fifties, larger than the average Amazonian, and not a weak man. According to Daniela, he owned a store. He probably hefted plenty of crates.

The man who sold Daniela to Rosa.

Ian clenched his jaw so hard, his teeth hurt. He pushed to his feet.

Pedro looked up, startled, then his gaze slid over Daniela, once quickly, then once again, more slowly. His face lit up. "*Querida!*"

"We leave now," Ian whispered to Daniela, "or I'm going to start beating up people. Your choice."

She shook her head and stepped forward, a hint of unsteadiness in the step and in her voice as she said, "*Olá, Pedro.*"

Ian shot a look that warned *clear and present danger up to and including murder* at Pedro, but the bastard only had eyes for the woman in front of him.

"Daniela!" Pedro reached out and put a hand on her shoulder, ran his palm down her arm. And said something Ian thought might have been a question about why Daniela was here, followed by a statement that Senhora Rosa would not be happy.

As Pedro reached for Daniela's waist, Ian stepped forward, but Daniela was faster. Pedro hit the mud, flat on his back the next second. *Oomph.* He flopped in a quickly forming puddle like a trapped fish, yelling at Daniela, or trying, the air knocked out of him so the words came out wheezy.

Daniela stood over him, rain streaming down her face, and the scene reminded Ian of the first time he'd seen her, as she'd emerged from the river with that giant black eel. He half expected her to pick up a stone and bash in Pedro's head.

And maybe Pedro did too, because he stopped struggling and lay still on his back in the mud, staring up at her, his gaze reflecting surprise and confusion, then flickers of fear. The balance of power had shifted, and he knew it. The victim was victim no longer.

Ian wasn't going to stop her if she wanted to kick the shit out of the son of a bitch. He had a hard enough time stopping himself from doing it for her.

But instead of kicking Pedro in the face, Daniela grabbed Ian's wrist and drew him away, back toward the river, the metal box held tightly under her arm. "He's just an old man."

Because she wouldn't kick a man who was down. She was bigger than that. She was bigger than anyone in the small village who'd looked the other way while she'd suffered through hunger and worse.

She let go of Ian to walk in front of him on the narrow path.

Pedro rose and moved to grab after her.

Ian hit him. Just once. Hard enough to break the man's jaw.

Pedro went down again with a keening sound.

Daniela looked over her shoulder.

"He's overcome with remorse," Ian said as he followed her, the deepening mud doing its best to suck off his boots, but he kept up.

She walked barefoot toward the Içana, straight and tall, all that black hair streaming down her back past her waist, her steps graceful. *A river goddess.* She didn't look back at the hut or her village.

* * *

Carmen

Carmen stood in the middle of the empty house in Santana, her gaze returning to the bloodstained floors. Nobody seemed to know what had happened. But people in the neighborhood confirmed that a young woman fitting the description of the girl who'd gone missing from the brothel upriver *had* lived here, having shown up in the middle of the dry season. The timing matched.

"I think she was sold to someone that same morning that we wanted to rescue her." Carmen's voice rang hollow even to her own ears. "If only we'd acted a day sooner."

"You can't blame yourself for this." Phil shoved his fingers through his spiked hair. "God, I hate that we're late again." He looked like he wanted to punch a wall, but, Phil being Phil, he wouldn't.

Late.

The neighbors said the house had stood empty for at least a week now. The girl and the foreigner who'd lived here had up and disappeared.

Carmen looked away from the rust-color stains on the floor. "Do you think the man who was with her killed her?"

They kept bouncing the same questions between them, and kept coming up with the same infuriating lack of answers. But there was no one else to talk to.

They'd called the police. One officer came. Looked in. Said maybe someone had cleaned fish in here. Then he left. He couldn't have been less interested. The people who'd disappeared hadn't been local anyway. *How was this his problem?* his parting expression asked.

Phil drew Carmen into his strong, capable arms. "We couldn't help her, but we'll help others."

Carmen needed to believe that. She looked up at the man she loved, hot tears rushing into her eyes. "Promise?"

"Promise." Phil brushed a gentle kiss over each teary eye. "This is what I want to do. For the rest of my life. With you by my side."

If she wasn't head over heels in love with him already, she would have fallen right then and there.

Phil led her out of the house. Led her into town. Next to the market square stood a two-hundred-year-old Jesuit church. He stopped in front of that, pulled Carmen into his arms, and kissed her. "Let's get married."

"I told you I can't—"

He silenced her with another kiss. And he kept her silent for a good long time before he pulled back and said, "I told you I don't care about that. I love you. Everything else is negotiable. Marry me no matter what."

She stared at him, dazed, her heart filling with love and joy. "Here?" She still couldn't grasp it. "What? Now?"

"As soon as it can be arranged." And then he kissed her again. "Marry me, and then we'll tackle everything else that comes our way."

PART
TWO

CHAPTER
SEVEN

Four years later.

Daniela

"What are you doing later, Dani?" Bobby Olson asked Daniela as they walked across the George Washington University campus that buzzed with life, a jungle in its own way. "How about lunch?"

He'd been a graduate assistant in one of her classes—international human rights law. Since then, every time they ran into each other, he asked her out.

"Got lunch plans already."

Crystal, on her other side, snorted, "Get real, Bobby boy. She's got Ian Slaney to go home to."

Bobby bristled like a capuchin monkey whose papaya had been stolen. "Okay, I'm going to say it. It's weird that you're living with a middle-aged man."

Bobby was a full foot taller than Daniela, blond and fair, with the lean body of a college athlete—he'd been on the tennis team. Boy-band material. Except that he was also seriously smart. He'd finished law school since they'd first met and was now working at a law firm, but still showed up on campus periodically. He liked GWU's law library.

"Ian is not middle-aged," Daniela grumbled, while Crystal said dreamily, "I'd live with him."

Bobby kicked the gravel walkway, sending a spray of small stones flying in front of them. "You're not related to him, and you're not going out with him." He shot her a look he'd perfected for making people on the witness stand squirm. For when he got that far in his career. "Are you?"

"No way," Crystal cut in. "Ian Slaney is saving himself for me. I'm going to have his babies."

Daniela rolled her eyes. All her girlfriends were in lust with Ian. He'd come on campus to drop her off or pick her up often enough that they all knew him. During the academic year, she'd lived on campus, but she spent pretty much every weekend, summer, and holiday at his apartment. Now that she had graduated, she was going to live there permanently. And, hopefully, be paying half the rent soon.

"Hey, you know how the copper wire was invented?" Bobby angled for a change of subject, trying to cut Crystal off at the pass before she could launch into an ode to Ian's manliciousness.

Daniela shook her head.

"Two lawyers fighting over a penny." He grinned. Then asked again, "So lunch?" all charm and lighthearted fun. "Come on, Dani."

"Can't. I just popped in for my transcripts. I'm applying for a job."

"Why don't you take the summer off? Hey, a friend of mine is renting a house on Virginia Beach. Want to come?"

"Thanks. But I really need to find work."

She had a driving need to learn, to do, to help. Sometimes, in the middle of the night when she couldn't sleep, memories from Senhora Rosa's house pushed into her brain. How many of the other girls were still alive? Half? Less than half?

But Daniela *was*. And she was filled with gratitude for that, and a burning need to make her life count. As corny as it sounded, she wanted to make a difference. She volunteered with homeless kids, but handing out food and clothes and playing games wasn't enough. She wanted to do more.

"Good luck." Bobby immediately switched back to full support mode, a good friend. "I'm sure whatever you apply for, you'll get it. I'll take you out to celebrate. And if they're idiots and don't want you, I'll take you out to drown your sorrows. Dani, you'll get in if they have any brains."

Crystal linked her arm with Daniela's. "We'll all take you out."

Girlfriend to the rescue. For which Daniela was grateful, until Crystal added, "But you'll be paying. Because if you get a real job, you'll be able to afford it."

"I hope." She was making next to nothing at the campus bookstore, and that job would end in a week. The university liked to hire current students, and she was done here.

Summer classes were already in session, students everywhere, chatting lazily on the lawn or hurrying to and from classes on the walkways. They were of every size and shape, every color.

Bobby was Minnesota Viking. Crystal, her roommate for the past two years, was black, from Tennessee, her right leg a titanium prosthetic. She'd been injured in the army. She never tried to hide it. She wore a ridiculously hot, short orange-and-peach dress that molded to her curves.

Daniela liked jeans and T-shirts, the latter sometimes borrowed from Ian. Because she looked young for her age, she kept her hair in a sleek bun at her nape, for a touch of grown-up sophistication. She was about average height, average weight, darkly tanned compared to Bobby, pale compared to Crystal. The GWU campus was pretty diverse. She fit in.

That fitting in, the acceptance, the fact that nobody thought her strange, not even when, at first, she'd spoken with a heavy accent, was one of the things she loved about living in this country. People were all different, and it was okay.

Of course, nobody here knew what she'd been. She'd left Daniela and all she'd done behind in the jungle. Here, she was Dani—just another young, carefree student.

Four years ago, on the airplane from Rio, when she'd been suddenly scared of leaving everything she'd ever known, scared of what would become of her in a new, unknown world, Ian had said, "You're as good as anyone else. And you can be anything you want to be."

Back then, she hadn't believed him. What you were used to, no matter how bad, always seemed the safest. Because a new thing, an unknown thing, could be even worse. Like a monkey jumping from a snake in a tree and landing in the open razor-toothed mouth of a caiman.

But Ian had been tireless in convincing her. He'd woven a cocoon around her with his words and protection, months of teaching and coaxing. And when Dani emerged at last, he'd sent her off to college so she could spread her wings.

"Penny for your thoughts?" Bobby flashed a dorky grin. "I promise not to stretch it into copper wire."

Daniela rolled her eyes and smiled.

Crystal groaned. "God, you're hopeless, Bobby. Friendly advice. You ever find yourself in a courtroom, no jokes. The judge will hold you in contempt."

"I have an excellent sense of humor."

"Who told you that? Your cat?"

As the two bickered, they reached Daniela's clunker of a car.

She quickly slipped behind the wheel so Bobby wouldn't try to change her mind about lunch. "See you guys around."

She could have gone out with him; she had little else to do this afternoon. He was attractive. Kind. Funny.

She'd gone out with other boys, guys from her classes. She'd even slept with two. The first one because she hadn't fully understood yet that she could say no when somebody pushed. The second because she chose to, because she'd wanted to know if it felt different when it was chosen.

It hadn't.

She barely reached the entrance of the parking lot before her phone pinged. She glanced at it. Text from Bobby.

How about lunch tomorrow?

She didn't respond. Driving and texting was stupid. She'd tell him no when she got home.

Bobby was a great guy.

But she wanted…*more*. And she didn't feel more with Bobby. She wasn't even entirely sure what the *more* was, if it even existed. She'd seen love in movies, but movies made up a lot of things.

All she knew was that at her core coiled a longing, almost like hunger, a wistful feeling, an expectation of something, or the promise of it.

But sex just didn't really work for her. She wasn't sure she'd ever want a man—not the same way that Crystal talked about her dates. Maybe that part of her was irrevocably broken. Or taken away as punishment for all that she'd done.

She headed toward the Beltway. The last couple of months in school had been hell, trying to complete all the requirements so she could graduate. She anticipated spending the summer with Ian after he watched her walk across the stage in her cap and gown.

Ian was her best friend.

He still had a strong streak of protectiveness toward her. He also made sure she kept up with the self-defense lessons so she could take care of herself.

She liked his dry humor, that he got her and she never had to explain herself to him. She liked that he'd seen where she'd come from and yet her past never for a second mattered to him.

She liked the gruffness at his core, and even his somber moods, a contrast to the happy-peppy glaze of her college friends. When kids in her classes said *anything is possible*, they meant *anything good*. But Daniela knew that in life, bad things could happen, and Ian too understood that. Crystal also did, which was probably why she was Daniela's best friend.

She drove across town to Ian's 1900s three-story apartment building, went up to his third-floor apartment, let herself in, passed the IKEA hall table piled high with mail. "Hey, I'm home."

No response, nothing but silence in the apartment. The living room and eat-in kitchen stood empty, and so did the two bedrooms. She could see the whole place from the entry; all the doors stood open.

Maybe Ian had to go into work.

She texted Bobby back with a quick sorry, then dropped her bag, adding it to the general mess. Over the past week, she'd stuffed her college paraphernalia in every corner of the place, a beanbag here, an extra computer desk there, then all her potted plants—she'd found she couldn't live without being surrounded by green. But at least the place looked lived-in. When she'd moved out every September, the apartment went back to looking empty and lonely. And still Ian wouldn't budge about letting her stay.

He'd insisted on the dorms. He wanted her to have all the normal experiences any twenty-something in college would have. He wanted her to date, join clubs, go to parties, eat cold pizza with friends at three in the morning.

She dropped her paperwork in her room, then padded out into the kitchen. She'd learned American dishes, soups and stews, and spaghetti, knew how to flip a burger. But most of the time, she made something lighter, something with coconuts or plantains, something with fresh fish. She'd found a grocery store that sold cassava and sugarcane. The lighter food was better for Ian's stomach. God knew, he ate enough greasy takeout when she wasn't here.

A knock on the door, and Iris, Ian's mother, popped in, a jeans-and-T-shirt girl like Daniela. Her only nod to city life was exchanging her rubber boots for sneakers. She'd moved to DC a year ago. Connecticut winters had become too much for her. And she was getting too old for farming, so she retired.

"Daniela! I'm so glad you're here." Iris always gave a long, warm hug. Her hair was short and magenta this week—she liked experimenting now that she didn't have to worry about scaring the cows. She had a face like sunshine. Her smile never dimmed. Ian's occasional dark moods were completely absent from her.

Sometimes Daniela wondered if they were really related.

She hugged the woman back. Ian and Iris were her family. "Just in time for lunch."

Iris sniffed the air. "Are you sure I can't talk you into coming to live with me? That smells like heaven. But I can't stay." She gave a tragic sigh. "I only stopped by because I left my knitting here the other day, and I have a knitting club meeting tonight."

She looked around. "I see my reprobate son isn't home yet. I texted him that I was coming over. He texted back that the shop called that his car was inspected. He went to pick it up. I thought he'd be here by now."

She grabbed her purple knitting bag from beside the couch. "I'm keeping my eye on the weather for your graduation party. I can't wait. It'll be the first big party at my place. I'm praying hard that we won't have any rain so I can do barbecue on the balcony." Her eyes filled with moisture, but she never lost the smile. "I'm so proud of you, I could burst."

That was Iris. She radiated love like the sun radiated heat.

"Any news in the romance department?" she asked.

Daniela thought of Bobby and shook her head.

"I'm telling you what I told my son," Iris said. "I refuse to die without grandchildren. I'm prepared to live to a hundred."

She hugged and kissed Daniela again before she left, with a reminder that the following week they had a double shift at the activity center for homeless children. They did that together at least once a week, their girl time.

After Iris left, Daniela went back to cooking. Lunch was almost ready when Ian walked in.

"Hey." He stopped inside the door, filling the doorframe. He wore jeans and a black T-shirt that had been washed a hundred times and softly draped over his muscles. "I thought you'd be at the school today."

Ian wasn't college-boy handsome, but he did have a certain harsh, hard-edged masculine beauty that came partially from his well-built physique and partially from his eyes that were dark but not black, more the color of strong coffee, the color of the Rio Negro and the Içana.

As she looked at Ian in the doorway, a peacefulness fell over Daniela, a floating kind of feeling as if she was in the river, or that bliss of swinging in a hammock when rain pitter-pattered outside and all was well with the world.

She had the sudden urge to walk into his arms, lay her head on his chest. She blinked the odd thought away.

"I didn't have as much to do as I thought I would," she said.

He sniffed the air as he moved forward, scoping out the stove. "That smells good. Let me take a shower first."

And as he passed by her, she caught a faint trace of perfume.

Nicole.

Daniela hadn't met her, but she knew of her. Nicole was Ian's ex-neighbor from his previous apartment. They weren't going out, but they hooked up from time to time.

An achy soreness spread through Daniela's limbs; her stomach cramped. She'd been bitten by a poisonous bug once when she'd been a child. She'd known it at once, feeling just like this, like she was about to be deathly sick.

"I'm leaving tomorrow," Ian called from his bedroom. "Flying to Jordan. Just got a case assigned. Missing American tourist."

After they'd come to the US from Brazil, General Roberts, someone Ian used to know in the army, offered him a job at a new DOD department the retired general had put together. Civilian Personnel Recovery Unit. They found and rescued US civilians who disappeared abroad.

He popped his head back out the door. "I'm going to miss your graduation. I'm really sorry."

He looked sorry. Serious. Concerned for her feelings.

She turned back to the stove and said, "No big deal," over her shoulder.

"It is. And I want to be here. But there's no one else available to go to Jordan."

And how could she ask him to stay? He'd saved her. Now he was saving others. Daniela, better than anyone, understood what that meant.

She appreciated and admired what he did. She wanted to do the same thing with her life: help people. But…

Ian gone. Maybe for the whole summer.

She gripped the bamboo spoon a little harder. She didn't ask when he'd be back. He wouldn't know, couldn't predict whether this'd be a hard case or an easy case.

She stirred the food and didn't understand why she felt like crying. She touched her free hand to the middle of her chest, pressed her palm against the pressure building inside. The air felt too thick inside her lungs, like at the beginning of the rainy season, before the storms descended to shake the world.

Carmen

"I can't wait to be back in Brazil." Carmen Heyerdahl held her six-month-old daughter, Lila, on her lap as the plane flew over endless green.

She kissed the little girl's head. *So much for expert medical opinions.* Against all odds, Carmen was a mother.

Her happiness was a nearly tangible bubble around her, filled with that sweet, irresistible baby smell.

"Let's hope we won't get kicked out this time." Phil grinned at her, then winked at Lila. "You might as well know, my love. Your mother is a troublemaker."

Carmen cleared her throat and patted Lila's chubby little leg. "There were extenuating circumstances. When you grow older, you'll understand."

Four years before, they had busted a house of prostitution and saved two dozen girls. The local powers that be, however, had not appreciated their efforts, so they'd been asked to leave.

They'd gone to Africa, only returning to the States when, out of the blue, Carmen had gotten pregnant. Two sets of overeager grandparents had demanded the relocation back to the States and wouldn't take no for an answer.

Carmen looked out the plane's window, over the green ocean of the Amazon rain forest. "I want Lila to grow up traveling like this. I want her to know the world. I want her to know what's at stake."

They were going to Manaus on a volunteer vacation—a lovely concept of people visiting distant places that needed help, donating some time working while they were there. A good way to do some good while traveling inexpensively, since housing and food was usually provided at a reasonable cost.

Phil pulled a blue plastic fish from the diaper bag and handed it to Lila, who immediately stuffed one fat fin into her mouth. "She is going to love this trip."

Phil's book on the rubber soldiers had been a moderate hit, possibly going on to bigger fame now that some Brazilian lumber baron, Raul Morais, had decided to finance a fictionalized Hollywood movie based on the story.

Carmen smiled, content, relaxed, happier than she'd ever been. "If this goes well with See-Love-Aid, if it looks like we can handle things with a baby in tow, maybe we can come back full-time."

She'd missed the lushness of Brazil. Brazil was in her blood. They wouldn't have to go back to the same little town that had kicked them out. Manaus was a big city. If they liked it, they might come back to Manaus permanently.

Lila tossed her plastic fish, and when Phil snatched it out of the air, the baby giggled, kicking her little feet as if she were riding an imaginary bicycle.

Phil handed the toy back to her, then flashed a handsome, confident smile at Carmen. "We'll barely be here for any time at all. I don't see what could go wrong in two weeks."

***

Eduardo

As Rio pulsed with crowds of tourists and noisy traffic rushed on in the summer heat outside, Eduardo Morais pumped into his wife, the frigid bitch, in their equally frigid, air-conditioned apartment. If she still wasn't pregnant in another six months, he was going to get rid of her and try another. He'd been plowing her for close to six years already. For nothing.

The boring, docile daughter of a business associate, she'd been handpicked by Eduardo's father, Raul Morais. Eduardo had always done his duty by her, but he had his fun with his mistresses.

His father—fully recovered from the stroke four years ago—was forever on his case about a grandson. *An heir.* The old man required one male child from each of his sons. He didn't have any specific instructions on female children.

Unfortunately, neither Eduardo nor his older brother Marcos had been able to deliver the desired grandson yet. Marcos had two daughters. Eduardo had nothing to show for his efforts.

His father was almost as frustrated about the lack of grandsons as about Eduardo's and Marcos's lack of ability to produce money with honest work. Because, merda, even though the old man had broken every law to build his empire, he expected his sons to be above reproach and pillars of the community.

They were never going to be that, but they *had* come up with the money! Eduardo pounded away, fury propelling him as he thought of the past four years, he and his brother trying to find what had been stolen from them.

He slammed into his wife and tuned out her whimpering.

He had taken care of the thief. But the thief had had accomplices. If Eduardo ever laid hands on the bastards…

As he imagined, in great detail, what he would do, the blood that would flow, he came in a blinding rush.

He collapsed on top of his relieved wife, caught his breath, rolled off. "Get dressed."

She scampered away.

They were expected at his father's estate. Raul Morais was giving a dinner to honor one politician or another. Morais Timber held inconceivably large swaths of rain forest. Raul Morais often needed an easement or a way to slip around an annoying environmental protection act. Political friendships were carefully cultivated.

Eduardo cleaned up and put on his tuxedo. As he headed out to the elevators with his wife, he spared her only a cursory glance. She'd come from money and looked it. Her dress was a peach-color froth of silk, probably a gift from her sister, who was married to Hugo Romero, who owned a major international luxury boutique chain.

Down by the curb, a car waited for them. Eduardo's father had sent the chauffeured limousine that efficiently whisked them straight to Jardim Botânico, an upscale neighborhood in the south zone.

Raul Morais could easily afford a residence in nearby Leblon, the most expensive neighborhood in South America, but he didn't want to live in a skyscraper, not even if it came with a three-story penthouse that had its own rooftop pool and garden.

Not that the house in Jardim Botâanico lacked anything. At fifteen thousand square feet—not including staff quarters—it held every imaginable luxury, including a spa with a sauna and live-in masseuse. The grounds featured an elaborate pool, an equally impressive pond with a twenty-foot waterfall, and a small forest of palm trees.

By the time Eduardo and his wife arrived at the residence, the party was in full swing, the guest list a testament to Raul Morais's wealth. The politicians came to angle for campaign contributions. The business owners came for access to the politicians. The singers and actors had been invited to lend an extra layer of glamour to the evening, and eagerly accepted. Movies needed investors. Musicians too always needed backers. The strands of connections wove through the crowd, creating the fabric of money.

Eduardo set his wife loose and went to find the old hyena. Must greet him first. The king would want his due. And he always got what he wanted.

Raul Morais stood near the elaborate parrot enclosure, surrounded by politicians who courted his favor. The stroke he'd suffered four years ago had left its mark on his once-powerful body. He listed slightly to the left, and he'd grown thinner. Yet without doubt, he was the most powerful man present. His eyes were the same bottomless black, his gaze sharper than a machete.

As Eduardo joined the group, his father nodded at him. "Excuse me, gentlemen, I need a word with my son."

They were, of course, all smiles, patting Eduardo on the shoulder, dear-boy this and dear-boy that.

Eduardo followed his father into the house, into his mahogany-paneled study.

"Marcos," the old man said to one of the staff, and the guy hurried off to fetch the older son.

Joaquim, the butler-bodyguard, stayed with them. He'd done a stint with the 1° Batalhão de Forças Especiais, the 1st Special Forces Battalion, the rough equivalent of the US Delta Force. He was at least two meters tall and over a hundred kilograms, dark skin, close-cropped hair, square jaw, kind of a horse face. He looked like a death machine and was incredibly loyal.

"A drink, senhor?" Joaquim asked Eduardo.

"No, thanks." He'd best keep his wits about him.

Marcos walked in with a full glass already in hand.

"Father." Then he shot a what's-this-about look at Eduardo with "Brother."

Joaquim poured the old man some cachaça, a Brazilian liquor made from actual sugarcane juice—unlike its poor stepbrother, rum, made from the leftovers of the main sugar removal process. The glass replenished, Joaquim stepped back into the corner. He did his best to blend into the furniture, but he was about as invisible as a water buffalo at the ballet.

Raul Morais sank into the leather chair behind his ornate mahogany desk that sat in front of equally ornate matching bookshelves. The entire study had been bought from the castle of some Portuguese nobleman, in the north of Brazil.

Looking at Raul Morais now, nobody would guess that he was a son of the favelas, the miserable slums of Rio. Or that his father had been one of the *soldados da borracha*, "rubber soldiers," men who'd been taken to the Amazon during World War II to produce rubber. Some said a hundred thousand men had been taken into the rain forest, some said more. Few made it home. Eduardo's grandfather had been one of the survivors—the toughest of the tough.

His son had taken after him.

By the time Raul Morais was sixteen, he'd thieved, prostituted to rich tourists—both male and female—and killed, in self-defense. By the time he was eighteen, he'd fallen love with a girl, Maria, who'd done all the same things to survive. When, a year later, one of their favela's famed gangs had beaten Maria to death for poaching on their territory, Raul killed again. This time in a hot fury that left three gang members dead.

To escape being hunted down, Raul had gone as far as he could from Rio, two thousand miles, up to the Amazon his father had escaped, then up the Rio Negro, up the Içana, and joined a small logging operation.

"Back when I started," he said now, "going into the rain forest and coming out with whatever you found was still legal. You cut it out—it was yours. You dug it out of the ground—you got to keep it. Not that I ever found anything. Rumors would fly about gold in one river or the other, but I never had any luck with that. I stuck to logging."

Eduardo exchanged a look with Marcos and leaned against the richly carved column behind him. Sounded like they were in for some serious reminiscing. The old hyena got like this from time to time, usually a precursor to lecturing his sons. First the tale of his long, arduous rise to riches, then his disappointment with his useless sons, who weren't fit to follow in his footsteps.

"Living off logging was as miserable as living in the favelas, except even harder work," the old man said with a pointed look. "Back then, loggers worked with mules instead of heavy machinery. Between the snakes, the bugs that carried disease, and the frequent accidents…" He shook his head.

His hard gaze pinned Marcos first for an uncomfortable moment, before moving to Eduardo. "I've done all the hard work. And now it's your turn to prove to me that you are worthy of taking over the empire I created from nothing. Do either of you have something to tell me?"

Eduardo and Marcos wouldn't look at each other. Eduardo hoped Marcos would say something. Marcos was probably waiting for him.

The old man's tone carried a warning as he said, "There isn't much time left."

No, there wasn't. Less than a year. Barely six months, in fact.

It'd been nearly a decade ago that Raul Morais had laid down his ultimatum. He'd paid for his sons' educations, then after college—which had taken them a number of extra years to complete due to a shared tendency to get distracted—he'd given each a million dollars to start out. Eduardo had been twenty-nine. Marcos had been thirty.

The deal had been whichever of them turned their starting capital into enough money to be able to purchase just two percent of Morais Timber within the next ten years would inherit the entire business.

But if neither of them succeeded, the business was going to the old man's younger brother, their only uncle.

Raul Morais put down his glass. "I didn't build Morais Timber to leave it to useless sons who'll run it into the ground after me. You are going to need to prove that you can handle a business. And that you can handle it honestly."

He let a weighty pause hang in the air before he finally went on. "I did all the dirty work. I did whatever I had to. I have reached as high as I can. But my sons can reach higher. A senator or president. Your dealings must be impeccable."

"We are running an honest business, Father," Marcos pointed out, speaking through gritted teeth.

The old hyena snorted with derision. "A worthless little security outfit. It's not the scale I'm looking for." He fixed them with an unforgiving look. "Can either of you come up with the money I require before I can consider letting go of the reins?"

"Yes, Father," Marcos said.

And Eduardo added, "I certainly will."

They *would*, somehow, together.

No time for another grand scheme. Which meant they had to go back to one of their failed schemes and somehow fix it.

Raul Morais dismissed his sons with a wave.

They walked out together but didn't talk. The servants always listened.

The brothers communicated with looks. They'd always been able to do that, had grown up as close as if they'd been twins. They'd always shared everything growing up. And they continued the practice into adulthood, sharing money, drugs, even, on occasion, a woman.

The old man had thought his challenge would make strong, honest men out of them. He thought competition would make each try harder. He'd pitted them against each other. Only one could inherit. The old hyena would not split his empire.

They, however, hated being in competition against each other, so right at the beginning, they agreed to work together. Their chances of coming up with enough money together were a lot greater than doing so separately. Then one of them would take the money to their father, receive the entire business, and share with the other brother at that point. There'd be nothing the old man could do but hiss and spit.

Diamond mining was big business in Brazil. They'd begun there. They'd invested everything.

Within two years, the small mine they'd financed—along with a number of other investors—went under, taking most of their money with it. They'd gained nothing but experience, a fair grasp of the industry. They'd learned, for example, that mines invested most heavily in equipment and in security. The labor itself was cheap.

The Morais brothers hadn't had enough capital left to get into equipment manufacturing. But they had enough—once they'd borrowed from all their friends with promises of immense returns as soon as they had Morais Timber—to start a company that specialized in mining security.

Getting into that side of the business was a whole new kind of education. The men in their employ were mercenaries who administered the law of the jungle: you stole from a mine, you died.

Surrounded by tough men, having tough men like that answer to them, Marcos and Eduardo began to feel tougher themselves. They were the lords of life and death. After years of prep schools and colleges and all the usual rich-boy pursuits, they felt like real men at last. After partying aimlessly through Rio during their twenties, now, in their thirties, finally, they began to feel like true macho men.

They spent most of their time on location, at the mines, with their mercenaries. They grew stronger, rougher. Their grandfather's survivor genes and their father's favela blood prevailed. The brothers took to the work of intimidation and violence like caiman to water. Began providing security for other industries.

The business was actually turning a profit. But not fast enough. They had to accept that they were not going to have the capital they needed from honest work.

So they'd stolen what they needed. But then, infuriatingly, it'd been stolen from them.

While they'd been tracking the foreign thief four years ago, the old hyena had had a stroke, and they'd thought all their problems would be solved.

Once their father was dead, the brothers would simply contest the will. But the old man had pulled through. And his security was tighter than an anaconda's asshole. Impossible to have him killed.

"Morais Timber goes to us," Marcos said under his breath once they reached the other side of the pool, where party guests were a little thinner on the ground.

Eduardo nodded. "We have six months left. I say we throw everything we have at finding the thief's little friends."

The American and the whore.

Somebody had to know where they went.

CHAPTER
EIGHT

Carmen

"Should we take her down?" Carmen looked at her daughter sleeping peacefully in the crib at long last after an endless, fussy night.

The full humidity of the rain forest filled the room, while city sounds—cars, busses, shouting vendors—filtered in from outside.

Phil cast a bleary-eyed look of disbelief from across their small room at See-Love-Aid's Manaus facility for abandoned girls. "Do. Not. Wake her up."

Carmen checked the crib, the mattress covered with a snug sheet, the baby sprawled on top. The room was too warm for a blanket. A mosquito net hung from a hook in the ceiling, tied to the corners of the crib. No way could it cover the baby's face.

"All right," she said. "I'll just go and grab something and bring it up. You can stay down, if you want."

Phil yawned, then pushed his fingers through hair that no longer stood up in spikes. He'd begun thinning on top. And still as sexy as ever, Carmen thought.

"I'm going to park myself next to the coffeepot and stick by it until it's empty," he said as he shuffled out of the room, scratching a fresh bug bite on the back of his arm.

Carmen followed behind him, leaving the door open a crack.

Heather was coming down the hallway—a petite brunette wearing a sarong made of a colorful local print—balancing two plates of eggs in one hand, two coffees in the other. Heather and Hannah, sisters from Oregon, were part of the permanent staff. They shared a room two doors down from Carmen and Phil.

"Lila is sleeping," Carmen told the woman. "Would you mind keeping an ear open for her?"

Heather smiled. "You go have breakfast. If that precious little girl fusses, I'll pick her up. It's a treat. You want me to sit with her?"

"You go have breakfast with Hannah. I'll be back in a few minutes."

She felt comfortable leaving Lila with Heather. Other volunteers were in their rooms too. Carmen knew that if Lila cried, half a dozen people would jump to make sure the baby was okay.

Lila was See-Aid-Love's first baby in residence. All the staff, the volunteers, and even the girls they took care of, were in love with her and spoiled her rotten. When the baby wasn't napping, she was passed from hand to hand and cooed to, sung to, rocked, danced with.

Carmen followed Phil down to the cafeteria, a sprawling room filled with tables and chairs, breakfast passed out through a window that connected the space to the kitchen. Carmen accepted a plate with thanks, then grabbed a cup of coffee.

Out back, girls were having a basketball game, from the sounds of it. The *pat, pat, pat* of the ball filtered in, along with the occasional wild cheering. They must all be out there; the cafeteria held only adults: most of the permanent staff and all the volunteers who weren't upstairs.

But then some girls did come in, four of them, carrying a small sisal mat and heading straight for Carmen and Phil.

Rafaela, Gabriela, Camila, and Luiza. Carmen had been memorizing the names. They wore Salvation Army T-shirts decorated with the logos of US sports teams, and looked like typical American high school kids. Except their noses were not in fancy phones.

"For Baby Lila." The oldest girl, Camila, presented Carmen with the mat, woven in intricate patterns, a jungle scene with lianas and birds.

"Oh wow. This is so beautiful." The design's lines were all exact and tightly woven, not something Carmen could do in a million years. "You guys are real artists. I'm going to hang this above the crib."

The girls looked at each other and giggled.

"It's not a picture," Luiza said with the exaggerated patience teenagers had for adults. "It's a changing mat for the baby."

"No way. It's way too nice to mess up. I'm going to treasure this. Thank you, girls."

Since Carmen had her hands full with breakfast, Phil took the mat. "I'll bring it up in a minute."

They both thanked the girls again, then Carmen headed up, listening for Lila as she plodded up the stairs. So far, so good. The baby wasn't screaming.

The hallway too, when Carmen reached it, was quiet.

She walked into their room silently, not wanting to wake her daughter, hoping to eat her breakfast in peace.

The crib stood empty. Oh well, Lila *had* woken up, then. Maybe that wasn't a bad thing. If she stayed awake during the day, she might sleep a little more tonight.

Carmen put her breakfast on the nightstand, cast the plate a last longing look, then headed to Hannah and Heather's room. Their door stood open a crack. Carmen knocked and peeked in.

The sisters were both reading the local paper, drinking coffee. Heather glanced up. "She didn't fuss."

And since they didn't have Lila, Carmen asked, "Do you know who took her?"

Heather frowned. "No. Not us. She didn't make a single noise. We've been listening."

Carmen went from room to room. Some stood empty, others had people getting ready for the day. No Lila. Nobody had heard her cry or seen her.

Maybe she'd fussed and someone had taken her down to the cafeteria to find Mommy and Daddy. Carmen went back down. She'd bring the baby back up so at least Phil could eat in peace.

But Phil was sitting at the end of the table with a handful of other volunteers, no baby. He looked a little perkier. He was probably on his second cup of coffee.

"What is it?" he asked as Carmen headed for him.

"I can't find Lila. Have you seen her?"

He shook his head. "I'm sure somebody has her."

"Not upstairs." And not in the cafeteria. The place was half-empty now, easy to scan at a glance.

Carmen's heart began to race.

Phil stood. "Let's check the rest of downstairs."

They searched, just the two of them at first, then the staff helped, then the girls. They checked every inch of the building.

Nobody had the baby.

CHAPTER
NINE

Ian

In Washington, DC, Ian headed to Karin Kovacs's office—his boss at the Civilian Personnel Recovery Unit, a new department at the DOD that dealt with recovering US citizens who'd gone missing abroad. He was back from nine weeks in Jordan and was about to be assigned a new case. He wondered where he was going next.

Maybe Brazil.

Four years ago, when he'd come back to DC with Daniela, returning to work as a bouncer at a bar wasn't an option. He'd quit drinking. And he'd needed a paycheck that could support two people. CPRU seemed perfect. When he'd been hired, he asked to be considered for any Brazilian assignments. He wanted to get back down there, wanted to take another look at Finch's murder.

He hadn't given up on that. He hadn't told Daniela, but he was working the case through the Internet and phone calls. The cell phone dropped by one of the men who'd attacked him and Daniela in Santana hadn't panned out—a burner phone—but Ian was moving heaven and earth to find another clue. The bastard who'd taken out Finch was a dead bastard; he just didn't know it yet.

But maybe he'd find out sooner rather than later. Fingers crossed for a Brazilian case.

Ian knocked on his boss's office door, then opened it and stared at the woman sitting across the desk from Karin.

Professional black pumps. Sharp, professional gray suit. Hair in a sleek, perfect coil at her nape. Daniela lowered the manila folder she was holding to her lap as she turned to look at him.

He froze in the door. "What are you doing here?"

Last he'd seen her, this morning, she'd been eating cereal in her pajamas in the kitchen. Although, she *had* acted weird. Preoccupied. He'd felt her staring at him, but every time he looked at her, she'd looked away.

"Ian, why don't you sit, and we'll catch you up." Karin gestured to the empty chair.

Tall, pale, and blonde, the boss was Daniela's opposite. She could have been a *Vogue* model, but she would never do anything as frivolous as that. She was brisk, incredibly intelligent, a consummate professional, dedicated to assisting Americans around the world.

Ian lowered himself into the seat next to Daniela as carefully as if the seat cushion was stuffed with scorpions, his every instinct screaming that he wasn't going to like what was about to happen.

His instincts didn't fail him.

Karin said, "I just hired Miss Wintermann."

Ian's blood pressure shot into the two hundreds.

He gritted his teeth and flashed a we'll-talk-about-this look to Daniela, and that was all he had the time to do before Karin landed the next punch.

"I'm teaming you two up for a recovery op in Brazil. Leaving immediately."

Over his dead body.

He was going to take the case alone, like he always did. CPRU didn't partner up its investigators anyway, except under the rarest circumstances.

"Who is the recovery target?" He fought to remain professional. He couldn't exactly argue with the boss, but he *could* make Daniela withdraw her application. They were going to discuss it as soon as they got home.

"Lila Heyerdahl, a six-month-old baby, stolen from US aid workers, Carmen and Phil Heyerdahl. Time is of the essence. She has to be recovered before she gets sold into the illegal adoption circuit, or…"

She didn't finish the sentence and didn't have to. Ian had worked a number of human trafficking cases since he'd come to CPRU, including sex trafficking. He knew damn well the industry had no lower age limit. He didn't even want to think about that. The depravity of some of his fellow human beings made him sick to his fricking stomach.

Karin went on with "I was trying to decide what to do with the case when Miss Wintermann called me. She's perfect for the job. We're lucky to have her."

Daniela called CPRU for a job? When?

"She hasn't had her training." Ian ground out the words, pain blooming to life behind his right eye, making him wonder if he was going to have an aneurysm before this meeting was over.

"Which is why she's going with you as your partner. She requested you specifically. I understand you know each other fairly well."

Did she know that, for the moment, they lived together? Maybe not. Karin had no reason to memorize Ian's home address. Even if Daniela had put the same address on her application, probably nobody would make the connection.

He gave a curt nod. And he felt the need to punch something. He'd been so good about that. Barely beat up anyone lately. Just the odd kidnapper.

Karin must have seen something on his face, because she said, "Miss Wintermann is from Brazil, so she knows the country, and she's fluent in Portuguese. She's a woman. A lot less threatening, large, and obvious than you are. She can pass for local. She'll be able to get into places, talk to people you might not be able to reach. I'm bending the rules here, but I'm not letting a six-month-old baby be lost. After having talked with Miss Wintermann, I'm confident that she can be a valuable asset to this mission."

"I'm aware of Miss Wintermann's experience." Ian clenched his jaw so tightly, it wouldn't have surprised him if he spit out teeth when the meeting was over.

Karin handed him a folder that looked identical to the one Daniela was holding. "The details are in here. Your flight leaves tomorrow. I suggest you both go home and start packing."

He nodded as he got up and didn't say anything else, because he didn't trust himself to speak.

He strode out into the office bull pen, which was—*thank fuck*—empty, since it was late in the day. He couldn't handle chitchat at the moment. Even Elaine the office manager had gone home, her desk by the entrance deserted, the wall next to it wallpapered with grandbaby pictures.

Daniela followed Ian out into the hallway. "Please don't be mad."

He didn't reply. He marched up the stairs and kept going. He didn't open his mouth until they were in his car in the parking garage. "I want you to call Karin and quit. I'll take the case."

He flashed her the look he usually saved for kidnappers. And that showed just how serious the situation was, because for as long as he'd known her, his driving need had always been not to intimidate her but to protect her. Today, for the first time, he *wanted* to scare her.

And of course, she decided not to be scared.

A stubborn light came into her eyes. "No."

"What do you mean, no?"

They were friends, but it was more of a guardian kind of relationship, where he guided her and protected her, and she did as he asked, had almost always done as he asked, from their first meeting.

Daniela put on her patient face. He disliked that look. It made her seem all mature and always made him feel juvenile, as if somehow they'd had a sudden role reversal.

She said, "Remember back in Santana when you were teaching me how to protect myself and you said I'd never again have to do whatever other people told me, including you?"

"*Except* me. I'm pretty sure, I said *except* me."

She shook her head.

A couple of cars passed. Nobody paid any attention to the two of them.

"Don't be stubborn about this."

She kept the patient look. "I'm declaring my independence."

If she began talking in Cantonese, he wouldn't have been more taken aback. "You've always been independent. I never tried to—"

"You didn't. You made me independent. But now I'm declaring it for myself. Because I'm an adult."

"You're twenty-two."

"Exactly my point." She flashed a confident smile. "I graduated from college."

"Yes!" He grabbed on to that. "You finished pre-law, and now you're going to apply to law school. You want to study international law. You want to be a human rights lawyer."

"You want me to be a human rights lawyer." Her eyes and voice held gentleness, as if she was trying to let him down easy.

What the hell was happening?

"I want to help people in bad situations," she said. "I want to be there with them. I know you'd rather have me safe in an office. But that's not my dream."

"Since when?"

"You saved me. I want to do that for others. It's important to me."

He let his head drop onto the steering wheel. Tried to think. True, he had been the one to send away for law school information packets. But only because law school had been her dream. Hadn't it?

"At first you wanted to be a teacher."

"That's because the missionary was the most respected person I knew. I wanted to be respectable. It's not like I had a wide variety of occupations to choose from in my village."

He clamped onto that as he sat up and faced her. "See, you wanted to be like the missionary because that was all you knew, and now you want to do what I do, but only because it's the one thing you've seen up close and personal."

She gave him another patient look. "Give me some credit, Ian."

And he had to, because, God, she was so damn bright. She'd gotten her GED and was in college within a year of him bringing her to DC. And she finished pre-law in three years. She had a brain that, once set free, soared like the harpy eagles over the Amazon. She could be anything. She didn't need to risk her life in some damn hellhole halfway around the world.

His forehead beaded with sweat. He needed to turn on the car, blast some AC, and get out of here. He didn't.

He couldn't make his brain work.

He could not, absolutely could *not* tolerate the thought of Daniela being in danger. The idea made acid bubble up in his stomach, and he didn't have stomach problems anymore, dammit. He wished, for the first time in years, that he had a drink handy.

"Do you want me to drive?" she suggested softly.

"No," he barked back, despite knowing that she could drive as well as he could. He'd made sure she'd taken defensive driving classes—at the same level as Secret Service agents did. He had a buddy in the business and called in a few favors.

Just like he'd made sure she'd had the best weapons training a civilian could get short of joining the military. And she had self-defense training to the point where the only reason she couldn't beat him was the extra eighty pounds he had on her.

He accomplished what he'd set out to achieve: Daniela Wintermann would never be anyone's victim again. What he hadn't ever dreamed was that she would use her self-confidence to disregard his advice, advice he was giving for her own good and safety.

"Where is your car?"

"I took the subway. I don't have a parking pass yet."

With resignation, Ian backed out of the parking spot and drove out of the parking garage. Part of him liked that she had grown into a strong woman, strong enough to stand up even to him. But, now what the hell? Because no way was he going to let her rush headlong into danger.

"We're going to make a great team." She was smiling.

He grunted.

She laughed, and the soft trill of her laughter filled the car, filled the space all around him, and maybe even inside him.

God, he had a hard time staying mad at her when her laughter was his favorite sound on earth. He'd known her for over a year by the time he'd first heard her laugh. And she still did it too infrequently.

"Okay, so no law school, but why not something else here in the US?" he asked as he drove into the bright sunlight from the dim parking garage. "Even in the government." He grabbed his sunglasses from the visor. "You speak three languages fluently."

She grew up with Portuguese, learned English, then she'd taken up Spanish in college. She soaked up languages like a sponge. If there was something she couldn't learn, he hadn't seen it.

"I'm grateful beyond words for what you've done for me." Her tone turned serious, her eyes solemn. "You ever need a kidney, Ian, you say the word. But I'm going to start making my own choices."

She managed to be gentle and firm at the same time. And completely adult. While he felt like throwing a fit like a kid.

He drew a slow breath and tried to dial back his frustration a notch. "I thought you were applying for positions at a couple of nonprofits."

Only a flinch of her eye betrayed her frustration. "The best they had was making photocopies in some tiny cubicle on the twenty-fourth floor of an office building in the middle of the city."

He watched her. *No, that's not for her.* She was all life and sparkle. She needed to be out there, needed to be free.

"I can't believe you went behind my back to apply for a job at CPRU." He winced. *Shit.* He was playing the guilt card now? He was turning into an old housewife.

"I can't believe I had to," she responded.

She always had an answer for everything.

"You need to listen to me on this—"

"Stop acting like you're my father!" She didn't exactly snap, but her tone was tighter than it had been so far.

Then, as he opened his mouth to answer, she stopped moving and just stared, the light slowly going out of her eyes until she looked stricken. "Is that how you see me? Like a stupid kid? Because I have never thought of you as a father figure, ever. I'm an orphan. I've always been an orphan. I don't need a father. I don't want a father. I don't want a big brother. I want..."

He waited for her to finish, but she didn't. She looked out the passenger-side window, away from him.

A black limo cut in front of them, diplomat license plates. Typical mid-day DC crazy traffic, everybody in a rush, tourists darting across the road to provide an extra level of difficulty. Ian focused on that to keep himself from saying something he might regret later.

"I didn't go behind your back to be sneaky," Daniela said. "I just—I wasn't sure if I'd get in. I didn't want to tell you until I did. I wanted you to be proud of me."

She still wouldn't look at him.

He'd hurt her feelings, and he hated that he had. But he hated the idea of her overseas, on dangerous assignments even more. "You don't know the first thing about this kind of work."

"Karin has been giving me an orientation for the past three hours." She tucked a stray lock of hair behind her ear. "And you can teach me the rest. You'll be with me every step of the way."

"No."

She finally turned to look into his eyes. "I already have an idea how we can approach this. When you and I get into Manaus, you could get in touch with the local trafficking network. We could pretend that you're selling me to them. We'll lie about my age."

His turn to look away. He stared straight forward. He pressed his lips together so hard, he was losing feeling in them. And he didn't say another word to her all the way home, which made him feel like a fricking drama queen, but he didn't trust what he might say if he opened his mouth.

Selling. Her. To traffickers.

The acid in his stomach grew into a lake. With piranhas that chewed on his stomach lining.

He pulled into the condo parking. She could probably tell that he was having a silent shit-fit, and she was waiting him out, maturely. And he *tried* to calm down as they marched up to the third floor. He didn't succeed.

He rented a two-bedroom condo for them in a safe neighborhood. Each bedroom had its private bath. Lots of sun, big kitchen. Lots of IKEA furniture, because she loved the store. She was like a kid at a playground there, trying every armchair and every bed. And she'd put together most of their furnishings, loved the puzzle, loved building things, her face shining with the pleasure of accomplishment.

He loved watching her when she was like that.

Right at this moment, however…The top of his head was about to blow off. He couldn't remember ever being this scared and mad at her.

We could pretend that you're selling me…

"Can we talk now?" she asked.

"We. Are. Not. Pretending to sell you to anyone." He ground out the words. "Ever!" His voice rose on that last word.

He wanted to grab her by the shoulders and—The tension in the room was throwing enough sparks to catch the curtains on fire.

Before he could say or do something he might regret later, he marched off. "I'm taking a shower."

He needed time. He needed some ice-cold water to cool his anger. He needed a lobotomy.

He let that cold water pound him. *Okay. No big deal.* She was an adult. She was a very capable person. He'd always known that eventually she would assert her independence by refusing his advice. He could live with that. He wanted that for her. He wanted her to be happy.

He just didn't want her anywhere near a human trafficking case in Brazil.

By the time he was toweling off his hair, padding naked into his bedroom, he almost convinced himself that they could have a reasonable conversation, after which she was going to make the reasonable decision.

She was waiting for him inside the bedroom door.

They never entered each other's bedrooms.

He hadn't set it as a rule, but he never entered hers, and she'd taken his lead. Until now.

"What the hell, Daniela?" He snatched the towel from his shoulder and wrapped it around his waist as he jumped back into the bathroom.

* * *

Daniela

"Well, that's one stupid rule broken." Daniela couldn't move.

Her body felt as if she was in the last mile of one of their ten-mile runs. When she was here, they often went for runs in the morning, to the Lincoln Memorial and back, up one side of the Reflecting Pool and down the other.

Her heart pumped harder; her blood raced.

She'd seen other women stare at Ian when he wore running shorts and no shirt, but to her he'd always been just…Ian.

And now…Now her heart wouldn't slow down.

"What rule?" His words came out winded.

She could see him through the open bathroom door. He was facing the mirror, hands braced on the sink, his back to her.

She couldn't look away from his wide shoulders, from his naked, muscled back. She was as bad as Crystal. When did that happen?

Over the summer. While he'd been in Jordan, and she'd missed him so much, she'd slept in his bed. And dreamt of him.

She'd dreamt of men before—those had always been nightmares.

But her dreams about Ian…

On impulse, she strode up to him, pressed against him from behind, and let her hands slide around him and up his chest, her palms resting against his hot skin.

She laid her cheek against his bare back. "Remember when you said we were never ever going to see each other naked? I think I hate that rule. I'm glad it's over."

She couldn't touch anyone else like this, but she could touch Ian. She trusted him to the bottom of her soul.

"Daniela." His voice carried warning. He was vibrating with tension.

Everywhere they touched, her body burned. She almost laughed out loud. She wanted Ian the way a woman wanted a man. Because she was…*normal!*

The pure, sweet desire that tingled through her was a thrilling surprise and an incredible relief. She wanted him, and she wanted him to want her too. She wanted to make him see her not as a waif, but as a woman.

If he didn't want her because of her past, she could accept that. But if the only reason they weren't together was because he insisted on seeing her as his responsibility, someone who needed his protection…

"Daniela." He sounded strained as if he was struggling to move some great weight. "Please leave my room."

"I want us to be lovers." She tried on the thought by saying the words.

"Christ. No." He twisted away from her and nearly ran through the room, dragging on jeans under the towel, grabbing a T-shirt to take with him, dashing out the front door barefoot.

The door slammed shut behind him.

Daniela leaned against the doorframe of his bedroom and looked out into the empty living room.

That had *not* gone well.

She didn't know what to do with Ian's reaction any more than she knew what to do with her physical attraction to him. But now she at least understood why her attempts at dating had been a disaster. Of course, the boys at college had never been enough. Because all along, she'd been comparing them to Ian Slaney.

Subconsciously, Ian was her measure of a man.

She didn't want anyone else.

He'd always supported her in everything, understood her. So why not in this?

For a moment, she was hurt. And then she was angry.

She grabbed her gym bag. She needed to work off some of her confusion and frustration. *Capoeira* would help.

Of course, even the sport was something Ian had given her—one of a million gifts.

When she'd moved to the US, at first she'd wanted to leave her past completely behind. She loved America; she just wanted to be an American. Ian had encouraged her to be proud of her rich heritage.

There's not one thing wrong with you, or bad about you, he'd repeated to her daily when she'd felt like she was just a dumb, backward girl from a bamboo hut in the middle of nowhere.

He was the one who'd first encouraged her to keep cooking Brazilian dishes. And sometimes they spoke to each other in Portuguese. When Ian insisted that she take up some kind of self-defense training, she'd chosen Brazilian capoeira and had fallen in love with it.

Capoeira combined martial arts with dance, acrobatics, and music. She took to it like a monkey to climbing. She'd even placed in a competition. Ian had told her he was proud of her.

Ian who'd just run from the idea that she was a grown woman who wanted him.

And yet...

As she drummed down the stairs, a slow smile spread on her face, and she had to suck in her bottom lip and wrap her arms around her gym bag so she wouldn't start laughing like a lunatic.

She had just seen Ian naked!

She texted Crystal to let her know that she got the job, and was going on assignment, so they wouldn't be able to hang out for the next couple of weeks.

Crystal texted back her congratulations, and a promise to take her out to celebrate when she got back.

Daniela put her phone away as she reached her car. Before getting in, she glanced around to make sure nobody was watching, and she did a little dance.

She was going on a mission with Ian!

CHAPTER
TEN

Ian

Ian said, "No, thank you," to the flight attendant when she offered him a glass of *Caipirinha*, the national drink of Brazil, even if at the moment he was more tempted to go back to drinking than he'd been in the past four years.

Daniela slept next to him, her dark lashes fanning her cheeks, a picture of innocence. As if she would be no trouble at all. *Sure.*

God, he desperately wanted everything to go back to normal.

She wanted the job, and she wanted a relationship with him. He'd had a stern talk with her, but she'd refused to give up both. Technically, she'd refused to give up either. But, magnanimously, she'd given him time to think about the relationship.

She negotiated like a pro. She knew him too damn well, and that was the problem. She'd known his arguments before he'd made them.

Christ. A relationship. Between the two of them. In what universe would that ever be right?

Not that she wasn't a beautiful woman. Men kept looking at her. When they did, Ian glared them down. Even so, some little fucker had managed to sidle up to her at the airport and buy her coffee.

Ian wanted her to have a boyfriend. He wanted her to have a normal life. Just not with that guy.

Truth was, she was stunning. She'd filled out, grown curves, kept her black hair long, and had a wild beauty, a certain Mother Earth kind of wholesome way about her. She was *very* clearly a grown woman. Some guy was going to be damned lucky to end up with her.

But she wasn't for Ian.

Wanting her would be fricking damn wrong, and that was the end of it.

She was as bright as a torch in the night jungle. She was all youthful energy and beauty and innocence. And he was a worn-out, jaded soldier. He had no right to her. She'd already brought him more happiness these past four years than he deserved.

They were going to find the missing baby, while he kept Daniela safe, then they would go back home, and he'd get started on the task of finding her an appropriate boyfriend.

She needed someone. She'd had a few dates in college, but nothing serious, nothing steady.

And Ian needed to start seeing Nicole again.

Without his drunken binges, his one-night stands had disappeared long ago, and he wasn't going back there. Nicole and he were on the same page, wanted the same thing. No feelings. No complications. He needed Nicole. Because if he didn't have someone in his life, it'd be as if he was saving himself for Daniela, which would be just plain wrong.

Also—he grabbed on to his next thought with the desperation of a drowning man—if he found Daniela the right kind of boyfriend, then she'd have someone else to watch over her, and Ian could go back to the house in Santana and finally figure out what had happened to Finch.

Ian kept his thoughts firmly on that topic for the rest of the flight.

They got into Rio in the late afternoon, an hour past their scheduled arrival since the pilot had to fly around a major storm. At least they didn't have to wait for luggage claim since they'd each brought a single backpack, which they'd taken as carry-ons. He didn't know where they'd end up in the course of the investigation, and they couldn't exactly be running around in the jungle with suitcases.

Once they passed through customs, they went straight to their hotel, some local chain, midpriced, a place that fit in the DOD's budget.

He'd called the local investigator from the plane, and the guy called him back just as they were checking in at the front desk, so Ian walked away to take the call and left Daniela to handle check-in.

He was still on the phone when she headed for the elevators. He followed her, ending the call.

"Everything okay?" she asked.

"We have an appointment first thing in the morning."

They got off on the sixth floor—beige walls, green tile floor. He followed her to room 605.

As she opened the door, he held out his hand. "My key?"

"We're sharing a room." She sailed inside without looking at him.

He stood in the doorway and felt a headache coming on. "I reserved two adjoining rooms."

She dropped her backpack on the king-size bed...the *only* bed. "The storms last night damaged the roof. They had to close off the whole top floor."

He followed her into the room, but not without caution.

The lobby *had* been hopping. With unhappy guests? But still, he couldn't shake the feeling that this was some scheme of hers in her sudden, unreasonable quest to change their relationship.

Then he heard distant clanging somewhere above them. The barely there whine of a drill. *Right. Repairs.* And he felt guilty for suspecting her of dishonesty. She wasn't manipulative.

The room was medium size, just the bed, two nightstands, a dresser with TV, and a desk with a chair.

He dropped his backpack in the corner by the window, as close to the air conditioner as he could get. "I'll take the floor."

She smiled at him, her jungle-green eyes as innocent as a baby dolphin's. "We'll take turns."

She might not have arranged for the shared room, but the turn of events didn't make her unhappy.

She sat on the middle of the bed cross-legged and opened her laptop. "I'll sign into the Wi-Fi and keep going with the online research."

They'd spent the first half of the flight gathering information on the missing baby's parents and on the organization that had brought them to Brazil. See-Love-Aid was a nonprofit that took regular people on international trips that were part vacation, part charity work. Lasting two weeks at the longest, the programs fit into most people's vacation schedules. *Micro Missions*, their home page said.

Not the worst idea Ian had ever heard. See-Love-Aid might be on to something. From what he'd seen on their web site, they'd taken a quarter million people on helping-hand vacations last year alone, and their numbers were growing.

Daniela bent over the laptop in the middle of the bed, all beauty and grace, her long black hair loosened from its usual strict coil and falling over her shoulders to touch the beige coverlet.

Ian rubbed the back of his neck, some weird nervous energy buzzing through him. "I'll go out and look around."

Before she could respond, he was out the door, and, in another few minutes, out of the hotel.

And then he could finally draw a full breath.

God, the two of them spending the night in the same room was the worst idea ever. Hopefully, by tomorrow night, the hotel could give them an extra room.

He wiped his forehead. He felt as if he was swimming in heat and humidity instead of walking.

The city was loud and colorful and alive, more so than any other city in the world. Rio had an undefinable, mesmerizing quality. The streets pulsed with life. Even the air smelled different, lush and fruity, salty from the sea breezes.

Four years ago, he'd been here briefly, looking for Finch, then he'd found Finch's trail and followed it north, to Santana.

Finch had come to Rio to work security for the headquarters of a sugar-cane conglomerate, Lavras Sugar and Ethanol.

Ian hadn't really looked into the business the last time he'd been here. He'd hurried off to catch up with Finch. Back then, he hadn't known that by the time he'd catch up with Finch, Finch would be dead.

Finch had been killed in Santana in the house by the Rio Negro, but he'd been in Rio when he'd left that message for Ian about having to go on the run. So it stood to reason that Finch's troubles had begun in Rio de Janeiro.

On impulse, Ian took a cab to the headquarters of Lavras Sugar. He'd spent an insane amount of time researching them on the Internet but hadn't found anything in the news, in legal reports, or on the employees' social media pages that could explain what had happened to Finch.

"How would I go about getting a job with security?" he asked the mustachioed guard at the gate.

He was shown to the HR department.

The woman behind the desk, still a beauty in her mid-fifties, smooth skin, deep brown eyes, long dark hair—handed him forms to fill out. After the question, *How have you heard about our company?* he put: *Recommended by former Lavras employee, Ronald Finch.*

He didn't have time to go undercover here right now. The best he could do was throw bread on the water and see if he got a quick nibble.

For a phone number, he gave his cell. For an address, he gave the street and number of an apartment building he'd seen on the way over. Since Daniela was at the hotel, he didn't want to lead anyone there.

If Finch had been running from somebody at Lavras, and the bad guys wanted to talk to Ian, they wouldn't find him at the address he provided. They'd have to call him. They'd have to make an appointment, probably pretending a fake job interview. At least he'd know when he'd be meeting them and where, and he'd be prepared.

On the way out of the building, he pretended to get confused and got off on the wrong floor.

Offices, offices, and more offices, drab gray industrial carpet, neon lights, cubicles. Damned if he saw anything worth killing for, or even anything interesting. So he went back to the elevator, as someone who'd just gotten lost would, and left the building.

Sugar.

He wasn't aware of any big conspiracies involving the sugar trade. Ethanol had more potential. Ethanol, or ethyl alcohol, was a drinking alcohol. However, it was also beginning to be used as alternative fuel. The fuel industry was cutthroat. That had possibilities.

Instead of taking a taxi, Ian decided to walk awhile, give himself time to think.

Did Finch get involved in something like industrial spying?

Finch had headed straight north from Rio. Probably trying to get out of the country but not daring to go to the airport for fear that whoever was after him would be watching for him there. That they had pursued him likely meant that he'd taken something, confirmed by his own words "sweet little package" in his phone message, and also by the fact that his house on the Rio Negro had been searched.

Ian turned those thoughts over and over in his head. He ended up walking longer than he'd intended, all the way back to the hotel. The room was dark, Daniela sleeping in bed. He breathed a sigh of relief.

He cleaned up in the bathroom, then went to lie down in front of the window where she'd made up a bed for him from the bedspread, a pillow, and a sheet.

The cover was plenty; he didn't really need anything. Even with the air-conditioning, the room was warm. If he'd been alone, he would have slept naked. As it was, he kept on his boxers and pulled the sheet up to his waist.

He lay on his back, staring at the ceiling.

She shifted on the bed.

"Linda was twenty-one when you married her," she said.

Christ. His shower must have woken her. "We're not talking about Linda."

"There's a lot we're not doing," she grumbled.

He closed his eyes. He was going to turn gray by the time this mission ended.

A romantic relationship between the two of them would be a mistake. He was determined to save her from that blunder.

When they'd first met, they both had been a mess, just in different ways. And he'd thought, what the hell, one of them should be put back together. He'd helped her fit into her new environment in DC, helped her lay down the foundations of a good, safe life, a life she would enjoy living, where she could reach her full potential.

And what a woman she was now. If he'd helped her, it'd been the best thing he'd done in his miserable life. But he wasn't going to cling to her. She was the rocket, destined for the stars. He was the fuel tank on the rocket booster that propelled the rocket for a while, but then fell away, fell back to earth.

He willed himself to sleep, reaching up for a moment to rub the ache in his chest. Apparently, falling back to earth hurt.

***

Daniela

Daniela waited for Ian to give up on the hard floor and come to bed. She pulled the sheet to her chin. She was excited about this next step, but that didn't mean she wasn't nervous.

Sleeping in the same room with Ian somehow made even the air different, thinner, and full of tingly tension. Daniela lay on her side and watched his shadowy shape as he lay in front of the window with his back to her, his wide shoulder outlined by the barely there moonlight.

When she'd first met him, she'd been scared of him.

Then he'd become her safe place.

And now…

She felt different around him. *Happy. Confused.* She felt full of possibilities. Another door had opened. She wasn't sure if she deserved another door—another new thing, another good thing.

In college, when she'd gone out with a guy and he touched her, she'd been an observer. She'd felt as if she was having an out-of-body experience. She'd been evaluating what it felt like—good or repulsive. She'd been trying to figure out if she could handle it. She'd been trying to tune out the emotions those touches brought back, so she didn't run screaming and make everyone think she was a lunatic.

With Ian…

She wanted him to be next to her. Just feeling his skin against hers, having her head on his shoulder would have made her happy. She wanted to lay her palm over his ribs and fall asleep feeling his heartbeat.

Lately, the tension she felt inside her chest when they were around each other was nearly unbearable. She was aware of every move and sound he made. She wanted him to look at her, then when he looked at her, she didn't know what to do with herself, what to do with her hands, what to say.

"Ian?" she whispered.

He didn't stir.

She'd tried to talk him into getting off the floor. He wouldn't. She'd tried to switch places with him, but he wouldn't do that either. He was like a great boulder, unmovable.

Maybe she was crazy to try. Except a tiny spark deep inside her heart told her she wasn't.

This trip was it. She'd graduated from college. She had a job. The same job as he had. They were partners. If he didn't finally see them as equals, he never would.

So the next morning, as they sat in the office of the head of the human trafficking division at the Departamento de Polícia Federal, Daniela was determined to be extra professional and useful.

"The Heyerdahls arrived in the country on July second," the federal commissioner, *delegado*, said from behind his metal desk, reading his notes.

He was an attractive man, swarthy good looks, close to forty, tall, well proportioned, well-spoken, with nearly accent-free English, someone who would come across well at press conferences.

"Carmen and Phil Heyerdahl," the delegado went on, "along with baby Lila spent one day in Rio for their See-Love-Aid orientation, then they flew to Eduardo Gomes International Airport, in Manaus."

All that checked off against Daniela's notes.

"I understand they were with a group," Ian said.

The delegado consulted his papers again. "Twenty-one people."

"Is it common for volunteers to bring their children along? As young as six months?" Daniela asked.

"I'm not certain," the man said. "You would have to ask See-Love-Aid."

"Then you don't mind if we stop by their offices this afternoon?" Ian asked in a deferential tone that was a lot more subdued than his usual growl.

The man flashed a photo-op quality smile. "Not at all. We have investigated thoroughly, you understand. But we would be, of course, very happy if you found something we hadn't. The United States has our full cooperation."

Daniela liked the sound of that.

Brazil and the US were negotiating some kind of a trade treaty, Ian had told her on the airplane, so they would likely get the full benefit of the spirit of cooperation. Looked like he hadn't been mistaken.

They talked with the delegado for another amicable half an hour before Daniela and Ian left.

"That was a waste of time," she said in the cab. "We didn't learn anything new."

"Courtesy meeting." Ian looked at his phone, probably to see if anything new had come in from the office. Two seconds later, he put his phone away. "We just needed to check in and have the federal commissioner's approval. Now the real investigation begins."

They didn't wait until that afternoon to visit See-Love-Aid. Ian gave the cab driver the address, and the man took them straight to the organization's headquarters.

A graying woman in her fifties met them, Cristina Luiza Sousa, Vice President of Operations. She spoke perfect English, with an accent only slightly heavier than Daniela's. She had warmth in her smile, fierceness in her eyes, and toughness in her carriage, the kind of woman who could rule the world given half the chance.

When Daniela got around to posing her question again about children on the tours, the woman said, "We do have children in nearly every group, but usually teenagers. Toddlers or younger children are pretty rare. Lila Heyerdahl was the youngest we've ever had. Her parents are experienced. They've worked both in Africa and South America before. This is their second time in Brazil, actually. They missed the work after the baby was born, from what I under-stand, but didn't want to commit to something more involved, so they decided to do two weeks with us. We anticipated no problems."

"And they're still in Manaus?" Ian asked.

"Yes. They don't want to leave without their daughter. Understandably." The woman smoothed down her skirt. "We put them up at our See-Love-Aid lodging. We'll do whatever we can to help them and the investigation." Her voice wavered. "We are all heartbroken."

Daniela thought she was telling the truth. That haunted look in her almond-shaped brown eyes couldn't be faked. Cristina Luiza Sousa really did care, wasn't just concerned with how it looked for her organization or how she could fend off a lawsuit.

Daniela liked the woman on the spot. Senhora Sousa was a strong, self-possessed female who'd dedicated her life to helping others. Daniela had very similar plans for her own future.

Ian asked a few more questions. Senhora Sousa answered all of them.

He treated the woman with respect and deference. And Daniela thought, *Is this what I would have to achieve for him to see me as an equal?*

They didn't uncover any great clues at See-Love-Aid headquarters, but Senhora Sousa gave them a list of everyone in the group the Heyerdahls arrived with, and the three-page application each volunteer had filled out. She already had signed releases from the volunteer visitors to hand over to the local police. Everyone had agreed to fully cooperate with any investigation that might recover the baby.

Ian and Daniela also received Senhora Sousa's permission to visit the See-Love-Aid project in Manaus and interview the employees. Senhora Sousa would call ahead and make sure that the US investigators had everyone's full cooperation.

"How do you feel about going up north?" Ian asked in the cab on their way back to the hotel.

Daniela shrugged. "I knew we'd end up in Manaus. That's where baby Lila disappeared."

He half turned toward Daniela, his full attention on her, his voice soft as he said, "We'll be close to your village."

"I don't want to go there," she answered his unspoken question.

Maybe she should want to. Maybe he'd expected her to want to go home. But to her, *home* was Ian's condo.

"I'm not the same Daniela that Pedro took down the river to Rosa's."

"I know."

"I just feel…" How could she ever explain this? "It's as if my mother's hut and the people I grew up with…they belong with a different Daniela in a different world. If I go back, then I'll be that Daniela again, the one that did all those things." She rubbed her arm, her skin feeling too tight and dirty. She pressed her thumb into a spot below her elbow until it hurt.

"You haven't done a thing wrong." Ian's tone was certain and fierce. "Wrong was done to you. You are as good and pure as anyone I know. There's not one thing wrong with you or bad about you."

"You don't know all that I—"

"I don't need to."

They both had topics they never discussed, and never even thought about if they could help it. Ian never brought up Linda and his twin sons, Connor and Colin. He'd told Daniela about them once, briefly, just the facts. And refused to have any kind of conversation about them since.

Daniela felt the same about her life in the village and at Rosa's. Growing up, she hadn't understood what she'd done was bad. She'd simply grown up in that life. Her mother, Ana, had been…what she'd been. The village had accepted them that way. And all the girls at Rosa's had been the same as Daniela.

When, in her childhood, the missionary had talked about "sin" during sermons, Daniela hadn't truly grasped the concept. Only after she'd moved to DC did she discover that most people would find her past shocking and wrong and shameful. Thinking about her childhood made her feel…if not worthless, then certainly worth less than others. So she'd locked her past away. *All that* had happened to someone else, someplace far away.

Except, now she was returning.

There is not one thing wrong with you, or bad about you, Ian had told her probably a dozen times a day at the beginning when she'd shared her doubts with him. And he made her repeat the words, *There is not one thing wrong with me, or bad about me,* until she'd believed them.

In the cab now, in Rio, the memories of those days with him made her heart swell. She smiled.

He raised an eyebrow. "What?"

I want you to see me as a woman. "Nothing."

Was this what lust was, this unbearable ache, this need to be with another person, the need to have him see her, truly see her, all the way to her heart?

An odd thought, because, as it was already, Ian saw her more truly than anyone ever had. How could she want more?

She set that question aside to concentrate on the kidnapping case.

Once they were back in their room at the hotel, she connected to Wi-Fi and tried to get them on a flight to Manaus, but the last flight for the day was sold out, so she arranged for tickets on the first flight in the morning.

The thought of spending another night together in the small hotel room had her stomach doing cartwheels.

They had a working lunch in their room, organizing notes, reading through the visiting volunteer profiles they'd received. Who knew, maybe one of the Heyerdahls' fellow travelers had something to do with the baby's disappearance.

"Just because human trafficking and illegal adoptions are a large problem in South and Central America, it doesn't mean that's the only possibility," Ian said as he looked up from the printouts he was holding. "Plenty of little kids disappear in the US every single day for a whole bunch of reasons."

She nodded. "We just need one clue."

"We'll find it. And then we'll find the baby." Ian's eyes held a fierce glint, his entire being focused.

Six months old. Daniela's breath caught. Baby Lila was the same age as Ian's sons had been when he'd lost them. That knowledge had to cut him.

"Ian? If you ever want to—"

He held up his left hand to stop her, while flipping through the printouts with the right.

Of course, he wouldn't want to talk about it…Daniela watched him for another few seconds, then turned back to her laptop.

They worked until six, until they squeezed every ounce of information from the material they had.

If any of the visiting volunteers had anything shady in their pasts, they hadn't put it on their application forms. Zero clues there.

"What do you want to do with your evening?" Ian asked.

She wanted to get out of the room for a while. "Can we go down to the beach?"

CHAPTER
ELEVEN

Ian

Ian had a bad feeling about the beach, and his premonitions were justified. As soon as their feet hit sand, Daniela's yellow summer dress flew off, leaving her in nothing but an indecent bikini that turned an alarming number of male heads.

Ian looked at the blue water of Guanabara Bay instead, at the hulking shape of Sugarloaf Mountain in the distance. But then he stole another glance.

Okay, fine, the scraps of golden fabric she wore actually covered more than what most women had on around here, the bottom not a thong—thank God, or they would have had to take him out in an ambulance. The top too covered…everything.

Yet somehow, Daniela still managed to draw every eye within a square mile. Or at least that was how it felt to Ian.

He dropped to the sand. Burned his ass. Welcomed the distraction.

"Aren't you coming into the water?" She came to stand right in front of him.

He looked at her small feet. Did not raise his gaze above the ankles. "I didn't bring my swim trunks."

He wore cargo shorts and a T-shirt, as undressed as he planned on getting.

The small tanned feet turned. She ran away from him into the waves and laughed in delight as the warm ocean hit her.

Now that she was far away, it was safe to look.

She was something in the water, always had been. Water was her element. All her insecurities melted off her there. In the waves, she was still and forever a river goddess.

She frolicked. Carefree like this, she was more beautiful than ever. Ian couldn't take his eyes off her.

Neither could any other man.

A blond surfer yuppie made his way over to her to chat, trying to talk her onto his surfboard from the looks of it. The guy was tall, with *some* muscle, and bronzed skin.

Without a single glance back at Ian, Daniela headed farther into the waves with him.

Now Ian wished he'd brought swim shorts. Because the little bastard was putting his hands on her. Maybe the help was necessary to get her on the board, maybe it wasn't. Christ, the guy knew her for what, half a minute?

Is this how pickups work now? "Hey, wanna ride my board?"

Ian felt about a hundred years old all of a sudden, and pissed enough to want to drown surfer dude in toilet water.

He wanted to go back to the hotel, but no way in hell would he leave Daniela alone with the guy. And if noodle dick put his hand on her one more time, Ian swore to God…

She laughed, the water carrying the sweet sound straight to Ian.

He closed his eyes. Drew a deep breath.

The guy with her looked to be in his early twenties. Daniela needed this, to be around boys her age. Back when she'd been in college, Ian had hoped she might bring home a boyfriend eventually, but she never had. He'd been prepared to be *completely* open-minded.

She was twenty-two now. She deserved romance in her life, someone who adored her, treated her the way she deserved to be treated. And Ian was *not* to get in the way when that young man showed up. But no way was it going to be this surfer dude. *No way.*

This one grinned like an idiot.

Daniela was way more mature. She could do better than this one. Hell, ten times better would still not be good enough for her.

She'd been sharp as a whip today at both interviews, asked all the right questions, paid attention, took notes. The op was going to go a lot easier because of her presence. Under different circumstances, Ian wouldn't have minded being partnered with her permanently. They complemented each other.

He was more the silent type, better at action then interaction. She was all smiles and able to pop out one question after the other. People responded to her youthful eagerness.

He watched her play in the waves, happy. Idiot boy's hand on her lower back now, *dammit*. Ian glared. Once she was back in the room with him, they were going to have a talk about touchy-feely little bastards.

Ian kept a close eye on the guy.

When they came out of the water, they sat on the sand some distance from Ian, chatted. Too far to hear. Then they went back into the water again.

This went on until the sky turned dark.

Ian's mood was darker.

Finally, surfer dude said good-bye. Then asked something. Daniela shook her head. He kissed her on the cheek.

That brought Ian to his feet.

But the guy was walking away already, and Daniela ran up to Ian, laughing.

"You didn't have to wait here. You could have gone back to the hotel."

"I like looking at the water. It's relaxing." His jaw hurt from being clenched for the past hour. His blood pressure was probably in the stratosphere.

Daniela kept grinning, falling in step next to him as they walked off the beach. "He asked me to go and have a drink with him. I told him I have to get up early in the morning."

The truth. They did have an early flight. But was that the only reason she hadn't gone with the boy? Did she want to go?

If she'd decided to go, could Ian let her?

Those questions and more like them buzzed around in his brain all the way up in the elevator.

Since she'd been wet when she'd pulled her yellow dress on, the fabric clung to her. Ian looked straight ahead, at the doors. Was this elevator smaller than the one they'd ridden down earlier?

He was ready when the damn doors opened, practically jumping out into the hallway. He strode into their room, then into the bathroom, straight into a cold shower.

When he came out, Daniela went in.

Ian moved to the window and stood in front of the air conditioner as he looked out over the city. He turned his thoughts to the actual reason why they were here.

Baby Lila. Kidnapping.

He tried to remember as much about Manaus as he could from his one previous visit. The biggest city of the Amazon stood on the banks of the Rio Negro, the black river, bursting with two million people. A sizeable crowd in which they had to find one six-month-old baby.

And Ian was also going to keep investigating Finch's death. Finch had spent some time in Manaus—a major port for ocean vessels, fifteen hundred kilometers from the ocean—on his way up the river to Santana, where he'd finally, fatefully, settled.

Ian checked his phone. *Nothing from Lavras Sugar and Ethanol.* No missed texts, no missed calls. *Early days.* Probably nobody had even read his application yet.

Now that Ian was back in Brazil, Finch was on his mind all the time. Not that he'd forgotten his friend these past years. He just hadn't been able to take off from work. The assignments kept coming, one after the other, and he was glad for the pay. His larger, two-bedroom apartment cost more than his old shithole of a place. And he insisted on helping Daniela with college, which she swore to pay back the second she finally got a job that didn't pay minimum wage. She'd been working at the campus bookstore for the past four years.

A perfectly safe job. Instead of moving on to CPRU, she should have tried working for a library.

Ian didn't care about the money. He wanted her to be safe and happy.

He kept his back to the bathroom door so he wouldn't have to see her come out in her skimpy nightgown. But he couldn't not hear the water running.

He shoved his hands in his pockets and stared intently out at the city, at the million lights.

I want us to be lovers. She'd actually said that.

Christ.

Ian squeezed his eyes shut. They were going to bring him out of the Amazonian jungle in a straitjacket.

***

Carmen

Seventeen hundred miles to the north, Carmen Heyerdahl sobbed in Phil's arms, her heart breaking. "We should never have brought Lila here."

The night bugs bounced off the window screen. They had the light off, but the bugs knew where they were anyway and seemed determined to breach the barricade. *Ping, ping, ping.*

The room had been a little too small for the three of them, but now without the baby, it seemed oddly smaller yet, suffocating, like being trapped in a coffin.

Phil wrapped both arms tightly around her, as if afraid that if he let her go she too might disappear. He kissed the top of her head. "It's not your fault. See-Love-Aid was supposed to be safe. Nothing like this has ever happened here."

"I'm not going to give up until I find her."

"I know." He kissed her again. "You've never given up on anyone in your life. I know you're not going to give up on Lila. Neither will I. We'll find her. The police are looking."

"And we're getting help from the US." She glanced up at Phil in the dim moonlight. He looked black and white, a shadow image of himself.

"That will make a difference," shadow Phil said. "And we'll keep searching on our own."

She laid her head back down on his chest as she nodded. His chest was reassuringly real. He wasn't really fading.

They'd been out every day, walking the city, walking the various harbors, the markets, looking at every child, hoping to see that sweet familiar face. They showed Lila's picture around tirelessly, put out printed posters, offered a reward.

Any day now, something would bear fruit. Any day now, they would have Lila back.

***

Daniela

Since Ian was sitting by the desk with the laptop when Daniela came out of the bathroom, she went straight to the makeshift bed on the floor by the window and lay down.

"You can take the bed," he said without looking away from the screen.

"I don't want to. It wouldn't be fair. We are on business here, and we are partners in the investigation." *Equals.*

A stifled groan escaped him.

"The bed is big enough to share," she pointed out. "But if you don't want to, then I'm fine here."

He said nothing, so she closed her eyes and pretended to sleep.

He stayed up another hour before he went to lie down on the top of the covers, fully dressed.

She turned away from the air conditioner. The frigid blast of air was about to blow her eyebrows off. She pulled her blanket to her chin. She wasn't a big fan of air-conditioning. She didn't mind heat.

"All right. Fine," Ian said. "Get up here."

She didn't make him ask twice. Her skin tingling—maybe from the AC, maybe from his sudden change of mind—she eased into bed. She kept at least two feet of empty space between them. If she moved closer, he might go and sleep on the floor again.

She was in the same bed with Ian, a start. No sense messing it up right off the bat.

He was the one who'd taught her, back when he'd been tutoring her for her GED, how to set goals, then how to break down big goals into manageable steps. Didn't he realize that she never forgot a single word he said?

She stretched and luxuriated in the idea of having gotten this far. She briefly considered "accidentally" rolling against him in the middle of the night so she could wake up in his arms, but she cast the thought aside. She didn't want to push him over the edge.

"Go to sleep," he ordered. "We have to get up at six to check out and catch the flight at eight."

She tucked herself in and lay looking at the dark ceiling, listening to him breathe right next to her.

"Are you scared?" she asked.

"I'm not scared of a damn thing."

"I'm scared a little," she admitted.

He turned onto his side, facing her. His voice gentled as he said, "Of what?"

"Of never finding my place." She turned on her side too, facing him. She couldn't see his expression in the dark, and maybe that was for the best. "I am from the Amazon, but I don't feel like I belong in the Amazon anymore. I don't feel like I'm going home. I feel like a grown turtle, trying to wiggle back into the egg it came from. I don't fit."

He listened.

Her lips tugged into a half smile she knew he couldn't see. "I'm very American now. I think I can chose my destiny and my place in the world. I want to control my fate."

He still didn't say anything.

"Back in the village, everything just was. I never even thought of myself as a prostitute. Never thought the word. I thought I was like my mother, and I loved my mother. She was a good woman. It was okay to be like her."

"You were an exploited child," Ian spoke at last. He didn't use the other word. He'd never used that word in relation to her, ever.

"Sometimes," she spoke her deepest fear into the dark, "I'm not sure if I deserved to be saved."

"Nobody has to deserve to be saved." His voice roughened. "And your place is with me."

"But you want me to go off and make my own life." And lately, every time he talked of her having that future life, separate from him, the words throbbed and hurt inside her chest.

"You'll have your own life. You'll have a husband and kids and a great job. But you'll always have a place with me."

"You think I deserve happiness."

"I know you do."

"Americans think everyone deserves to be happy. The people I knew before, they just hoped they'd survive from one day to the next."

He fell back into silence.

"I think you deserve happiness too," she said carefully. "I don't think you should punish yourself for Linda and the twins anymore, Ian."

And he did what she knew he'd do. He turned on his back and closed his eyes, ending the conversation.

***

Ian

The flight to Manaus, in the heart of the Amazon, ate up four hours, the plane booked full, people pressed together, so Ian and Daniela couldn't discuss the case.

They couldn't discuss the previous night either, because somehow, in the fricking two minutes that Ian actually slept, he managed to roll over to her side of the bed and had put his arms around her.

He didn't know which one of them was more surprised when they woke. He'd never shot out of bed that fast in his life, not even in his army days.

Letting Karin Kovacs pair them up on this case had been the worst idea ever. This could never happen again.

Ian looked out the plane's window at the meeting of the rivers. The Rio Negro converged with the Rio Solimões just below Manaus, the Rio Negro's nearly black water meeting Rio Solimões's light brown. The colors stayed separate where the rivers met, didn't mix, as if some fancy barista had drawn a cream line on coffee.

All that water made Ian think of the Potomac.

The Potomac had taken away Linda and the boys.

The Rio Negro had given him Daniela.

One river had swallowed his heart; another river, halfway around the world, had gifted it back. A different heart, beaten up, scarred, but a beating heart at least.

He shut off that line of thinking and examined the city below them instead as they came in for landing.

Manaus spread on the side of the Rio Negro, surreal in every way. You didn't expect to see a metropolis of almost two million people, bigger than Philadelphia, in the middle of the Amazonian rain forest, in a region with the population density half of Mongolia's.

As they left the airport, stepping into the noise of a group of boys playing drums on the sidewalk, Ian watched Daniela slow and take a sniff. Even here, in the city, the earthy smells of the rain forest were in the air, mixing with the smell of fish from the river, and the harsher smells of civilization like car exhaust. But you could tell, just from the smell, that you were in the Amazon.

A disturbing thought that hadn't occurred to Ian before gripped him.

Daniela said last night that this was no longer home for her. But maybe she'd feel different now that she was here. She could take a boat back up the river. She could stay, be anything—a teacher or start a business. She'd always been a river goddess.

What if the Içana calls her back?

She turned and smiled at him. "On the way home, I want to pick up some souvenirs for my friends at the airport before we leave."

And something Ian hadn't even known was knotted inside him slowly relaxed.

Cabs lined up by the curb. The cab driver at the head of the line opened the back door for them. Daniela gave the address for See-Love-Aid's Manaus headquarters in Portuguese and chatted with the man as they got in.

She watched the city as they passed through. Ian watched her.

They didn't go all that far. Less than half an hour later, the cab stopped in front of a building that might have been a shipping warehouse once but had been converted into See-Love-Aid's sanctuary for displaced girls.

Mrs. Frieseke, a fifty-something American woman with softly graying hair and warm brown eyes, showed them around. She was the site manager. She reminded Ian of the director of the organization in Manaus, both women brisk, confident, competent, like distant sisters.

"The older girls make sisal rugs, placemats, flip-flops, bags, and baskets." Pride bloomed in the woman's voice like a flower as she led them to a workroom filled with teenagers. "Basically everything and anything that can be made from sisal. Then See-Love-Aid sells what we can through the Internet via fair trade channels. It pays for the children's housing and education. And we're able to set aside enough money for them to get started in life once they graduate out at eighteen. At that age, they're mostly too old to be dragged into the sex trade."

Ian raised an eyebrow, thinking he misheard.

But Mrs. Frieseke said, "Unfortunately, sex tourism is a booming industry here. People come from North America, Europe, all over the world. But they mostly want what they can't get at home. Children."

Ian glanced at Daniela. Sadness sat in her eyes. Obviously, this was no news to her.

Ian must have looked ready for murder, because Mrs. Frieseke patted his arm. "We're working on it. Giving girls a safe place is one aspect. We're also working on changing politics. Politicians, in general, don't care. Sex tourism brings money into the region. The better the economy, the more likely a politician is to be reelected. And the girls are too young to vote, so they're of no use to the men in government. But we will change it somehow." She stuck her chin out. "I know we will."

Ian had seen army drill sergeants with less determination.

They crossed the largest workroom as Mrs. Frieseke explained more about how the See-Love-Aid shelter in Manaus worked. The girls followed their every move, dark-haired, dark-eyed for the most, but a handful of blondes among them, skin every beautiful shade that God created. *Safe.* Ian liked that thought very much.

He glanced at Daniela and caught her watching the teens with a suspicious sheen in her eyes.

What is she thinking?

He didn't want to ask in front of Mrs. Frieseke.

Maybe Daniela was thinking about how different her life might have been if she'd ended up in a place like this instead of Rosa's. The thought slammed like a fist into Ian's stomach. He stepped toward her…To do what? He stopped a foot from her, held back.

He suddenly understood that bringing her here *had* been a mistake, but not for all the reasons he'd thought. Not because any investigation could turn dangerous. Daniela's presence here was a mistake, because being back, even a hundred miles away from her village, was hurting her.

He knew her well enough to know that she was struggling with her emotions, her face just a little too impassive. And the fact that she had to struggle made Ian's chest feel hollow, like the drums those boys had played outside the airport for tourists.

"Could we talk to the Heyerdahls?" he asked Mrs. Frieseke, to get them moving.

"They had to fly to Rio this morning. Their visas are expiring, so they need to renew them. They should be back tomorrow, or the day after, at the latest."

That would work too. Ian and Daniela could lay the groundwork, get a good idea for what they were facing, before the parents and their emotions were brought into the mix.

He followed Mrs. Frieseke up the stairs, Daniela close behind them.

The dormitories were upstairs, for both the kids and the volunteers. Two separate staircases led up—one to the kids' dorms, the other to a smaller area that belonged to the permanent staff and the visiting volunteers. The two areas were sealed off from each other, connected by a single steel door, to which, Mrs. Frieseke told them, she held the only key.

The adults' section had twenty rooms, each with two single beds pushed against opposite walls. Some rooms housed permanent See-Love-Aid staff, the rest went to the volunteers who rotated out every two weeks.

"We have only one empty room right now," Mrs. Frieseke opened a door for them and showed them in. "We're usually booked full. I hope this is okay."

Two beds, two chairs, a small table, and a nightstand. No dresser or wardrobe. Apparently, while the volunteers were here, they lived out of their backpacks.

Mrs. Frieseke said, "Bathrooms are at the end of the hall. Ladies to the left, gents to the right."

"This is great." Daniela swung her backpack onto the bed by the window, while Ian wondered if this was all a great conspiracy.

Separate rooms couldn't be found? Really?

Why did everyone keep assuming he'd be okay with sharing a room? Thank God, at least they wouldn't have to share a bed.

Waking up this morning… Daniela had her head on his shoulder, her arm across his chest. The way her eyes slowly opened to look into his. That moment when neither of them could look away…

That could not happen again.

"Thank you for the accommodations," Ian told Mrs. Frieseke when she looked at him with expectation, as if he might have missed something she'd said. He added, "We appreciate you putting us up here."

Being at the scene of the kidnapping would be helpful to the investigation, better than trekking over daily from a distant hotel.

"Could you please show us where the Heyerdahls' room is?" Daniela asked the woman.

Mrs. Frieseke pointed at a closed door at the end of the hallway.

A difficult spot, really, for a kidnapper. He or she would have had to stroll through the entire length of the dormitory to reach the room, then back, with a potentially crying baby. Yet, according to the original police report, nobody had seen anything.

But maybe the report didn't record everything the police had learned.

"I'd like to talk to the police, if you could point us in the right direction." Ian was itching to get started. They'd rested on the plane. He wanted to hit the ground running.

He had the name of the local detective he needed, so once Mrs. Frieseke told them where the police station was, they headed off that way. They took the bus they were told to take and stood in the back.

Within five minutes, Ian spotted two pickpockets. As the two youths headed toward them, Ian flashed a look of I'll-break-your-scrawny-necks. They glared at him but turned away.

"Impressive," Daniela said under her breath. Then, "Do you think the police will help us?"

"They should. The delegado from Rio said he would call ahead to make sure."

"They won't want to be shown up." She looked down at her sandals, then shifted on her feet. "They could be involved in trafficking."

And he bit back a curse, because he remembered what she'd told him about the red house on the river, how Rosa had been friends with the cops in her small town, and that they were frequent visitors to the girls.

He kept his eyes on Daniela, who'd already shook off her moment of hesitation. But still…Would she be uneasy with the local police? She had every reason to hate them. Meeting them might be the last thing she wanted to do. What if the uniforms brought back miserable memories?

Yet she stood on the bus now with her back straight, the angle of her chin pure determination, ready to face down whatever came her way. She was brave, perhaps the bravest person Ian knew, but even brave people hurt.

Oh, fuck it. He was hanging on to a support pole so the bus's jerking and swaying wouldn't knock him off his feet or into someone, but he reached out with his free hand and pulled her against him, her back to his chest, and held her there.

She immediately relaxed against him.

He didn't tell her that she didn't have to go to the police station if she didn't want to. It would imply that he thought her weak; he thought she couldn't handle it. He knew she could. But he would have spared her.

"I feel like I'm in a clothes dryer," he said, and made it sound like he was only hanging on to her so they wouldn't be thrown around as the bus turned, once again without slowing down, at the next intersection.

She responded with "I think the bus driver learned driving at a tractor derby."

She was tough both mentally and physically. No slouch in hand-to-hand combat either, but she felt small and fragile against him. And quickly, Ian learned the danger of holding her. Once he allowed his arm around her, letting her go was nearly impossible.

CHAPTER
TWELVE

Daniela

Daniela's body was still tingling as they sat at the police station. Ian had held her for the entire twenty-minute bus ride—which passed way too fast.

That kind of physical contact between them was new—a first. Okay, second. This morning, she'd woken up in his arms. He was finally seeing her as a woman and as his equal. She could have spent the rest of the day daydreaming about his arms around her, but they weren't here on a pleasure trip. Unfortunately.

They went through the case step-by-step with the investigating detective, Gustavo Santos, a man in his late forties who was graying at the temples and thinning on top. He wasn't overweight, but he did sport a respectable potbelly, a sign that he'd primarily been riding a desk for the last couple of years. He wore a wrinkled suit and a tie that had tomato stains on it and smelled like fish. Quite a bit sloppier than the delegado had been in Rio.

Santos had his own office, crowded with file cabinets, but a decent size. He had his own coffeemaker. *Must rank fairly high up. Probably the old fox of the department.*

One of the men who'd always beaten Daniela at Rosa's, the man who'd been the roughest, had been a policeman. But Santos was the picture of friendliness and cooperation.

He scanned through his own report, a copy of which they already had, but the printout in his hand was embellished with handwritten notes on the margins that he must have added since the official report had been filed.

"The call came in at nine thirty in the morning," he said. "We responded immediately, arrived at the scene at nine forty-seven."

He took a sip of his coffee, then went on. "We were told by the parents that they discovered the baby missing just before nine."

Ian asked, "Why wait half an hour to call?"

"The parents had gone down to breakfast. They left the baby sleeping in the crib. They thought it was safe. The whole group had been looking after her. In fact, a couple of people had said they'd look in on her if she woke up and started crying."

Santos sipped some more coffee. "So when the parents came up and saw the empty crib, they thought the baby cried and someone came in and got her. They went from room to room to see where she was. Some time passed before they realized that the baby wasn't on the premises."

"Do you have a list of who was upstairs at the time?"

The man paged through his notes, didn't find what he was looking for, so he went to his computer. "Four of the six permanent See-Love-Aid staff were downstairs, coordinating breakfast. Out of the twenty-one visiting volunteers, fifteen were downstairs, including the Heyerdahls, and six were upstairs, including the baby. The metal door between the girls' dormitory and the adults' section was locked."

"So seven people with immediate access," Ian said.

The detective nodded. "Although, somebody could have gone up without being seen. It's just a short flight of stairs."

"I assume you questioned everyone, the people upstairs and downstairs."

"We conducted extensive interviews. Nobody saw anything suspicious."

"What's your best guess?" Ian asked.

Santos pressed his lips together, clicking his pen a few times before responding with reluctance. "Trafficking for illegal adoption. A blue-eyed, blonde-haired baby girl in the private adoption circuit is worth her weight in gold, I'm sorry to say. With a forged birth certificate and adoption release, the fees start at twenty thousand dollars. That's big money here."

"It's big money anywhere." Anger choked Daniela at the thought of a defenseless little girl in the hands of conscienceless men.

When she'd been young, she'd thought this was simply how things were done. The strong made choices for the weak—the natural order of things. Everybody accepted it, the same way they accepted the start of the rainy season, the floods, and the fact that some snakes and bugs were poisonous.

But since then, she'd seen a different world. She'd seen freedom and justice, neither perfect in the US either, but better than here. She could no longer accept the "*this is how things are*" explanation. She had no intention of accepting it.

The detective leaned back in his chair and folded his hands over his large belly, over his rumpled jacket and stained tie. "I don't think the visiting volunteers were involved. I checked them thoroughly. They alibied out each other. And this was not a crime of opportunity. This is something set up in advance. You have to have connections for this sort of thing."

Daniela said, "You must know the people in town who are usually involved in activities like this. You must have looked into them."

He nodded. "We have suspicions about one gang in particular when it comes to trafficking babies. But we have no specific lead that points to them in this case. I had the gang watched for as long as I could justify it in the budget. They only have about a dozen members, but to watch that many…" He made a helpless gesture with his hands. "We simply don't have the manpower."

"What have you done so far?" Ian asked. "Just so we don't duplicate."

"We brought in as many gang members as we could catch for questioning, nine altogether. Believe me, we're working this case as hard as we can. A kidnapped American child is not good news to any city. All we need is for tourists to stop coming. The economy is in a crisis already." Resignation echoed in Santos's tone. "The police just went through budget cuts. Now we have fewer people to solve more crimes, because, of course, the worse the economy, the higher the crime rate. I'm sure things are done better in the United States."

"Don't bet on it," Ian said. "Some things are the same everywhere."

They talked another full hour before Daniela and Ian headed out, with a lot of new details but nothing that came remotely close to being a solid lead.

Instead of taking the bus again, they walked to get a feel for the city. To her, the place looked a lot like Santana only bigger and more crowded. Gritty. Poverty stared her in the face, while violence waited just under the surface like sharp-toothed fish in the Rio Negro's black water.

"Do you think a complete stranger could just walk into the hostel?" she asked. "Risky, isn't it?"

"Stealing babies is a risky business by definition, I'd think." Ian sounded lost in thought.

"But if everyone involved in the kidnapping were outsiders, why do it at See-Love-Aid? If the gang took the baby, they would have known about her because they saw her out in the city with her parents. So why not make plans to grab her out in the city, then disappear in the crowd? The streets are their turf. They know every inch. See-Love-Aid would be uncharted territory."

"True. Why give up home court advantage?" Ian turned to her. "Good point."

"I learned everything I know from you."

A genuine smile spread slowly over his rugged features. "Flattery will get you everywhere. Want some ice cream?"

He smiled very little, mostly when he knew she was looking, cheering up for her sake. *You deserve better than having to live with a morose old bastard*, he'd once said.

He'd improved over the years, whether he knew it or not. They both had.

He scanned the shops. "I think I saw a *sorveteria* when we got off the bus. Or is that sorbet?"

Anything cold sounded like heaven in the near triple-digit heat, and Daniela almost jumped at the offer before she had a chance to think on it. She was on the tips of her toes, grinning, but then lowered her heels back onto the ground as she reconsidered.

He flashed her a *Now what?* look. "It's not a trick question."

"Ice cream is something you buy for kids. Buy me a drink."

He seemed to be swallowing a sigh. "I don't think you're a kid. I swear."

Happiness spread through her, but she still couldn't stop herself from asking, "Have you ever bought ice cream for Nicole?"

"No. And I don't see Nicole anymore. Haven't in a while. But people have ice cream on a date all the time. Grown men buy ice cream for grown women. I swear."

"Is this a date?" she asked carefully.

All the good humor slid off his face. "No."

She wouldn't allow herself to become discouraged. At least she was working alongside him. At least they were together.

Four years ago, in Finch's house on the river, she'd spent two months with Ian, all day, every day. Then he'd taken her to the US and, shortly after, he went to work for CPRU. She spent her days in GED classes, then at the college. For the last couple of years, it seemed as if they barely saw each other.

But now…They were true partners. They were sharing a room. She wasn't going to complain.

"Ice cream sounds good."

"What are you grinning about now?" he said in a dry tone.

"I'm happy."

"That means you must be plotting my demise one way or the other." But he grinned back.

A dirty little boy sat on the curb in front of the ice-cream shop with a cracked plastic cup in his hand. Ian dropped a few *reais* into the cup.

Daniela glanced around and caught an older boy watching, a few feet behind Ian, leaning on a phone pole.

"You know this is just so his buddy can see which pocket you took your wallet out of, right?"

"We'll cross that bridge when we get to it." Ian stepped into the ice-cream shop.

He bought four large cones, giving two to the boy on the curb as they passed him again. "One for your brother," he said in his broken Portuguese. "It's a hot day."

The kid searched his face, looking for the catch. Was he a cop? What did he want? Was he trying to buy some kind of services?

Then, as they walked on, and Daniela looked back, the kid was shoving both ice creams into his mouth as fast as he could, melted goo running down his dirty chin.

"I'm sure if they had another way to make enough to eat, they'd do that," Ian said.

Probably a thousand out of a thousand people seeing those kids would have seen garbage. If the small boy came too close, some would kick him away. Daniela had seen that happen and worse.

Ian wasn't like most people. He had dark places he tried to hide from her, didn't let sunshine reach. But all his places, dark or light, were good and honorable.

After the ice cream, they decided to grab a bite to eat and ended up at a tourist dive, a bad choice, in hindsight. The place had a large tank in the middle filled with piranhas, which the tourists could feed with chicken wings for a few reais.

Ian ignored them. Daniela was appalled. She couldn't believe *this* was going to be their first unofficial date.

They couldn't even talk, since they couldn't hear each other over the tourists' horrified and delighted screams and squeals. They ate their fish stew, then got out of there.

Ian's cell phone rang.

"Yes," he said after he picked up, then, "That sounds great. I can be there tomorrow afternoon." He listened with his forehead in a frown. "Okay. Thank you."

"Who was that?" she asked when he hung up.

"I have to fly back to Rio tomorrow. I plan on being back before the end of the day, the following morning at the latest."

"For what?"

Instead of responding, he said, "Stick around See-Love-Aid. Plenty of people to interview there. That should more than take up your day. I don't want you out, wandering the city."

Her earlier optimism plummeted. *She* might be thinking they were equal partners, but clearly, he wasn't thinking the same.

"Why are you going to Rio?"

"A little side business."

She waited for him to say more, to explain. He didn't.

Why was it a secret? Either he thought she couldn't handle it, or he didn't trust her.

The fish stew sat in her stomach like a handful of river mud, her good mood washed away by a flash flood of darker emotions.

So Ian expected her to cower in the safety of See-Love-Aid tomorrow, did he? Doing what? Reorganizing the paperwork?

No. She was an investigator just like him.

She was going to investigate. She could go to places and talk to people that he couldn't.

***

Ian

Looked like fish were nibbling on the bread Ian had thrown on the water at Lavras Sugar and Ethanol. They'd called him for an interview. He wished he could fly back to Rio right away, but he wanted another look at See-Love-Aid, wanted to talk to as many people as possible. That way, while he was in Rio, all that could percolate in the back of his head.

So he called in flight reservations for the following morning.

When they got back to See-Love-Aid, Mrs. Frieseke was more than helpful, once again. She gathered the permanent staff together in the empty downstairs dining room.

Other than Mrs. Frieseke, three women sat around the largest table, and two men. Mrs. Frieseke made the introductions.

Ian had read the original police interviews. He was going to ask most of the same questions. A full month had passed since the child's disappearance, so he expected to get slightly different answers.

The staff would have talked about the case a lot in the intervening month. This was a major tragedy in their midst. With time, their recollections would grow more and more similar to each other as certain aspects were reinforced, others forgotten. Investigating a crime with a month's delay was not ideal. But even if they'd forgotten some of the details, maybe someone had remembered something new. That was Ian's best hope here.

He didn't even want to think about Finch's case, the four-year delay there. He should have gotten to it sooner. Some friend he'd turned out to be. If he'd been alone, he would have taken a few months off from work long before now. But with Daniela in college, he'd needed every paycheck. And, with her spending every break with him, they'd needed a two-bedroom apartment.

He was a damn fool, unable to let her go. No wonder she'd gotten some strange ideas. When they returned to DC, he was going to make serious changes.

He'd been half listening to the conversation Daniela initiated around the table, but now, his mind made up about her future and feeling better for it, he turned his full attention to the six people who sat around with somber faces.

"First, maybe you could just tell us where you were when baby Lila went missing," Daniela said, looking at each person in turn, smiling at each, sincere gratitude on her face that they were here.

Mrs. Frieseke began. "I was at the hospital with one of the girls who broke her arm while they were playing basketball outside."

"Did all the girls come in after the accident?" Daniela asked.

"No, they stayed to finish the game. Pierre was watching them."

Pierre Avy, a Frenchman in his early twenties—with the kind of too sym-metrical, unlined puppy face Hollywood was so fond of—nodded, making love to Daniela with his eyes, showing way too many teeth. Ian wondered if the guy would still be that confident with a couple of those teeth knocked out.

"When it's not raining here," Pierre said in an irritating French accent, "it drizzles. So anytime we have a dry court, we take advantage of it. Mornings are great for games, before the worst of the heat hits."

According to the police report, Mrs. Frieseke's presence at the hospital had been confirmed. The ER had a sign-in sheet. And the girl she took also backed up the site manager's alibi. All the other girls were either playing bas-ketball or watching the game. According to them, as was well-documented in the police report, Pierre Avy hadn't left the court the entire time.

For now, tentatively, Ian was prepared to cross Mrs. Frieseke and Monsieur Avy off the suspect list.

Daniela turned her attention to a pregnant woman who'd introduced herself as Carol Peterson. She was blonde and tall, very Midwestern, from Wisconsin, according to the report Ian had.

"I had post office duty," Carol said. "I volunteer to go into the city, since I like the walk. Helps to work the kinks out of my back. I want to do as much as I can now before the baby is born. And I like going out in the relative cool of the morning. The post office is nearby."

"Will you be staying here for the baby's birth?" Daniela asked.

"Of course." Carol patted her belly. She carried a smile around the table. "These people are my family."

According to the report Ian had, she'd begun working at See-Love-Aid with her husband two years ago. Seven months ago, her husband had died of a snakebite he'd suffered on a fishing trip upriver. Neither of them had family back home. Carol stayed.

She looked drawn, exhausted, still grieving, but putting on a brave face.

Back when Linda had been pregnant, this had been Ian's worst fear. If he had been killed in the army, Linda would have been left alone to raise the babies. *Never* had he imagined that it could be the other way around, his family gone and he still here.

"It's important to have people you care about around you," he told Carol. And because she reminded him of Linda too much for comfort, he focused on the two middle-aged women who sat next to her—thin noses, thin lips, short brownish hair. Hannah and Heather. Sisters.

"We were having breakfast in our room," Hannah said.

And Heather added, stricken, "We had the door open to a crack to listen in case the baby cried. She never made a sound."

The second male staff member was the only person who hadn't talked yet. Early thirties, nearly white-blond, tall, Scandinavian looking, from Cleveland, Ohio. His name was Henry Stubner.

"I was fixing the dripping faucet in the men's room. My room is right next to it, and the dripping kept me up at night." Henry barely glanced at Ian. His full attention was on Daniela, who was smiling at him.

"Sounds like you're very handy to have around," she said.

He flashed a grin that was decidedly not modest. "I do what I can. I'm here to help."

He kept holding Daniela's gaze.

Ian cleared his throat. "What does everybody think of the parents?"

For crimes of murder and disappearance, investigators always looked at the family first.

Several people began to speak at once.

"They're heartbroken, and so are we." Mrs. Frieseke was the loudest, or maybe she was heard over the din because her voice carried the most authority. "I never could have imagined anything like this happening here. In our dormitory. We haven't even needed security beyond Henry and Pierre."

Her mouth drew tight. She probably blamed herself, at least partially. She confirmed that by saying, "If I had thought to put at least one security guard into the budget…" She shook her head. "But we have Pierre and Henry. They're strong young men. I never thought…"

Carol put her arm around her and hugged her, as much as she could with her giant belly.

Both Henry and Pierre drew themselves straighter in their chairs, everything about them resolute, from their hardening gazes to the angle of their chins, as if saying, *it might have happened once, but we're alert now; nothing like this is ever going to happen again.*

As the only two men on staff, they probably felt responsible too, probably fancied themselves the protectors of the others. Ian wasn't impressed. They'd done a shitass job at protection.

Of course, the repurposed warehouse held no riches and was always full of people, so it probably didn't draw thieves. And as far as taking one of the girls for trafficking went, the city was full of girls just like them, living on the streets. Nobody would notice if they went missing. So the traffickers didn't need to court trouble by coming here and tangling with an international aid organization.

Ian sat back and let Daniela conduct the interview since she was good at it. She seemed to know instinctively just what tone to use when asking a question, how to respond, whether with admiration or understanding or commiserating. She excelled at handling people.

And he hated to think where she might have learned that, back at Rosa's, where reading a client right would have meant the difference between life and death.

For the past few years, Ian had barely thought of Daniela's past. Her past had nothing to do with her present, would have nothing to do with her bright future. But since they'd been back in Brazil, the past kept pushing into his thoughts. And what he hated even more was that Daniela probably experienced the same.

He watched her ask her questions to the people around the table. They all responded. Nobody seemed to be holding anything back. But as good as Daniela was, the group interview didn't net any new, actionable information.

After they finished, Mrs. Frieseke took them to see the older girls and talk to them. Work was in progress in the three separate workrooms, and they visited each in turn.

The girls worked, laughing, chatting, listening to music. They didn't put their work down even while answering questions. They worked hard. Most of them had come from the streets, so they knew the alternative.

None of them had been in the visiting volunteers section of the building. They weren't allowed up there, a rule that Ian thought sensible.

They visited the young girls' schoolroom next and received the same eager-to-please but unhelpful answers.

"Maybe you could conduct one-on-one interviews tomorrow," he told Daniela when they were back in their small room after a surprisingly satisfying cafeteria dinner of fish and fruit, settling in for the evening.

She sat on her bed, watching him with what he thought was a guarded expression. They had the lights off to keep the bugs away from the screen that had a small tear in it. Moonlight dusted her with silver.

"I want you to tell me why you're going back to Rio," she said. "Please don't treat me like a child."

She wore a thin, strappy nightgown.

He lay on his bed, on his side, wishing for air-conditioning. He was immensely grateful for that five feet of distance between them. *No*, she was most definitely not a child.

So he told her about Lavras Sugar and Ethanol. "Finch was working for Lavras in Rio at the time he got in trouble. Maybe the trouble he got in was at Lavras. If I interview, I'll probably meet the head of security, the guy Finch worked for. I want to find out what happened."

"Whoever Finch ticked off either killed Finch or had him killed," she pointed out. "I don't like it that you'll be going into possible danger alone." She rubbed a narrow hand over her eyes. "You didn't see him."

Finch's body. Tortured.

She dropped her hand but was still for only a second or two before her fingers began worrying the edge of her nightgown.

Ian hated that he'd made her upset. "They're not going to knock me off in the middle of the HR department. It's a professional building, headquarters of an international corporation. I'll be safe. I'll poke around, then I'll be out of there before they can so much as come up with a plan."

"I wish I could come with you."

"We came to Brazil to investigate baby Lila. Even I shouldn't be going. I'll make up for the missed time when I get back."

"I don't want you to stay in Rio overnight." She fixed him with a hard look. "Pierre asked me out. He wants to take me to the opera. If you don't come back, I'm going to go with him."

No way was Monsieur French Casanova getting anywhere near Daniela. "I won't stay the night."

He couldn't tell for sure in the semidarkness, but she looked a little on the smug side. Probably was. She was probably playing him like a fricking fiddle.

CHAPTER
THIRTEEN

Ian

"So you and Senhor Finch were close friends?" Marcos Morais, the head of security at Lavras Sugar and Ethanol asked. He was almost as tall as Ian, freshly cut dark hair, expensive suit, shifty eyes.

"Finch and I were in the US Army together," Ian said. "Last I talked to him, he liked it here in Rio. When I lost my job back home, I figured I might as well head down here. He kind of disappeared. Maybe I'll track him down."

"You used to talk with him often?"

"Called each other once a month or so. You know, checking in."

"Have you been in Brazil before?"

"Not recently."

They'd already discussed Ian's qualifications and were just shooting the breeze as the interview was winding down.

"Seems like Lavras is a great place," Ian said. "I bet you've been here forever. What's not to like about sugar, right?"

"Easy job." Marcos stayed laid-back, twirling his pen on the desk. He played the whole interview that way. *Hey, we're all friends here.* "I had a small company protecting diamond mines before this. Believe me, you wouldn't like that."

Ian had some understanding of the private armies that protected diamond mines. "I believe you. Guarding an air-conditioned office beats being out at the mines, in malaria-infested backwoods, doing cavity searches on laborers to make sure they aren't stealing anything."

Marcos's hand stilled on the pen. "Been in the business?"

"Had friends who were."

"Here?"

"Africa."

Marcos nodded as he pushed to his feet and held out his hand to signal that the interview was over. "Thank you for coming in. You'll be hearing from us shortly. Make sure your contact information is correct."

"Definitely. If you think of any other questions, just call," Ian said as he left the man.

He walked out to the elevators, didn't accidentally-on-purpose get lost this time. He had what he'd come for. Whatever had happened to Finch, Marcos had been part of it. He'd brought up Ian's friendship with Finch way more times than was necessary. And every time they talked about Finch, the pulse in Marcos's neck beat a little faster, his gaze turned a little sharper.

Once baby Lila was safely back with her parents and Ian returned to Rio, he'd start his investigation with Marcos Morais.

He walked out of the building, thinking about various ways he could dig into Morais. Then he reached the sidewalk and scanned the street. He didn't have to wait long for a cab.

"Airport," he told the cabbie, then relaxed back in his seat.

"Big accident on the highway, senhor. You American?" When Ian nodded, the guy cranked up the air-conditioning. He grinned in the rearview mirror. "I want to be New York City cabbie someday." He looked as eager to please as if Ian had the power to make the guy's ambitions come true. "I'll take the backroads. Sim?"

"Sim." Ian's mind was on other things.

What did Finch find at Lavras? What did he take?

Was Lavras doing something illegal? Did Finch find proof? But then why not take it to the authorities? Was Finch blackmailing Lavras with whatever he found? Finch was a good kid, but he'd always been impulsive. And he hadn't had the best track record at resisting temptation.

He'd almost gotten court-martialed in the army when he'd crushed a beer bottle with his bare hand on a bet and cut his palm to shreds. *Destruction of government property.*

Finch had gotten in trouble more than once for drinking and doing stupid shit. Once, in the middle of the night, he'd colored their superior officer's uniform pink with Kool-Aid.

As Finch's past fiascos circled in Ian's head, he failed to notice that the cab wasn't going towards the airport at all, until they were on a single-lane road somewhere in the outer suburbs and the cabbie drove into a weed-infested tunnel.

A white van blocked the cracked concrete of the road ahead of them.

Ian reached for the gun tucked into his waistband.

The cab stopped.

Another white van stopped behind them, blocking them in.

The cabbie jumped out and ran from the short tunnel, scrambling up the embankment to their left, then disappearing over the rise.

Shit.

Ian dove for the front seat. Too late. Bullets were flying already.

"Throw your gun out," somebody was shouting.

He had no other choice. He was hemmed in. Enemy before him, enemy behind him. He had no real cover. And if one of the idiots hit the fuel tank…

Ian tossed his weapon, an old Taurus .357 Magnum, through the open driver's side door. Hadn't had it long, dammit. He'd bought it off a kid on the edge of the favelas after he'd gotten into Rio this morning. He'd planned on stashing it someplace safe before he flew back to Manaus. Couldn't take a gun on an airplane these days.

As soon as he tossed the revolver, the shooting stopped.

"Get out of the car. Hands in the air."

He did as they told him. If they wanted him dead, they would have blown his head off already.

Right now, right here, he'd been outmaneuvered, plain and simple. He needed to gain time, and he needed to gain a sense of the enemy he was facing.

Marcos Morais, head of security at Lavras, got out of the van behind the taxi and strode forward, a Taurus PT92—Brazil's response to the Beretta 92—in hand. Better by a long shot than Ian's weapon had been. Next time, he'd buy a gun off someone like Morais instead of a street kid.

The man walked toward Ian. "I thought of a few more questions."

He looked confident about getting answers. He had every reason to be. A four-man crew stood behind him, with weapons drawn.

***

Daniela

Ian hadn't returned by midnight. He wasn't answering his phone either.

Daniela called Iris after dinner to check in, but hadn't told her about her missing son, just that Ian was out investigating. She didn't want to worry Iris. Iris was having enough trouble with her bingo partner, who was lording five grandchildren—and a sixth on the way—over her.

Exhausted from scouring the worst slums of the city, Daniela finally went to bed, to *his* bed—to make sure she couldn't possibly miss Ian if he came back. But she couldn't fall asleep.

By five in the morning, she was on a GOL Linhas Aéreas flight and reached Rio by noon since she only had one quick stop in the city of Brasília—the seat of the Brazilian government, the federal capital of Brazil. She made herself sleep on the flight so she wouldn't be completely beat when they touched down. In Rio, she rented a car because she was pretty sure someone had taken Ian, and she was going to rescue him, so she'd need a getaway car, not a cab.

The thought that, like Finch, Ian was dead, *killed*, floated at the edges of her consciousness no matter how hard she fought to beat it back. The possibility of this worst-case scenario made her chest feel crushed, as if a water buffalo had sat on her.

Images of Finch lying in a pool of blood on the kitchen floor flashed into her mind, and she broke out in cold sweat. She refused to accept that she was too late to save Ian.

But she couldn't believe the best-case scenario either, that Ian had simply lost his phone and missed his flight last night. She hadn't had the kind of life that gave her that kind of optimism.

She settled on the most likely scenario: Ian had run into trouble.

She could track his cell phone with hers through GPS, same as he could track hers. He'd insisted on that years ago. At the time, she'd rolled her eyes and called him overprotective. Now she was glad she'd agreed.

As far as she could tell, he was in a large building at the edge of the industrial district. A sugar refinery, she realized when she finally reached it. Two men stood at the gate, two more security guards at the entrance of the main building.

If they thought they could keep her from Ian, they had another think coming.

* * *

Ian

"Where are the diamonds?" Marcos Morais asked.

"At the diamond mine?" Ian guessed.

The man pistol-whipped him, knocking his head to the side.

Ian stood against the whitewashed cement-block wall, his hands tied to steel pipes on each side of him.

Marcos and he had spent the previous evening in a conversation exactly like this. Then Marcos had left for the night, leaving Ian alone in the small utility room to the rats and his worries about Daniela. He'd spent a couple of hours trying to undo the ropes, but Marcos must have been some Boy Scout extraordinaire. The ropes held.

And first thing in the morning, Marcos was back, fresh and ready for round two.

Ian braced himself against the wall behind him, as if nothing but the wall was holding him up. His nose was bleeding. Stars danced in his vision. He didn't have to pretend hard that he was in bad shape, about to fold.

Marcos finally stepped closer. Ian was careful not to grin. The idiot was now close enough for a head butt or for having his legs swept from under him. Once Marcos was on the ground, Ian could crush his scrawny neck under his boots, finagle Marcos's knife away from him, and then Ian would be out of there.

He decided to wait a little longer. He was still hoping Goat Man would show up. Marcos wasn't Goat Man. He didn't have a scar on his nose. Ian wanted both bastards. He hoped to hang in there as long as he could, just in case.

He figured Marcos might call in reinforcements for the final beat down. *Come on, Goat Man.*

But instead of Marcos calling anyone, he drove his fist into Ian's stomach. "You tell me where the diamonds are, or I'm going to take you apart into small little pieces. Have you ever seen the machines that grind up the sugarcanes?"

Ian hadn't, but he could easily imagine. He tried to suck in air. At least yesterday's lunch was long gone, so he wouldn't vomit again.

"Who killed Finch?" he asked, more breathless than he liked, but at least he could still talk.

"Fucking idiots." Marcos drove his fist into Ian's stomach again.

He doubled over. Coughed. Several seconds passed before he could straighten. "Tough having partners...who don't know...not to kill a man... before he gives up the information."

Marcos punched him in the ribs next. "Don't worry. That's not going to happen here. First you talk, then you die. I'm clear on the order."

Ian spit blood. "It's a pleasure...doing business with a professional."

To hell with waiting for Goat Man.

Ian prepared to lurch forward, but the door opened, and a man in his early twenties hurried in, dressed in a security uniform.

The guy didn't look at Ian but kept his gaze studiously on Marcos Morais. "Senhor."

Marcos snarled at the interruption but went out to talk to him. After a moment, the lock clicked.

Which meant Marcos had been called away for a time.

Ian tried to blink away his double vision. His head swam.

Time to blow this popsicle stand. He just needed a minute to recover. He slid to the ground into a sitting position, his back to the wall, his arms stretched to the side, suspended by the ropes.

He tried to catch his breath as he scowled at the door—solid steel, and not a damn thing in here to pick the lock with. He glanced at the small window. That had potential.

Except, the window darkened even as he watched. Someone moved past.

A guard?

Okay, one guard he could handle.

As pain pounded through him, Ian focused on his ropes again but didn't get more than three seconds. Then the glass was kicked in, and the second after that, Daniela's head appeared in the gap.

For a moment, her face was a study in tension, then she relaxed and smiled at him. "Hey."

God, let this be a hallucination. She could *not* be here.

"Are you okay?" She examined the room, then slipped in, careful of the broken glass, landing on her feet with a small bounce like a cat, looking more curious than scared. She wore black hiking boots, tight black shorts that ended mid-thigh, paired with a black tank top, her hair in a tight bun at her nape.

He growled at her. "What are you doing here?"

"Isn't it obvious?"

She was saving him. *He* was supposed to be *her* protector. How in hell had they ended up with their roles reversed?

She walked up to him. Stopped. Took in the ropes.

"Can you untie me?" The pain in his ribs was abating at last.

"How badly are you hurt?"

"Not enough to stop me from getting out of here."

"Good."

Instead of cutting him loose, she straddled his lap, one knee braced on the ground on each side of him. "Just give me a moment to be relieved, okay?"

She put her arms around his chest and lay her head in the crook of his neck.

He couldn't move away, nothing but wall behind him. "Marcos could come back any second."

"If you're talking about the guy who just walked out of here, he jumped into a car and drove off. I think he'll be a while." She pulled back to examine every inch of Ian's face.

"Daniela?"

She brushed back his matted hair from his temples with her slim fingers, her green eyes filled with concern. "I was afraid that they killed you."

Her voice was tender and…sexy, and he couldn't think about that, couldn't think how intimately they were pressed together.

"Untie me. Please."

She lifted up his shirt and carefully wiped the sweat and blood off his face. And then she lowered her head and brushed her sweet lips over his in a move so erotic and so innocent at the same time, that hot need shot though him out of nowhere, so strong that it made him dizzy.

Thank God, his hands were tied. Because there was no way he would have been able to keep them off her.

He held completely still.

She brushed her full lips back and forth over his. She was smiling as she whispered, "You're mine now, and there's nothing you can do about it."

Right, because he so wanted to run. But he said nothing. He absolutely could not encourage her.

He didn't have it in him to reject her yet again either. He hated putting pain in her eyes.

She nibbled his bottom lip gently. Then she licked the corner of his lips. Ian was glad Marcos had focused on his midsection. His face was all right, other than what he thought was a split eyebrow.

He was harder than the steel pipes he'd been tied to, and she had to feel it, sitting on him as she was. He didn't dare move a muscle.

She licked a slow, delicious line across the seam of his lips. Not kissing her back took every ounce of strength that he had.

She had passion. He was glad in a way. He'd been worried it might have been brutalized out of her—but he really wished she pointed her newfound passion somewhere else.

Of course, then he'd want to murder the guy.

She kissed him a little harder.

And then his control was gone, as fast as if it'd been shot from a cannon. He was probably going to hell, but he didn't care, because he would happily spend all eternity burning in flames for the chance to kiss Daniela back.

So he did, taking her sweet mouth, feeling as if he'd been underwater for years, and was just now coming up for air. All the pain of his body was gone. He could barely even remember it. He couldn't remember anything but her.

And that thought pulled him back to sanity.

This was not the time and place.

There *was* no time and place for anything between them.

He drew away, both of them breathing hard.

She folded against him once again, her arms around his torso, her head coming to rest on his shoulder as she softly whispered, "Ian," her warm breath tickling his skin.

His heart stumbled in his chest.

"Could you please untie me now?" Even to his own ears, his voice sounded strangled.

She took one last second. Then she moved off him and untied him, without looking at him, focused on the ropes.

While he strode to the chair in the corner to pick up the phone that Marcos had taken from him the day before, she hurried to the window. She was up and out before he could offer her a boost.

He had a harder time. His shoulders were wider, so he scraped against some of the broken glass, ended up losing a little more blood, not that he cared at this stage. Daniela was in the middle of enemy territory. He needed to get her the hell out of there.

Except he barely had a chance to brush the glass off his shirt before they were discovered. The security guard who'd interrupted Marcos's questioning was running toward them, gun in hand.

CHAPTER
FOURTEEN

Daniela

As more guards followed the first one, Daniela and Ian ran for the chain-link fence at the back of the factory lot.

Panic rattled Daniela as she stumbled on the loose gravel, then caught herself. Her lips still tingled, her heart a confused mush, but she had no time to think about that now.

The fence is too far.

They wouldn't be able to get away before the men caught up with them.

Rain had begun to sprinkle while she'd been inside. She prayed it wouldn't turn into a serious downpour. At least the guards weren't shooting. But why? Had they been ordered not to kill the prisoner?

To avoid getting caught halfway up the chain-link fence, then being dragged down by their ankles, Daniela and Ian stopped short of the fence and stood ready to take down the four guards who were quickly catching up, shouting at them to halt.

"The two on the left are mine," Ian said.

Which implied the two on the right were hers.

What, he wasn't even going to try to shove her behind him?

She glanced at him from the corner of her eye. He looked grim and ready to fight. And he was letting her fight by his side like a real partner. Then she had no more time to marvel, because the men reached them.

That they apparently weren't allowed to shoot made all the difference. They turned their rifles in order to use the butt of the weapons to knock Ian and Daniela down, but before they could get that far, Ian knocked one unconscious with a roundhouse kick.

Daniela attacked the skinniest guy, the one nearest to her. She went for a punch to the solar plexus, like Ian had taught her, ducking under the rifle, swinging her right arm back and putting her whole body behind the punch, aiming not at the guy's chest but about a foot behind it, as if wanting to put her fist *through* him.

The guy didn't take her seriously, didn't try hard enough to block. Big mistake. She knocked him back on his ass, where he stayed, gasping for air.

The next guy approached her more warily, but she knocked him down too, with a well-aimed roundhouse kick just like Ian's—thank God for the heavy-soled hiking boots she'd brought on the trip in case they needed to go into the jungle.

Ian's two were down too, and he turned to help, but she was already lunging at the fence. The rain made the aluminum links slippery, but she'd been born to climb trees in any kind of weather. A little water wasn't going to defeat her.

Ian was right behind her. Then they were over the top, jumping the ditch outside the fence, then in the rental car that waited where she'd left it on the shoulder.

She slammed behind the wheel, and he didn't argue as she got them the hell out of there.

"Are you hurt?" he asked instead, checking her over.

"No. You?"

"A couple of bruised ribs from last night. I'll live."

He flipped down the sun visor and checked out his face in the mirror. He pulled up his shirt and wiped off the last of the blood with the inside of the shirt before tugging it back down. Then he ran his fingers through his hair to comb it back into order.

When he was finished, he flipped the visor up. "How do I look?"

Like the man I'm falling in love with. God, she couldn't say that. "Your eyebrow is cracked. You have a black eye to put all black eyes to shame. And your knuckles are busted."

"If airport security questions me, I'll say I've been in a car accident."

"Or beat up by someone who wanted your wallet. They'd definitely believe that." Then a different problem occurred to her. "Do you have your passport? You can't get on a flight without ID."

But he nodded. "They only took my phone and gun."

"What gun?"

"I bought some protection before I went to see Marcos at Lavras. I got it in the building without trouble. It's a sugar company, not a courthouse. They don't have metal detectors. But they caught up with me later."

He told her what happened as she drove straight to the airport.

That he let her drive was new. Before, Ian always drove when they were together. He really was beginning to treat her like a fellow investigator.

"Did you find out anything?" she asked.

"Our buddy Finch stole diamonds."

She took her eyes off the road for just a second to stare at him. "No way."

"Sadly, yes. Marcos used to work for the diamond mines. I'm guessing he stole a couple, somehow Finch saw them, and he lifted them."

"Why? How could he be so stupid? Didn't he know they'd come after him?"

Anger and disappointment laced Ian's voice as he said, "He probably thought he could outrun them."

Silence settled on the car as she thought of Finch, who, whether he'd realized it or not, had saved her from Senhora Rosa. "Why didn't he leave Brazil right away?"

"Who the hell knows? Maybe he had a buyer lined up in Manaus." Ian's hands fisted on his knees.

Then they were at the airport, and they got through without trouble. On the plane, full as always, they couldn't really talk about Finch and the diamonds, so they had to shelve that conversation.

Ian drifted off in the aisle seat. Daniela stayed quiet next to him. He probably hadn't gotten much rest last night. His neck bent at an uncomfortable-looking angle as he slept now. She should have given him the window seat, should have thought about that when they'd sat down. He was going to wake with sore muscles.

She slipped her hand between his head and the headrest and tilted him toward her, until his temple rested on her shoulder. As he settled against her, she smiled with satisfaction, a lot more relaxed now that she was leaving Rio with Ian.

He was safe.

And *she* had saved him.

Now he'd definitely see her as a strong, grown woman.

She couldn't wait until he kissed her again.

***

Eduardo

Eduardo Morais watched as his father drank one glass of cachaça after another in his study.

The old man had called in both his sons, but Marcos was off tracking the American who might have their stolen diamonds.

Eduardo was almost glad Marcos had lost the guy. At least now, in comparison, Eduardo didn't look so stupid for Finch's premature death. Now Marcos had made a mistake too. The brothers were once again on equal footing.

And maybe, if luck was with Eduardo today, he'd be the one to deliver checkmate to his father.

The old hyena behind the desk had to make do with his younger son today, and his squinting, disapproving eyes said he wasn't happy about it. He didn't appreciate losing half his audience when he was in the mood to pontificate.

Joaquim the butler-cum-bodyguard stood unobtrusively in the corner, stepping forward only when his boss's glass needed to be refilled.

"You and your brother give me nothing but grief lately," Raul Morais grumbled.

"Yes, Father."

"I should have had more children," the man said moodily, staring in front of him. "I wanted to, with darling Maria. But Maria…" He sighed. "I could have with the others, but…" He shrugged.

Thank God you didn't. But Eduardo nodded.

"After Maria died and I ran north," his father said, "I went into the rain forest at the end of the rainy season with the loggers, and we didn't come out until the beginning of the next one. At night, I dreamt of Maria. For months and months, I never got closer to a woman than that."

Eduardo said nothing. When the old man got into a mood like this, he just needed an audience. He didn't require a response.

"Then logging season ended," Raul Morais said, "and we floated the logs down the river. I stopped at the first village, went straight to a hut where I heard a woman would take care of me. I could only imagine—some old whore who could no longer hack it in the bigger towns downstream." He gave a strangled laugh. Shook his head. But then a fond, almost affectionate look came over his face, so unusual that it made Eduardo actually pay attention.

"Instead," the old man reminisced, "I found a beautiful young girl, a mix of some Indian, some white, some black. Large brown eyes, long dark hair down to the back of her knees, nothing but a scrap of cloth wrapped around her hips, her budding, firm breasts bare..." He sighed. "I felt a tenderness that I thought I'd buried with Maria."

Eduardo shifted in the chair and swallowed back a groan. Would he have to sit through a listing of all the prostitutes his father had ever slept with?

"The girl told me her mother wasn't home." Raul Morais kept going. "I wasn't interested in her mother." A faint smile softened his harsh mouth. "I asked her name. Ana. She was a virgin."

Eduardo had his doubts, but he didn't voice them.

"I didn't pay her before I left," his father said. "It wasn't like that between us. I didn't want her to think that I made her into a whore. I was going to make her into my wife. I'd float the logs down to Manaus with the crew. Get my pay. Then I meant to go back."

"But then you met Mother," Eduardo said to hurry along the tale.

"In Manaus, I met the geezer who owned the logging operation. He had no sons, just one daughter, a round, bucktoothed girl who wanted me as soon as she set eyes on me. Your grandfather's house was a revelation, let me tell you. The nicest place I've ever been inside, and they only let me as far as the foyer, hat in hand, waiting for my pay."

Eduardo had a hard time picturing his father as a humble laborer. He'd never known the man as anything else but a proud, confident, heavy-handed dictator.

He seemed to be lost in the memories. "Tile floor, antique furniture, a chandelier overhead. And a whole second floor at the top of a wide staircase. Just for two people and their servants. Your grandfather had other businesses besides logging. He had two small ships that ran goods and adventurers up and down the Rio Negro."

"And you thought, someday you'd be like that," Eduardo said dutifully, resigned to having to hear the whole annoying story.

"I saw then what was possible." His father's eyes shone. "Your grandfather handed out the pay personally, magnanimously, bald and overweight, huffing just from having come down the stairs.

"*Hasn't swung an ax in decades*, I thought. Yet there the man stood, having all the money, while us poor bastards who broke our backs and risked our lives would get just enough money to eat and whore through the rainy season, then be broke and desperate enough to sign up for another go when logging season started up again."

Eduardo didn't point out that his father paid his own workers just as little, or less.

"After we got our pay," Raul Morais said, "we were sent around to the kitchen in the back for a meal. The daughter came in. To me, the kitchen alone seemed like a palace. And the girl, Rafaela, seemed like a princess—even if bucktoothed and plump as a stuffed pigeon. And the princess wanted me.

"I spent the rainy season seducing her, making sure that she was with child by the end. We married. When logging season started, this time, I went back up the river as crew boss. Maybe it was your grandfather's way of trying to get rid of me."

Not the first or last person to have that idea, Eduardo thought.

His father squared his shoulders. "I refused to die. I finally saw the light. I understood that riches don't come from hard labor. Riches come from leaping on opportunities. A successful man moves forward by leaps and bounds. So I leapt."

Eduardo reached nonchalantly into his pocket and fingered the small capsule there—a jungle poison that would mimic a heart attack.

If only Joaquim, that gorilla of a butler, would turn his back. Or leave for a minute. *Doesn't the damn man ever have to piss?*

"By the time the next logging season came around," Raul Morais said, "I had a son, your brother. I named him Marcos to soften up your grandfather, then convinced the man to rest and let me take over the business. I never held another ax again either." His tone stiffened with pride.

"Then Grandfather died the next year." A suspiciously *convenient* death. Eduardo was familiar with this part of the tale.

His grandfather had died, and Raul had another son. This one, he'd named Eduardo, after the little brother he'd left behind in the favelas in Rio. And as Raul Morais held his new son, he realized he was rich enough to have his brother found, to have his brother brought to Manaus, so he hired an investigator to do just that. And now, Uncle Eduardo might end up with Morais Timber.

The younger Eduardo hated his namesake with the heat of the equator. He squeezed the capsule in his pocket, caught himself, stopped and pulled his hand out. He didn't want to burst the damn thing.

"Sometimes I think the happiest I've ever been were those years in Manaus," his father kept blabbering. "I thought all the hardship was behind me. I'd done all the starving, thieving, killing, so my sons would never have to. I wanted you and Marcos to live like the rich I saw in Rio, people I watched passing by in fancy cars when I'd still been a child of the favelas. I wanted to raise you to be princes." He sighed. "Have I made a mistake there?"

"Of course not, Father." The old man had given them everything. Except his love. And now, the Morais millions.

"I've been soft," Raul Morais said. "I didn't discipline you enough."

Eduardo swallowed back bitter anger. He was pretty sure the old man beating him and Marcos bloody with a bamboo cane a few more times would not have made them into better men. They both had plenty of scars on their backs.

Once, when he'd been ten, the old man had beaten him to the point of fainting. He could no longer remember why, but he could still remember the slicing pain. It had to be over idleness. The old man hated nothing more than any perceived sign of laziness in his offspring.

Eduardo reached back into his pocket, palmed the capsule, then took it out, resting his hand on his thigh, waiting. One second when nobody looked was all he needed.

"I should have paid more attention to you two, but I had too much work." The old man stared into his drink, reflecting. "All my time, all my energy I put into the business. Every *real* I made, I bought land with it. Not the rubber plantations that were going out of business already at that time. Just virgin rain forest. I'd buy as much as I could. The government was making noise about controlling its resources. Permits were needed for everything, and fees, and blasted taxes upon taxes. If you didn't have permission, logging was no longer legal."

"But you wanted to stay legal for your sons," Eduardo said. How many times had the old man told them that? Always expecting gratitude, even admiration. Did he expect to be worshipped?

Had he even done it all for his sons? Or because he'd wanted to build his kingdom in the sunshine, not in the shadows. A king needed a kingdom. That had always been his fantasy: the boy from the favelas who would be king. Or, at least, the father of senators, maybe even a president.

He shook his head now. "My new friends in business didn't understand me. They laughed at me. The land was dirt cheap. I bought as much as I could, and then I bought more." The grin he gave was pure favela, pure hustler. "And then I gave money to politicians to crack down on illegal logging. After that, I gave them more money to make national parks of large chunks of land I couldn't buy. It all made the lands Morais Timber owned more valuable."

He fixed his son with a steady stare. "Leap on opportunities. And if there are no opportunities, create them."

"Yes, Father."

"But never forget, it's a jungle out there."

Eduardo resisted rolling his eyes. What did his old man know about the jungle anymore? Morais Timber had moved its executive offices to Rio decades ago. Raul Morais wanted to be closer to the place where decisions were made. He was now a wealthy man. Politicians curried his favor.

Raul was on his third wife now. The first, his sons' mother he'd married to pull himself out of poverty. The second to gain admittance to the highest echelons of Manaus, a city that had been growing by leaps and bounds. The third, he married after moving to Rio. He needed a way into Rio society, a hostess with class and breeding who would host his parties when he entertained senators and millionaires.

Eleanora was currently in Switzerland for some kind of health treatment.

The previous wives, Raul Morais had simply discarded. The two sons he kept. He didn't have any other children. On purpose. He had the heir and the spare—enough. He was building a kingdom. He didn't want a bushel of offspring to fragment it into small slivers after his death.

He made his sons compete for the prize. Little did he know that they conspired behind his back.

If Marcos got back the diamonds, everything would work out. Or...if Eduardo succeeded here today...the competition would be off, and the Morais fortune equally divided between the heirs.

They had two chances. Marcos and Eduardo. One of them would succeed. Eduardo loved and trusted his brother, but he wanted to be the one.

He reached for his drink, knocked it over. "Sorry."

He looked at Joaquim, willing the man to come and clean it up.

But Raul waved off Eduardo. "Go. I'm tired. I can't make any decisions today."

So Eduardo had no choice but to stand.

Joaquim walked him out. Before opening the front door for Eduardo, the man produced a bottle of water from behind his back.

"I noticed you were holding a pill, senhor." The man's hard gaze held Eduardo's. "Perhaps you'd like to take it."

Sweat popped onto Eduardo's forehead. He cleared his throat. "Just some headache powder. But while we were talking, the headache actually got better."

Joaquim kept his horse face expressionless. He gave a measured nod, then opened the door.

Eduardo hurried out, a cold shiver running down his spine, as if death had brushed by him.

He shook off the disturbing sensation by the time he reached his car. As he drove away, he glanced into the rearview mirror. Joaquim still stood in the door, looking after him.

Eduardo swore and slammed his fist into the steering wheel. He's been so close. One minute, or, less than that, *a few seconds,* and he could have done it.

He hoped Marcos succeeded. Getting the diamonds back was their only chance.

* * *

Carmen

Carmen taped a MISSING CHILD poster onto the light pole on the sidewalk that edged the road, her daughter's sweet, chubby face smiling at her from the picture.

The heat and humidity were oppressive, Manaus with its two million inhabitants hopelessly large. Carmen ignored the sweat that rolled down her back, ignored the car exhaust that choked her.

Phil worked the other side of the street. They tried to cover as much territory as possible. The phone number listed went straight to the police, and Gustavo Santos, the detective on the case, had an officer assigned to it. Because of the reward, dozens of calls came in every day, but no real lead so far.

Carmen pushed on. *Maybe today.*

She trusted Ian Slaney and Daniela Wintermann, the US investigators, hoped beyond hope that they'd be able to find Lila, but she wanted to do absolutely everything that might help.

She taped up the next poster, then the next, bleary-eyed from crying all night and dizzy from lack of sleep. Then she somehow, stupidly, slipped off the curb and twisted her left ankle. She went down with a cry of pain.

Phil was next to her in a moment. "How bad?"

"It's nothing. A sprain." But when she tried, she couldn't put weight on the leg.

He helped her up. "Let's catch a bus back to See-Love-Aid."

"We still have all these posters for today."

"Then you take a cab back, and I'll keep on with the posters."

She held his concerned gaze.

She couldn't go back to their room, to the empty crib. She couldn't lie there on the bed, looking at Lila's empty baby bottles on the nightstand. She needed to be doing something. She needed to be doing *this*.

Thank God, she didn't have to say it. Phil nodded as if she had. He turned his back to her and bent his knees. "Piggyback ride. I'll carry you. You tape the posters."

Tears gathered in her eyes—a permanent state lately. "I love you."

Had she ever thought that maybe he wasn't a strong man, not enough of a warrior? How wrong she'd been. He'd been her rock through this whole ordeal. She couldn't imagine a stronger man than Phil Heyerdahl.

"I love you too, Carmen." He moved forward, carrying her easily.

People looked at them askance. But then the onlookers saw the posters she was taping up, and some came over to pat her on the back and wish them luck, others offered prayers.

The spectacle she made on Phil's back drew attention. Instead of hurrying past them, passersby actually looked more carefully. People were actually checking out the posters.

And Carmen thought, *Maybe this will help.*

They finished the block, then moved on to the next one.

***

Not far behind them, a young woman stopped, her chest tight. Her skin tingled as she read the poster on the side of the bus stop. The photo of a smiling baby was the largest thing on the poster, but the young woman could focus only on the numbers at the bottom of the page.

Ten thousand US dollars. The local currency was right under it, in smaller print: *thirty-six thousand reais.*

A fortune in Manaus.

She could think of a million ways to spend that money. That much money could save her.

Thirty-six thousand reais.

She chewed the inside of her cheek, shifting from one foot to the other, unable to stay still. *Too much.* The reward had to be a trap. If she went to the police, they'd put her in jail and keep the money.

She read the poster again.

Before she could read it the third time, the bus rolled up to the curb, huffing and puffing as it stopped. She hurried up the steps. Then the bus was moving again.

Through the window, she kept her eyes on the reward money for as long as she could make out the numbers.

***

Ian

By the time Ian and Daniela got back to the See-Love-Aid hostel, the Heyerdahls had also returned. They invited Ian and Daniela into their room, offering the two chairs. Carmen was sitting on her bed, her right foot up on the bed, elevated, with a wet cloth on her ankle. She kept one hand on the crib.

Phil sat behind her, a hand around her waist, supporting her.

They told their story, pretty much what the detective had related, but with a lot more tears.

The young couple were in their mid-twenties, collapsed, no other word for it. They looked as if they'd been through war, eyes red, faces pallid. Their gazes were dazed, as if they hadn't slept since their baby had disappeared.

Ian ruthlessly punched back every dark memory that tried to rise from his past.

"Lila is such a good baby," Carmen said. "She rarely fusses. That's why I knew I could leave her for a few minutes. We felt we were surrounded by friends." Tears poured down her face. "I thought it was safe."

Ian wished he had access to the other visiting volunteers who'd been here at the time, but when their two weeks had ended, they'd all gone home, scattered to the four corners of the world. Only the Heyerdahls remained. The new batch of volunteers currently in residence hadn't been in Brazil when the baby had been kidnapped. Ian saw little point in questioning them.

"Did anyone pay special attention to Lila?" Daniela asked gently.

The mother sobbed harder.

The father, Phil Heyerdahl, said, "Everyone did. She was the darling of the group. She was handed from lap to lap, entertained. We had no shortage of people offering to watch her, even change diapers." He pulled a little rolled-up mat from under the bed. "Even the teens. Look. They made her a changing mat."

Carmen sank against his chest behind her but kept a hand on the crib, as if needing that connection.

"How about when you were out in the city? Anyone come up to you? Did you ever feel watched?" Ian asked.

Phil dropped the changing mat onto the other bed. "I'm big and blond and blue-eyed. I stand out a little among the locals, but not that much. There are plenty of other tourists. So some people looked, but nothing unusual. Carmen looks local." He kissed the top of his wife's head, folded both arms around her. "We asked these questions ourselves a hundred times."

"We gave DNA to the local police," Carmen said. "Her hair from her little brush. So if any child is found…"

"That's very good," Daniela immediately reassured her. "If the police have DNA, they can identify her."

"Even if they don't find her right away." Tears rolled down Carmen's face. "Babies change so fast."

A knock came on the door, and Carol stuck her head in. "Sorry. I'll come back later," she said, then backed out and closed the door behind her.

Ian decided he'd check on her later, ask if she needed anything. He didn't think she should be here this close to giving birth, but that wasn't his decision. Best he could do was help with what he could. He remembered Linda at this stage of the pregnancy, feet swollen, heartburn out of control, general twenty-four-seven misery.

"That's Carol, one of the permanent staff," Phil Heyerdahl said.

"We've met." Ian drew his attention back to the man.

"She's about to have a baby." Carmen flashed a miserable look. "I feel like I should offer her the crib, but I just can't. When we find Lila…She's only six months old." Caught herself. "Almost seven now. But she still needs the crib."

Six months old. The memories overwhelmed Ian, the twins sitting up for the first time while he'd been home on leave, making all kinds of sweet sounds, but not words yet.

He'd had plans for their first birthday. He was going to order a rent-a-petting-zoo visit over the Internet, have them show up at the house. He'd found a place that did that. They had a pony, a goat, a piglet, and two bunnies. He'd wanted to make sure Connor and Colin would have a good time, even if he was half a world away.

He rubbed his eyes. Filled his lungs. Looked at the Heyerdahls.

He'd always done his best on every case he'd investigated for CPRU, but somehow, baby Lila was fast becoming personal.

He took in every detail of the room, the parents, the way they talked, the tone, the words, the body language. He watched and listened while Daniela asked questions and consoled the mother.

The Heyerdahls seemed ridiculously grateful that Ian and Daniela had come all the way from the US to help them. Ian didn't want their gratitude. Not until he brought that baby back.

After the interview, Daniela went to talk to the girls again, while Ian went outside. He needed some air, so he walked around the building, all the way to the back.

He scanned the ground as he walked, doing his best to ignore the heat and humidity. An idea was slowly forming in his head. Maybe the reason why nobody had seen anyone taking the baby out of the parents' bedroom was that baby Lila hadn't been taken out.

She could easily have been lowered from the window, in one of the large sisal baskets the girls wove right on the premises. Maybe whoever had stolen the baby had passed her over to his or her baby-selling connection right here.

Of course, a month later, finding any tracks was hopeless.

The back of the property stood knee-high in weeds. A row of small wooden houses waited straight ahead, their tiny backyards fenced except for a few.

Daniela was talking with the girls in the far corner of the yard. They were playing some kind of a game with rocks and empty food cans. She had her back to Ian. She had the girls' full attention, every face turned to her, every expression admiring. The girls seemed very impressed that someone so much like them could become an important American investigator.

The girls had been outside at the time of the kidnapping, but they would not have seen the area where Ian was standing, not from the basketball court. But…maybe not every eye had been on the basketball game. *And*, Ian thought now, *maybe one had snuck off back here for a smoke or a beer, or to meet a boy. Teenagers were teenagers the world around.*

He left Daniela to the girls and went to talk to the people who lived in the wooden houses. The police had done a door to door, according to their report, but Ian wanted a firsthand feel for the people who lived in the homes. They would see the aid workers coming and going. They would have seen the baby. Maybe one of them had come up with the kidnapping to make a little money.

Ian strode across the lot, crossed through a small backyard that wasn't fenced in.

Having a little distance between Daniela and him for a couple of hours wouldn't hurt either. That kiss back at the sugar factory…

He couldn't think about that kiss. Every time he did, he felt so guilty, he wanted to hand his own ass to himself, dammit. He'd spent the rest of the morning carefully maintaining professional distance. And maybe he'd keep investigating for the rest of their time here, without stopping, because he couldn't cope with the idea of sleeping in the same bedroom with her.

He strode toward the nearest house, the path to the steps overgrown with weeds. He gave it a try anyway, knocked on the door. Nobody responded.

At the second house, a harried mother with three little kids clinging to her legs opened up for him. He asked his questions: Where had she been a month ago? If she'd seen or heard anything?

He was glad that while he'd been teaching Daniela English he'd agreed to her teaching him Portuguese. They used to trade word for word after she'd moved to DC.

Daniela's English was way better than Ian's Portuguese, but he knew enough for basic questioning. And he must have gotten his questions right, because the woman in the cracked-open door responded.

"Sorry, senhor. I didn't see anything. I didn't know what happened until the police came."

He tried four more homes and received nearly identical answers.

"How about the empty house?" he asked on an impulse at the last place he visited.

"Essie?" The old, nearly toothless woman in the doorway wrinkled her forehead, which was so wrinkled already, Ian could just barely tell that she was frowning. "She moved to São Paulo."

"Do you know why?"

"New job."

"Do you know when?"

The old woman hesitated, sucking her only tooth as she tried to remember, so he asked, "Was it before or after the baby disappeared?"

The woman thought hard, scratching the mole on her chin. "Before, but not much, maybe a day or two. I only remember because Clara, the neighbor, said the police wanted her to let them into the house to make sure the kidnappers weren't there. Clara has Essie's key."

He thanked the old woman and went back, asked Clara for the key. The neighbor didn't hesitate handing it over—probably because Ian had flashed his CPRU ID card when he'd first questioned her. Likely she had no idea what the card meant, but she'd decided he was some kind of a foreign official. She gave him the key with the warning that the local police had already seen everything.

Ian went for a look anyway. The power had been shut off, but he didn't really need the overhead lights. Enough light still came through the windows.

Essie had left behind her furniture. Not unusual in itself. The furniture was cheap bamboo stuff. Moving it would probably cost more than buying something used in São Paulo.

Two bedrooms. One with an adult-size bed, the other one a kid's room, pictures of animals on the walls, a plastic ball in the corner. The sisal carpet still had dents in it where a crib had been.

Ian strode back to the neighbor. "Did Essie have a child?"

"Two years old," the woman said. "A little boy."

Ian thanked her, then walked back to See-Love-Aid. The police report didn't include an interview with Essie. Made sense, she'd moved before the incident. She couldn't possibly have seen anything. Yet something floated at the edges of Ian's mind, wisps of half thoughts he couldn't put together into a whole.

As he walked up the stairs to his and Daniela's room, he decided to visit Essie's neighbor again the next day and see if Essie had left a forwarding address or a phone number where she could be reached.

Daniela was back in their room already, sitting on her bed, organizing her notes.

"Anything?" he asked.

"The girls insist that they were all at the game. Nobody snuck off. They never sneak off. They're all perfect angels." She shoved an escaped tendril of black hair behind her ear. "They're probably worried that if they betray any bad behavior, they'll be kicked out. They just don't want to risk it." She stacked the papers into a pile and put it on her nightstand. "I'll keep trying. Every time we talk, they trust me a little more."

Something was off in her voice, something more than frustration.

"What is it?" Ian asked. "What's wrong?"

She dropped her gaze. "I told them I grew up around here, upriver, grew up poor like them." She picked at the bedspread. "But I didn't tell them what I've been. They might trust me more if I do. If I talk about that. If they don't see me as an investigator so much, but something else."

"You are an investigator," he said, because he knew how hard she'd worked to create a new identity for herself, because she deserved to be respected for what she'd achieved. "But you have nothing to be ashamed about your past either. You survived it. It doesn't make you a bad person. It makes you a survivor, an incredibly strong woman who could overcome extraordinary hardship."

She looked up with a half smile. "Calm down, mother hen. No need to have the talk again. I know, I know."

"Good." But even so, he knew that a break line existed between her past and present, a fault line between continents. And when those continents rubbed together, there was friction and earthquakes.

She stopped picking at the bedspread. "Found out anything new by walking around?"

"Not much. I talked to the neighbors out back. Nobody's seen anything." He had nothing but some unformed half thoughts, too vague to articulate. Instead of trying, he asked, "Want to go out for dinner?"

The food at See-Love-Aid was okay, but they were obviously on a budget and leaning toward vegetarian. He needed a damn steak.

Daniela was already on her feet, her melancholy shaken off. "Do I ever not want to go out to dinner? Do you even know me?"

Good question. Did he? *Because that kiss…*

He turned and strode out the door. No way was he thinking about that kiss while they were in a bedroom together.

Since there was a fried food place at the end of the street, they walked. Neither of them felt like taking a bus deeper into the city.

They bumped into Carol, coming out of a small convenience store.

She wasn't shopping for the girls at See-Love-Aid this time. She was carrying a bag of diapers.

"Getting ready for the baby?" Daniela asked.

Carol laughed. "Two weeks left, but you know how these things go. The baby could be early."

"Want me to take that back for you?" Ian offered and surreptitiously checked her ankles, relieved that they weren't swollen.

Carol waved him off. "Doesn't weigh anything. You two have fun out on the town." She winked at them as if they were going on a date.

Ian paused.

Was that what everybody thought?

He scowled as Carol moved on, and he and Daniela resumed their walk. Did the other aid workers think he and Daniela were a couple? Did they think he was some fricking old lecher who'd take advantage of a young woman?

All right, they were sharing a room. But they were partners!

And he'd never even…

All right, except for that one kiss.

He filled his lungs. He wanted this op to be over. Hell, he wanted to run for the hills.

Next to him, Daniela marched along happily, walking fast to keep up with his long strides. When she caught him looking at her, she grinned.

She pointed at the busy, grimy street, the air filled with car exhaust and the fishy smells of the river. "Hey, isn't this great? We've put in a good day's work, and now we're going on a date."

Swear to God, Ian wanted to jump in front of traffic.

* * *

Daniela

The call came just as Daniela and Ian got back to their lodgings. She was in a good mood, even if Ian had worked the word *friends* into the dinner conversation no less than half a dozen times. She didn't buy it. He *had* kissed her back in Rio. And there'd been nothing friendly about that kiss.

For the first time in her life, she felt desire, felt like a normal woman. She wanted. And she wanted to be wanted back. That kiss gave her so much hope, she'd been on the verge of breaking out in song every time she remembered Ian's lips on hers.

As Daniela watched, he answered his phone, then mouthed to her, *Gustavo Santos.*

The local detective.

Ian said, "Yes" and "Thank you" a lot, then hung up.

She was holding her breath. "What is it?"

"You know the gang that's been involved in illegal adoptions before? One of the women in the gang has been seen around with a baby. And nobody remembers seeing her pregnant. The police are tracking her down. Once they have her, they're going to bring her in. We are invited, as a courtesy, to the questioning, but the detective asked that we don't say anything to the Heyerdahls until it's certain that they have the right child."

Relief filled her down to her toes. "Thank God."

Please let this be baby Lila.

She wanted to rush straight to Carmen and Phil, but she understood Santos. If they were wrong, the Heyerdahls would be devastated.

As Daniela lay in bed that night, she thought about the case, and she thought about Ian. She cared about baby Lila more than she could put into words. And she *was* focused on the case. But her awareness of Ian was like constant background music these days. Or as if the TV was left on in another room. You did your business, but the sounds were there, woven into the fabric of your day.

And night.

She could never have imagined that sleeping in the same room with him night after night would be this disappointing. He didn't even kiss her good night.

How could Ian keep ignoring her?

Even after the kiss in Rio.

The kiss!

She couldn't believe she'd worked up the guts to do *that*. But, God, how good it had been. If they hadn't been in danger, she would have kissed him over and over again. She wanted to. Even now. Still. While he...

Out of the darkness, his growly voice said, "Thank you for coming to Rio for me. But, please, don't do anything like that ever again."

She turned to stare at him in the semidarkness. *That was it?*

CHAPTER
FIFTEEN

Ian

Gustavo Santos conducted the questioning in a large but plain conference room on the ground floor of the police district headquarters. Maybe the interrogation room was too small for all of them. Or maybe they had floggers hanging on the wall that he didn't want the Americans to see. Ian didn't know and didn't care. He watched the suspect.

She held a blond baby, nothing but hatred and contempt toward the police in the woman's drug-hazed black eyes that matched her stringy black hair. Tattoos covered her neck and both of her skinny arms. She could be anywhere between twenty or forty, impossible to tell. Too many years of hard living had left deep marks on her.

"You take my baby away over my dead body." She spat the words at them and looked ready to fight.

She didn't have a lawyer present.

"When did you have the baby?" Gustavo Santos asked.

The questioning went on in Portuguese. Ian didn't understand every word but got enough to know what they were talking about. And if he missed anything, he could always ask Daniela.

He sat back while Santos worked the suspect. He and Daniela were here only to observe.

The woman gave the baby's birthday, and the detective made a note. The date was seven months ago, so the timing matched. The baby was the right age.

"Where?"

"At the Hospital Adventista."

The detective produced a printout from the folder in front of him and pushed it over to the woman along with a pen. "I need you to sign the release of medical records form."

"No way."

"Then we'll take the baby for a DNA test, and you won't have her back until we get the test results."

Shooting them a look of murder, the woman scribbled what might or might not be a signature.

The detective walked the piece of paper to the door, called over a secretary, and instructed her to obtain the records immediately, have them emailed over. Then he strode back to his chair and sat.

"Is your boyfriend blond?"

The woman's chin came up in defiance. "What's it to you?"

"You don't see a lot of blond kids running around here."

"Maybe his father ain't from around here."

"Where is he from?"

Her eyes shot sparks of anger. "He's a fucking prison guard down in São Paulo. I got knocked up while I was in the can. Now you happy?"

The detective didn't look happy.

Neither was Ian. While the baby was the right sex, age, and coloring, she didn't look like the pictures Carmen Heyerdahl was showing around. Not that you could necessarily tell much from baby pictures. Fuzzy hair, no teeth, chubby cheeks—babies looked a lot alike at that age, at least to Ian.

The detective kept asking questions.

The woman answered, but with thorough contempt. You could tell from her tone that if she thought she could get away with scratching all their eyes out, she would have gone for it. She certainly had the nails for aggravated assault: long, ragged, with plenty of dirt packed underneath.

Should an altercation happen, Ian was happy to know that he'd had his tetanus shot just last year.

Santos moved on to questions about other gang members, to which the woman responded with stony silence. They went on like that for about twenty minutes.

Then the email finally came in from the hospital, and everything matched up. The little girl was hers.

She left with her baby, cursing them all the way out of the station, ending with a hearty *vai se fuder!* to Gustavo Santos. "Go F yourself" in Portuguese.

"I'm sorry." The detective looked ready to curse too, scratching at the hair that was graying at his temples. "I really thought this was going to be it. We'll keep looking."

Ian shook the man's extended hand. "We'll do the same."

He was grateful for the cooperation. The woman with the blonde little girl had been a long shot, but it could have worked. Better to try and fail than to leave any stones unturned.

Daniela was thoughtful as they got on the bus. "I'm glad we didn't mention anything to Carmen and Phil."

Ian held on to a plastic handle as the bus rattled on. He could have rented a car, but he wanted to get a better feel for the city and the people. For now, the buses and the cabs would do.

The traffic was crazy chaotic. If he drove, he'd have to keep his attention on that. This way, he could freely look around, watch the hustlers, the people selling drugs, the prostitutes, the shady element he was interested in. If he ended up needing a car, he could always rent one later.

Talking about the shady element...Ian watched as a pickpocket headed for them. Daniela stared the guy down. She could be seriously fierce when she wanted to be.

He'd always known she was tough, but on this trip, away from everything DC, he was beginning to see her in a new—or maybe old—light. Every once in a while, the river goddess came out, and he didn't know what to do with her.

Part of him couldn't wait until this mission ended. While the rest of him...

He was going to ignore what the rest of him wanted.

When they got off the bus in front of See-Love-Aid, the first person they saw was Pierre the French Casanova, fixing the front steps, filling the cracks with wet cement from a bucket. He immediately hurried over. He was watching Daniela as he asked, "Any news?"

"Not yet."

As the bus pulled out, a beat-up pickup truck with See-Love-Aid's logo pulled up to the curb in its place, and Henry, in the driver seat, lay on the horn before jumping out and tossing the keys to Pierre. "All yours, bro." The big, blond English teacher from Ohio paused. "Hey, and I fixed that knocking in the back. Loose exhaust pipe."

He seemed to be a jack-of-all-trades.

He turned to grin at Daniela, his gaze dipping to her purple sandals. "Nice shoes."

She smiled back. "Thanks."

Ian scowled. Henry was close to his age. What the hell did he mean by looking at Daniela like that?

As Henry disappeared inside, girls ran from the building to pile their crafts in the back of the pickup.

Pierre used up the last of his cement and stood, then stepped toward Daniela. "Want to come with me to the shops to drop off the goodies?"

She glanced at Ian.

He did his best not to grind his teeth. No way to tell her *no* without looking like an idiot. "Fine with me."

He wanted to canvass the neighborhood again anyway. He could do that alone. Daniela deserved a couple of hours off. It wasn't as if they were joined at the hip.

So she went, with Pierre the French Casanova, while Ian stayed behind.

Mrs. Frieseke invited him to lunch with her. She was alone at the staff table, the others already having finished. The older girls were back in their workshop, the younger girls in their classes.

"Oh, your poor face," the woman cooed, her plate of rice and fish nearly empty. "It hurts to look at you. Those thugs in Rio did a number. I was a nurse back home. Did I tell you that? In San Francisco. Nurse for a while, then when my back gave out, I became a social worker. Are you sure you don't want a butterfly bandage for that eyebrow? You'll have a scar there."

"My own stupidity," he said. "When they asked for money, I shouldn't have resisted."

"They didn't know you were the law. They don't respect the law anyway. Not in Rio and not Manaus. With the economy slipping, crime is going through the roof. I worry that, if it gets worse, we won't be able to get enough volunteers to come here." She sighed. "Where did you and Daniela go this morning in such a hurry?"

"Police station." Ian dug into the rice, cooked in coconut milk and flavored with a spice he couldn't name.

The woman brightened. "Do they have anything?"

"Thought they did, but it didn't pan out."

She stared into her soup, guilt filling her eyes. "I hope you find that child."

"We'll do our best, ma'am."

She looked up. "Is Daniela still out?"

"She's gone to the shops with Pierre."

Mrs. Frieseke raised a sparse eyebrow. "Heather won't like it."

Ian stopped eating. "Why is that?"

"They're an item, as they used to say in my day. Heather is already plenty jealous of Hannah. Pierre had a fling with Hannah last year. He's a handsome young man. The women enjoy him."

And it sounded like he'd enjoyed half the staff.

And he was out with Daniela.

A dark mood enveloped Ian and turned him off his food. He didn't even touch his fish. He waited politely until Mrs. Frieseke finished her lunch, then said good-bye and moved on. He went to see the few neighbors who hadn't been home the first time he'd checked out the small wooden houses out back.

He went from home to home, asked his questions, got plenty of answers, but nothing that helped. All the while, he kept an eye on the window of the room he shared with Daniela, but he didn't see any movement. She wasn't back yet.

Three hours had passed. How could going to the shops to drop off a load of souvenirs take three damned hours?

They were going to have a talk about the French Boy Wonder when she got back.

CHAPTER
SIXTEEN

Daniela

Pierre took Daniela to lunch after the shops, so they didn't return to See-Love-Aid until midafternoon. The time hadn't been wasted either. Pierre seemed to know everything about everyone and wasn't afraid of sharing.

He was twenty-two, her age, fun, entertaining, handsome. And still, for most of the time they spent together, Daniela had been thinking about Ian. She was glad when they were finally returning to See-Love-Aid.

Pierre looped his arm around her shoulders as they walked inside, and she let him, as an experiment. But neither Pierre's nearness nor his touch made her feel like Ian did. Her heart didn't race; her skin didn't tingle.

She was about to move away from him when she spotted Ian in the rec room, talking intently with Carol, the pregnant staffer, on the sofa in the corner.

"We're back," Pierre said. "Did we miss any fun?"

Carol and Ian turned toward them at the same time.

A quick look of annoyance flashed across Carol's face.

What's that about? Does she like Pierre?

Her husband had died seven months ago. Maybe Carol was lonely. If she was ready to move on, Daniela wasn't going to blame her.

But while Carol was annoyed at Pierre's hand on Daniela's shoulder, Ian's gaze was completely emotionless and flat.

Nudged by some little devil, Daniela stepped closer to Pierre.

Ian's expression grew tighter.

And even though Daniela knew she was being juvenile, she couldn't resist whispering to Pierre, "Hey, let's go tell the girls how much money they just made."

Pierre winked at her and steered her out of the room.

She didn't look back at Ian, but she hoped he was having a stroke. He deserved it. If he refused to admit that he wanted her, why shouldn't she have fun with someone else?

But as they found the girls out back and delivered the good news, Daniela soon became tired of Pierre's joking and messing around. He did a French mime imitation, then demonstrated some break-dancing moves to the girls' great amusement.

He was like a kid. He was immeasurably immature compared to Ian. Honestly, Pierre was even immature compared to Daniela.

She used the opportunity to chat with some of the teenagers she hadn't talked to before.

"Do people who don't work at See-Love-Aid ever come here?" she asked a sweetly dispositioned sibling pair, Gabriela and Fernanda, who took the initiative to show her the vegetable garden.

"Of course," Gabriela, the older sister, said. "We have foreign visitors, donors. Some of the shop owners come to negotiate with Mrs. Frieseke. Lots of people come here. Some girls have relatives who visit."

"Does anyone ever go upstairs?"

The girls shook their heads simultaneously, ear-length brown hair swinging around their tanned cheeks. "Visitors aren't allowed to go upstairs."

But then the younger girl, Fernanda, giggled.

The older sister, Gabriela, flashed her a warning look.

Daniela got an idea. "Has a boy ever snuck up?"

The girls took great interest in their matching red rubber sandals.

"It must be hard that there're only girls here," Daniela said, although it seemed pretty good to her.

Fernanda bit her lip, then asked, "Did you go to school with boys in America?"

"I went to college with boys, yes."

"Did you have a boyfriend?" The girl's eyes sparkled with mischievous curiosity. Both sisters watched her with rapt attention.

"I had friends who were boys."

The younger girl giggled again. "Gabriela has a boyfriend," she whispered.

Her sister shoved her. "Fernanda!"

And Daniela said, "I won't tell."

Gabriela shot a warning look at her sister. To Daniela, she said, "He only came upstairs once. When I was sick and I couldn't go down to work. He brought me fried piranhas."

Daniela remembered fried piranhas fondly. "Seems like a good guy."

Gabriela allowed a shy smile. "He is. He wants to marry me when I graduate from here."

Daniela smiled back, grateful beyond words that places like this existed.

She fanned herself with her hand as they stood out under the sun. She'd gotten used to the cooler climate in DC. Manaus was even hotter than the jungle village she'd grown up in. In the village, they had the tree canopy above to cast shade. The city was little more than streets and buildings. The blacktop radiated back the sun's heat, and the buildings trapped the sweltering air, kept it from moving.

Earlier, during the un-air-conditioned truck ride to the shops and back, sweat had dampened Daniela's shirt, and she was even hotter now, standing in the garden. The combination of heat and humidity was too much.

"So just one boy?" she asked. "No other outsider has ever been upstairs?"

But the girls just shook their heads earnestly, and as Daniela looked into their open and honest gazes, she believed them.

After she finished the garden tour with the sisters, she decided to go upstairs and wash off, put on a clean dress.

As she reached Carol's room, she slowed. Then, on impulse, she knocked.

She couldn't shake off the image of Carol so cozy with Ian on the couch downstairs earlier. What had they been talking about? Daniela wanted to chat with the woman, even if only for ten minutes, wanted to get a feel for whether or not Carol was maybe interested in Ian.

Because when Daniela had turned to leave with Pierre earlier, Carol hadn't been upset. She looked relieved. As if maybe she'd been upset not because Daniela had been out with Pierre, but because they'd come back and interrupted Carol's little chitchat in the rec room with Ian.

The thought made Daniela mad enough to choke a caiman.

She had no trouble seeing Carol being attracted to Ian. Who wouldn't be? And Ian…

Carol was older than Daniela. Ian had a hang-up about age. Carol had lost her husband. Ian had lost his wife. They had that in common. Carol was having a baby. Ian missed his sons, even if he refused to talk about them.

Is Carol what Ian looks for in a woman?

Daniela clenched her teeth.

As she knocked again, the door pushed open. It hadn't been properly closed.

She stuck her head in. "Carol?"

But Carol wasn't in there.

A printout on the small table just inside the door caught Daniela's eyes. A plane ticket confirmation for the day after tomorrow. Then she noted the half-packed suitcase in the corner.

Daniela pulled the door closed and walked toward her own room. Carol was leaving? Was that what she'd been talking to Ian about earlier?

Nobody could blame the woman if she'd changed her mind about having her baby here. Daniela was sure Manaus's hospitals were great and very modern, but she'd bet hospitals in the US were still better.

She washed, changed, then went back downstairs. Ian and Carol were gone from the couch. Daniela looked around, but when she didn't find him, she hopped on a bus, then another and another, and rode around the neighborhood. With Ian off somewhere, she was free to follow up on an idea she'd had earlier.

The Heyerdahls worked and lived at See-Love-Aid. Most likely the kidnapper would have first noticed them somewhere around here. That meant that the kidnapper lived somewhere around here.

Daniela wasn't sure what she was looking for. But she did look at every baby she spotted. Even the ones who weren't blond. Hair could be colored. She was pretty sure she would recognize baby Lila. And if she needed a reminder of the little girl's face, all she needed to do was look at one of the MISSING CHILD posters that seemed to be everywhere.

She didn't see Ian until that evening, back in their room.

Her bus trip netted nothing, but she told him what she'd learned from Fernanda and Gabriela about visiting boyfriends.

"So people we didn't previously know about do sometimes go upstairs," she said. "Except, there's no passage between the girls' dorms and the staff housing, not with that door always locked. The key had been at the ER with Mrs. Frieseke. So I don't think a boy sneaking in could have taken the baby."

Ian watched her thoughtfully. He'd already taken his shower. Water glistened in his hair. His clean T-shirt clung to his wet skin, outlining his muscles. "But if boys sneak up to the girls," he said, "it's possible that a man might sneak up to one of the female staff in the adult dorms."

She lifted her gaze to his eyes. "It's possible."

"So maybe somebody has a boyfriend on the outside. A boyfriend she's hiding from the others for some reason."

"Or," Daniela added, "someone has a girlfriend that he's hiding."

"First thing tomorrow morning, we're going to start looking into this. Talk to people one-on-one, discreetly. I'll start with Carol. She's been here for two years. She knows a lot about everyone."

Hating a pregnant woman felt wrong, but if someone decided to kidnap Carol, Daniela would have been only mildly anguished. This trip was supposed to bring *her* and Ian closer together. *Not* Ian and another woman.

Thank God, Carol was leaving.

"After Carol," Ian said, "I'll talk to Pierre. He gets around, from what I hear."

"I don't mind talking to Pierre." He was immature, but a fun guy. Simple and lighthearted. He might know some gossip.

Ian watched her as if he was trying to see inside her. "I'll talk to Pierre. You talk to Hannah and Heather."

***

Ian

They spent the following morning trying to discover more about the personal lives of the staff, but nobody seemed to have any romantic secrets beyond the fact that all the women appeared to be secretly or not so secretly in love with Pierre.

After lunch, while Daniela chatted up Henry, the last person they hadn't talked to yet, Ian went to see Clara again, Essie's neighbor. He wanted Essie's phone number so he could call and ask her if she'd seen anything suspicious before she'd moved from the house at the back of the See-Love-Aid property.

If someone had planned the kidnapping, they would have staked out the place days prior to the kidnapping in order to get an idea of people's schedules and movements inside See-Love-Aid. Essie might remember seeing a stranger lurking around.

Clara was more than helpful, once again. She wrote Essie's cell phone down on a wrinkled flyer and handed it to Ian.

"I had the strangest thing happen just this morning." She tapped her head with her knuckles as if saying she was going batty. "I could swear I saw Essie at the market. I tried to catch her, but she got on a bus. I'm sure it wasn't her, but whoever I saw looked just like her." She sighed. "I guess I'm seeing her everywhere because I miss her. She was like a daughter to me."

The woman stepped back to show Ian a picture on the hall table. The photo showed her with a younger woman at some kind of a festival, hugging, laughing.

Essie was pretty, if bony in the shoulders. As Ian leaned closer, he noted a scar on the younger woman's chin. Then another on her cheekbone, as if the skin had split—maybe from a mean punch—and she hadn't bothered to have it stitched, just let it heal on its own.

"Would you mind if I took a picture with my cell phone?"

The woman shook her head. Her eyes clouded. "I'm happy for her, but I miss her. Still, it's good for her to have that job in São Paulo."

Ian sensed something in the quivering tone of her voice. "Wasn't she happy here?"

The woman pressed her lips together. But, after a moment, she said, "That boyfriend of hers. Fabricio Melo." Deep lines of disapproval wrinkled her forehead. "He's not a good man. He's got harsh hands. It's good for Essie that she left. He's a poor fisherman. Essie gave *him* money." The woman's gaze held motherly worry. "He took money she needed for her baby."

"You know where Fabricio lives?"

The neighbor shrugged. "On his boat, mostly."

Ian thought about that on his way back to Daniela.

Essie's boyfriend was a no-good loser. Maybe the type of guy who could talk his girlfriend—whom he controlled with violence—into doing something criminally stupid.

Let's say Fabricio talked Essie into helping him steal the baby. Then the guy took the baby up north, maybe to Mexico, or all the way to the US for an illegal adoption. Essie might be waiting somewhere around here for him to come back with the money.

If the neighbor had seen Essie in Manaus, that probably meant they didn't have the money yet; the baby hadn't been sold yet. If they had the money, they'd be out of here. Why risk running into someone who knew them? If they suddenly came into money, people around here would wonder where it came from.

But in another city, they could easily start fresh.

Halfway up the stairs, Ian turned around and went back down again. On a hunch, he hopped on the bus that went to the nearest market, the one where Clara would most likely be doing her shopping. If Essie was seen shopping at that particular market, then she had to live somewhere in that direction.

As the bus pulled away from the curb, Ian called Essie's cell phone number.

The phone rang and rang before a woman picked up with a tentative, "*Alô.*"

"This is Dr. Ian at the Hospital Adventista," Ian said in his best Portuguese, but didn't bother hiding his accent. There had to be some foreign doctors who worked in Brazilian hospitals. "We have your boyfriend, Fabricio Melo. He's been in a car accident and has a concussion. We can't release him unless someone comes to pick him up. He gave your number as his emergency contact. Can you come and get him?"

Silence stretched on the line. Then muffled praying. "I can be there by three."

Ian glanced at his phone as he hung up. Two p.m. He was standing right behind the bus driver, so he asked the guy how to get to Hospital Adventista.

"Get off at the next stop, then take Bus 418," the driver said around some candy he was chewing, then yelled out the window to curse at a cab that cut him off.

Ian followed directions and was standing in front of the hospital in under thirty minutes. Then he settled in by the front doors and waited for Essie, visualizing the young woman he'd seen in her neighbor's photograph.

Essie arrived a few minutes early, jumping off the bus, rushing toward the doors, her narrow face pinched, thin shoulders hunched, her threadbare dress too large on her. She kept rubbing her arms in a nervous gesture.

Ian waited until she walked back out twenty minutes later, a lot less frantic but now with a puzzled frown. She crossed the road and got on a bus. He followed her.

She led him to a poor but fairly decent neighborhood of what looked like blue-collar apartments, up to a second-floor rental. Ian waited on the turn in the staircase while the door closed behind Essie, and she turned the key in the lock. Then he hurried up.

He listened at the door. Couldn't hear anything. He knocked.

"Who is it?" a tentative female voice called in Portuguese after a few seconds, the same voice as the one he'd heard on the phone when he'd called Essie.

"New neighbor. I'd like to introduce myself." Now he tried to hide his accent, but had a feeling he didn't quite succeed.

"My husband doesn't want me to open the door to strangers when he's not at home."

"No problem. I'll come by when he's home. Sorry to bother you."

He listened again. He thought he heard a baby making noises. Nothing suspicious there. Essie had a toddler.

But what if, at one point, she'd had more than one kid in that apartment?

Ian went downstairs, then across the street, settling in next to a smoke shop to see if she might come out, maybe with a stroller to take her little boy for a walk. Ian wanted a chance to talk to her, to ask questions. He wanted to get a feeling for her, what type of person she was. Capable of kidnapping?

From her neighbor's description, Essie wasn't a criminal. If she lied to Ian, he would be able to tell.

But Essie never reappeared.

Ian called Detective Santos. "Any chance you could pull me a police report on a Fabricio Melo? He's a fisherman. Young guy. Aggressive. I'm thinking he might have a record, possibly in domestic violence."

"You found something?" The detective sounded muffled, as if he was talking around his dinner.

"I don't know yet. He's the boyfriend of a woman who used to live behind See-Love-Aid. The woman took off just before the kidnapping. I'm just running down everything that even distantly resembles a lead."

A moment of silence on the other end, Santos probably chewing and swallowing. Then he said, "I'll send the report to your phone. But I probably won't have it until tomorrow morning."

"That's fine. I appreciate the help." Ian thanked the man, then let him get back to his dinner.

Once the sky turned dark, Ian headed back to See-Love-Aid. Essie was unlikely to go out now. The streets of Manaus weren't that safe at night, not in this neighborhood. The days might belong to working class people, but the nights clearly belonged to the criminals. As he waited for the bus, Ian picked up a discarded newspaper from the bench, rolled it up, and tucked it into the back of his waistband, pulled his shirt over it. He hated being without a weapon.

The bus came. Four teenagers loitered in the back, one openly dealing drugs, a nasty-looking knife hanging on his belt under his parted shirt. The little shit measured Ian up, marked him for a foreigner, whispered something to the others. They gave tough-guy laughs, like something they might have seen in a movie. Ian figured every one of them probably had at least a knife.

He knew he didn't look like easy prey, but there were four of them, and sometimes there was stupidity in numbers. So Ian half turned and let his shirt stretch a little over the rolled-up newspaper, gave an eyeful of what would look like a serious concealed weapon from ten feet away. The teens didn't approach.

Ian got off at See-Love-Aid at the same time as a middle-aged prostitute got on in a cloud of perfume. She eyed Ian with regret, the bus driver with hope, and the teens with a look of don't-give-me-shit-I-ain't-in-the-mood.

See-Love-Aid was locked up. Ian had to ring the bell. A minute later, someone shuffled forward to open up—Henry, with a baseball bat. *Now* he was stepping up security.

In his wrinkled T-shirt, his hair mussed, he blinked sleepily at Ian. "Anything?"

Ian shook his head. He didn't want to give false hope.

"Hey, Carol decided to go back to the States," Henry said. "We're giving her a send-off in the morning, if you want to be there to say good-bye."

Ian stopped. "Anything wrong with the baby?"

"Nah, man." Henry shrugged. "I guess she's getting close. Just decided she wanted a US hospital. I guess at this stage, the airlines don't like if you fly. So once she decided, she needed to get going. Or whatever. I don't know, man." He shrugged again. "Maybe what happened with little Lila…I think it spooked Carol."

Ian didn't blame her. "When is she leaving?"

"Crack of dawn. Sevenish."

"Thanks for letting me know." Ian drummed up the stairs as Henry locked the door behind him.

They'd say good-bye to Carol, then he'd take Daniela to Essie's apartment. Daniela sounded like the locals. And she was a woman. Essie wouldn't feel threatened by her.

He'd bet Daniela would have no trouble talking her way in. And then she could take a look around, see if there was any sign of a second baby having been in the apartment. She could ask why the sudden move from Essie's old place, when she had a good friend next door. Why lie about going to São Paulo?

That lie… That meant something.

So Ian was going back with Daniela to see Essie. First thing tomorrow morning.

* * *

Daniela

Daniela looked up from her laptop when Ian walked in deep in thought, his brow furrowed. She was sitting on the floor, her back to the wall, her legs stretched out in front of her.

"Anything new?" Ian looked her over, as if to make sure she was all right, then, satisfied, he moved to the open window that let in only the slightest of breezes through the screen, and stared out, back to whatever thoughts were flying around in his head.

She updated him on the staff interviews she'd spent her day on, finishing with "Not a single new clue. No one had an affair we didn't already know about. Nothing."

"Carol is leaving tomorrow," Ian said. "Henry just told me when I came in. I didn't realize."

"I thought she would have told you."

"You knew?"

"I saw the ticket confirmation in her room yesterday. I was looking for her and popped my head in."

He raised an eyebrow, silently asking why she hadn't told him.

She shrugged. She hadn't wanted to talk about Carol with Ian, for a variety of reasons. One being that Carol's leaving meant there'd be another room available. Ian would jump on the opportunity to move out of their shared accommodation.

Daniela made a point to relax the clenched muscles in her shoulders. *Focus on the investigation.*

But it seemed Ian wasn't yet ready to let go of the Carol topic. "I hope her baby is born safely. I'd like to catch her in the morning before she leaves to say good-bye."

Daniela swallowed her jealousy. "Where did you go today?"

Then she listened as Ian told her about Clara seeing Essie, the phone call that brought Essie to the hospital, then following Essie back to her apartment, finishing with "I wish I could take you there right now, but if we show up at her door at night, it'll make her suspicious. She's home alone with her child. She isn't going to let in strangers in the middle of the night."

"We'll go in the morning." Excitement over a possible clue made Daniela forget all about Carol. She popped up from the floor and settled on the middle of her bed with her laptop so she wouldn't be in Ian's way as he moved around. "I'll say I'm from the post office and she needs to sign for a delivery."

Ian went straight to his bed and sat on the end of the mattress, facing her.

She stifled a sigh. One of these days, she would dearly like to be in a bedroom together with him and be in the same bed again. She couldn't forget how she felt when she'd woken up in his arms in Rio, or when he'd held her on the bus the other day. She wanted his arms around her again.

"Essie lived within thirty yards of the Heyerdahls' window," he was saying, his thoughts clearly far away from the two of them in bed.

Because he was a professional investigator, and she was a twit. She forced herself to focus on what he was saying.

"Her boyfriend came to visit pretty frequently, from what the neighbor said. So maybe Fabricio saw the blonde baby girl out back at See-Love-Aid, maybe the Heyerdahls watched a basketball game with their daughter, and Essie's boyfriend figured he could make money. Right now, it's the best possibility I can come up with."

Daniela could see it. "He either talked or forced Essie into helping him. He needed Essie to take care of the baby. And if he passed the baby out the window, lowering her somehow, he needed Essie down on the ground. Probably with a stroller. Once baby Lila was in the stroller, if someone caught a glance, they wouldn't have given it a second thought. Essie must have been out there with her little boy all the time."

"So they plan out the kidnapping," Ian said, "then Essie moves, a day or two before. Perfect alibi. The cops never even thought to track her down."

"But she only moved into another neighborhood."

"She's waiting for the boyfriend to return with the money."

Maybe. "Or," Daniela said, "maybe the boyfriend is still here. And baby Lila too. Maybe they decided to stick around Manaus for a while, until the police stop looking for the baby. I doubt they can keep an intensive investigation up much longer, even for an American baby. They wouldn't have that kind of budget."

Excitement flashed across Ian's face for a second, then melted away. "Would Essie have run to the hospital if Fabricio was living with her?"

"Maybe he's living with her, but he hadn't been at the apartment when you called. He could be keeping up appearances, out fishing."

Ian gave a slow nod. "Or he could be off somewhere, trying to make connections, find the right person to pass Lila to. He's a fisherman. He isn't in the human trafficking business."

Daniela watched him. Did he see how good they were together? "A crying baby wouldn't be suspicious at Essie's new apartment," she said, "since Essie has her own child. She could move around with a stroller, the baby covered up, and nobody would think anything of it."

God, if they could bring back baby Lila tomorrow to her parents. She'd be willing to do anything to make that happen. But she also wanted to stay realistic. "And if the baby isn't there?"

Ian lay down on his bed and folded his arms under his head, but tension hung around him like mist around the river as he stared at the ceiling. "We call in Detective Gustavo Santos and the local police. A city as big as Manaus has to have some kind of a forensics team. They can sweep the apartment for DNA. Babies spit up and mess up diapers. If baby Lila has been in that apartment, she left DNA evidence, I guarantee it."

Daniela put away her laptop and lay down on her side. She'd already showered and had on her nightgown. She watched Ian in the light of the single table lamp on the shared nightstand between them. The sleeves of his T-shirt stretched over his muscles.

He was a strong man. Probably stronger than Henry and Pierre put together.

In her experience, the strong took what they could from the weak—the law of the jungle. But Ian protected the weak. He made her feel safe, but he made her feel other things too. He wasn't crazy religious, but to her, he was a better man than the village missionary.

He cared about the baby they were looking for. He cared about Carol and her unborn child. He cared about the girls. He cared about his friend Finch, and still would not forget Finch's death, no matter how many years had passed. He put himself in danger to get Finch justice.

He had a heart, but he refused to acknowledge it.

As she'd locked away her past, Ian had locked away his heart. The difference was that her past had to be locked away. The past was ballast around her neck, dragging her down to drown. And Daniela wanted to fly. She wanted to live the life Ian had promised her, being anything she wanted to be, because everything was possible.

She could live without her past. She was better off without her past. But Ian couldn't live without his heart.

"Hey," he said. "Before we leave town, do you want to take the girls out for ice cream? We could all take the bus, with the volunteers as chaperones. I'm not complaining about the cafeteria downstairs, but I'm beginning to think that they're unfamiliar with the concept of dessert."

Her heart jumped like a fish jumping from the river in the sunset, in a slow arc, tail flapping with joy, water spraying, sparkling. They had postcards like that all over the city, catching that perfect moment.

"Sure."

She stared at Ian as he stood and gathered up his small bathroom bag, preparing for his shower.

She'd always cared about him. Long before she'd become physically attracted to him. But as he left the room with an "I'll be right back," the truth hit her so hard, she felt flattened to the bed.

She wasn't just attracted to Ian.

She was in love with him.

The bed seemed to spin with her. She closed her eyes.

Love.

Was she brave enough for that?

Love wasn't something she contemplated often. Like physical desire, she wasn't sure she'd ever feel love. The college campus had been drenched in it, but to Daniela, it always seemed superficial. Her friends were in love with one guy this week, another guy the next. Most of the time, when someone said love, they meant sex.

She knew sex. She knew the difference.

But now her heart filled with a soft, warm, gooey, boundless feeling. Was she brave enough to give herself over to it?

Yes, she was, she decided.

And Ian?

Ian would have to be brave enough to acknowledge his heart. And he would have to get over his unreasonable ideas that he was nothing but her protector, that he was too old for her, that he was her mentor, that a deeper, more intimate relationship between them would be wrong.

When they found the baby, Ian would have to acknowledge that Daniela was useful in solving the case. He would have to see her as an adult, as his partner, as his equal.

As the perfect woman for him.

CHAPTER
SEVENTEEN

Ian

Daniela was ready to go at dawn, buzzing with excitement, but Ian held her back. They were going with the package-delivery idea, but the post office didn't open that early. He wanted to make sure their story was plausible.

So he made her eat breakfast, and they were there to say good-bye to Carol, see her out to the airport taxi. Everybody was there. The girls gifted her with a sisal diaper bag they'd made just for her.

Rain had fallen overnight, so the sidewalk was wet, humidity already probably close to ninety percent. But at least the worst of the heat was still a few hours away. Carol would be on the plane by the time the sun fully hit, comfortable in an air-conditioned cabin.

The staff and volunteer visitors gave Carol hug after hug, cards, small gifts that she had trouble tucking into her overflowing suitcase. The Heyerdahls embraced her the longest.

Ian wondered if they weren't a little relieved to see her go. Having another baby around would have been difficult to cope with while their own baby was still missing. Hearing a baby cry in the night...

But Carmen and Phil had nothing but sadness on their faces for losing Carol. They promised to keep in touch. Carmen promised to be on hand over the phone for any baby advice Carol might need.

Then the cab was moving off, everyone on the sidewalk waving.

When the others returned inside the building, Ian flagged down another cab and gave Essie's new address.

Next to him in the back, Daniela was chewing her bottom lip.

"It'll be fine," he said. "By the end of the day today, we'll know more, one way or the other."

She took his hand and squeezed it. He didn't have the heart to pull away.

By the time the cab pulled up in front of the right building, Ian caught her case of nerves. He wanted to find the baby as much as Daniela did. He couldn't stand thinking about a little kid in harm's way.

They went up. Knocked.

"*Bom dia!*" Daniela called a *good morning* through the door, then she went into her post office package-for-delivery spiel, speaking in rapid Portuguese.

No response.

Ian knocked again. He kept his voice low as he said, "I hope I didn't spook her yesterday."

He knocked a third time. Waited. Nothing.

Daniela tried the doorknob, then looked back at him as the door opened a crack. He gently pushed her aside and went in first.

He could see the entire small studio apartment at a glance. The bathroom door stood open. Nobody anywhere.

An empty box of baby formula sat on the table. He remembered those days. Pain sliced through his heart. He forced it back behind the hard shell he'd built and picked up the box, turned it over in his hands.

Daniela stepped up to him and looked at the formula. "What is it?"

"Essie's kid is two years old," he said carefully. "At that age, kids don't need formula anymore. They eat solid food."

Daniela's eyes flared with hope. "You think baby Lila's been here?"

He scanned the apartment again, noting the lack of belongings, the abandoned vibe of the place.

"They cleared out," he said through clenched teeth, holding back from punching a hole in the wall. "I might have spooked her with that fake call to the hospital. Then showing up at her door later."

He had to find them. He needed just one clue. He threw himself into searching the place.

While he looked around, checking for a single sliver of paper, anything that might give him a hint to where Essie had run, Daniela was staring at the garbage can overflowing with dirty diapers.

Ian stepped up behind her and looked over her shoulder. "Are you seeing something I'm not seeing?"

"Remember when we ran into Carol and she'd just been buying diapers?"

"So?"

"By that time, she already knew that she was going back to the US for her baby's birth. She had the ticket confirmation. I saw it. So why buy diapers in Brazil for a baby who was going to be born in the US?"

"What does Carol have to do with any of this?"

"Carol is your blind spot." Daniela's voice filled with sympathy, her gaze soft. "She reminds you of Linda."

"I don't want to talk about Linda."

"I know. And you don't have to right now. But just consider this…How do we even know that Carol is pregnant?"

He couldn't believe they were even discussing a fake pregnancy. "Because this is real life, not a sitcom. She looks pregnant."

"She could have gained weight."

"She doesn't look fat. She looks pregnant." God, he didn't have patience for this, not now, not when he'd screwed up. Last night, he should have found a way to get into this apartment, while Essie was still here.

Daniela tilted her head, then went still, as if holding her breath. "Have you seen Carol naked?"

A strangled laugh escaped him. But from the wounded look in her eyes, he realized she was asking seriously. "No. I didn't see Carol naked."

Daniela nodded and breathed. "So she could have a fake belly."

"Lila is almost seven months old. It's not like Carol could fake a pregnancy, steal Lila, then pass her off as a newborn."

But Daniela refused to see reason. "Carol is involved in this somehow. I know it. We need to go to the airport. Trust me."

So off they went, because, of course, he did trust her.

"She said she had a ten a.m. flight, right?" he asked in the back of the cab that flew through traffic.

He'd offered a big enough tip so the driver would take every slum alley shortcut available, shortcuts, Ian, if he had a rental car, would never have known.

Daniela held on to the seat in front of her with one hand, checked her phone with the other. "We have fifty minutes left."

"How far to the airport?" Ian asked the driver.

"Soon, senhor." As the man ran a red light, he began to sweat. He held on to the steering wheel with both hands, leaned forward, the determined look of a race car driver on his face.

They were doing well until they hit a roadblock.

"What's that?" Ian asked.

"Police, senhor. They must be looking for someone."

"We get off here." Ian paid the man, shot out of the car with Daniela, then they ran. They hurried past the police checkpoint and grabbed another cab on the other side of the barricade.

"Forty minutes left," Daniela said as they slammed in the back of the car.

Ian called Detective Santos. "Daniela and I need to get into the airport. Can you call airport security and get us a free pass?"

"You got something?"

"We suspect that baby Lila is still here in Manaus, about to be smuggled out on a plane. If a Carol Peterson tries to get on a flight, they need to stop her."

"I'll meet you at the airport," Santos said on the other end, a little out of breath, as if he was already running.

Ian had the money out and the door open by the time the cab pulled over in front of the airport. He shot out of the car while it was still moving, but somehow Daniela was already ahead of him.

But they only got as far as the first line of security, two armed guards who went for their guns when Ian and Daniela tried to push past them, ignoring the CPRU badges they held up, ignoring their shouted explanations.

So they pulled back.

"Twenty minutes," Daniela said as Ian pulled his phone again.

Santos picked up on the first ring. The sound of sirens came through the line. He was in his car. "I'll be there in twenty minutes."

"Too late. You have to tell them to let us in." Ian handed the phone to one of the guards.

The man listened. Objected. Listened. Objected again.

Then he gave the phone back to Ian and made his own call on his radio, probably to his supervisor.

He listened. Explained. Listened. Shooting Ian and Daniela pissed-off looks the whole time, his hand back on his weapon, same as his buddy's.

Then, *finally*, he ended the call and stepped aside, waving them through with a long curse about foreigners.

They ran to the departures board, searched the list of dozens of flight, lucked out when the overhead speaker system announced the boarding of Carol's flight for Miami. Gate 29.

They ran.

If the plane took off before they got there…

Could an ordinary detective stop a plane from taking off? Ian wasn't about to take chances. He didn't know Brazilian jurisdictions. He grabbed his phone and called the federal commissioner they'd met in Rio when they'd first arrived in Brazil.

To his credit, the delegado didn't ask many questions. He got with the program right away.

But could he get through in time? And did he have the power they needed?

***

Daniela

Daniela scanned every female in the boarding area, looking for Carol and anyone resembling the photo of Essie that Ian had on his phone. Ian was looking through the shops interspersed with the gates.

When Daniela couldn't spot the women, she held up her CPRU ID to the gate agent at the desk. "Has a Carol Peterson boarded already?"

The woman shifted uncertainly on her feet, glancing around for a supervisor and finding none. When Daniela didn't budge, at last the gate agent checked the passenger list. "We don't have a Carol Peterson on this flight."

But…the Miami flight had been the only ten a.m. flight to the US on the departures board. *If Carol isn't going to the US, where is she going?*

The loudspeaker system was announcing flights that were boarding. *Which one?* Daniela ran toward the long line of other gates, explaining to Ian as he followed that Carol wasn't going to Miami.

What if she was already on a plane? They'd never catch her before her flight took off.

When Daniela finally spotted Essie with a stroller, in line to board a flight to Rio, Daniela rushed forward. Only one child in the stroller. A brown-haired toddler.

"There," Ian shouted behind her.

She turned.

Carol was pushing another stroller from the direction of the bathrooms. This one held a blonde baby girl, six or seven months old, sitting up and blowing saliva bubbles. The exact baby they'd all seen in Carmen and Phil Heyerdahl's posters.

Ian and Daniela broke into a run.

Carol spotted them the next second, her eyes snapping wide. Then she was careening around a group of tourists with the stroller, and took off running, her long white linen skirt flapping behind her.

Unfortunately for her, airport security was finally rushing up to the gate. Ian had only to hold up his CPRU ID and point, and two guards were right there, grabbing Carol.

"Easy!" Ian ran forward. "She's pregnant. Be careful."

Baby Lila was crying, then crying harder, scared by all the people surrounding the stroller. Ian picked the baby up, held her against his chest, and patted her back with soft little taps.

"Hey," he cooed, something Daniela had never heard from him before. "Everything is okay now. We're going to take you back to Mommy."

The baby looked up at him, teary eyed and blotchy faced. Hiccupped. Then gurgled. Then smiled at the giant of a man who held her. And Ian smiled back.

As Daniela watched him, her heart suddenly felt too large for her chest. That sweet, achy pressure filled her, an indefinable longing that was so sharp, it stole her breath for a second.

Security was tugging a protesting Carol away. "Ian. This is not what it looks like. Help me."

Ian glanced at Daniela. "Can you hold the baby? I'll go with Carol."

So Daniela took Lila from him, with a squeak of protest from the baby, who, after a moment, was content to settle against Daniela and shoved her little fist into her mouth. "Go."

Because Carol was pregnant. And Ian would want to make sure the guards weren't too rough on her, wouldn't hurt her unborn child by accident. Because that was the kind of guy Ian was.

Exactly why Daniela had fallen in love with him.

***

Carmen

Carmen nearly dropped the phone. Their small room seemed to close in on her. She couldn't breathe.

Phil was by her side instantly. "What is it?"

Her body trembled so hard, she thought she was shaking the room. She put out a hand to steady herself on the doorframe. "They have her."

"They have our Lila?" He grabbed her gently by the shoulders, his gaze eagerly searching her face. "Who?"

Tears streamed down. "The police. We have to go to the station."

Her hair was a mess. Her clothes were a mess. She'd let Gabriela and Fernanda give her a makeover earlier, to the girls' great entertainment. Whenever she wasn't out on the streets looking for her daughter, she was with the girls downstairs. They kept her sane.

She glanced in the small mirror on the wall as she flew toward the door. Winced at her reflection. And kept going. Thank God she had clothes on, because if she hadn't, she wasn't positive she'd take time to dress. She might have run out in her underwear.

Phil ran right by her side, catching her when she tripped over her own feet, his voice tight. "What did they say?"

"It was Daniela. She said they had Lila."

"Is she sure it's Lila?"

"They've seen her picture enough." But Carmen didn't dare fully believe it either. Her heart was a soap bubble.

They ran into Pierre at the bottom of the stairs, sorting mail. "What's going on?"

"They have Lila!" Phil shouted as they passed the Frenchman. "We're going to the police station."

Pierre ran after them. "I'll take you. The truck is up front."

Mrs. Frieseke came running from somewhere in the back at the commotion, a wooden spoon dripping in her hand. "What happened?"

"The police have Lila!" Pierre called back. "We're going to the station."

Carmen kept running. Then she was in the truck, and if willpower could make trucks fly, they would have been in the air already.

Pierre took the wheel. A good thing, because Phil's hands were shaking as hard as hers. They held hands the whole way over, sometimes praying out loud, sometimes praying silently, and sometimes just sitting there and crying.

She didn't dare be happy. *Not yet. Not yet.*

What if it wasn't true?

God, let it be true. Please, dear God.

She barely registered when they arrived at the station. Or when they ran inside. Or when they were shown to the back. Everything passed in a blur.

Then they came to an office with a window to the hallway. A uniformed officer stood in front of the door. On the other side of the window, inside the room, a female officer rocked Lila back and forth as the baby slept.

The world stopped. Snapped into focus. Blood rushed loudly in Carmen's ears as she gripped Phil's arm. She was light-headed. She lunged toward the door anyway.

"I'm sorry, ma'am. No one can go in," the officer said.

She stared at him, barely comprehending the words, even though her Portuguese was excellent. "That's my baby in there."

Phil went nose to nose with the guy. "Look here—"

"It's okay." Detective Gustavo Santos hurried down the hall from the opposite direction. "Let them in."

As soon as the door opened, Carmen flew through, then she had to slow down so she wouldn't jostle Lila too much and wake her, scare her.

She didn't take a full breath until she had the baby on her shoulder, having to remind herself not to hug her too tightly. She buried her nose in the silky baby hair and breathed in her sweet baby scent, let the tears flow as Phil's arms went around them.

There wasn't enough air in the room. She couldn't breathe. She couldn't say a word. All she could do was stand there and hold her baby.

"Thank God," Phil said to the top of her head, his arms steady, his voice shaky.

Lila stirred. Opened her eyes.

Then those little baby blue eyes widened, and she went nuts, squealing and wiggling, smiling, grabbing for Carmen and her daddy. Some people thought babies this age didn't really know what went on around them, but Lila sure did. She was overjoyed to see her parents.

"We have some paperwork for you to fill out when you're ready," Detective Santos said from the doorway. "Take your time. Officer Romero will be outside the door. He'll let you know when the ambulance gets here. The baby will need to be checked out at the hospital and released by a doctor before you can take her home."

Carmen just nodded without looking at him, barely registering the words.

The man said, "She wasn't hurt, as far as we can tell. The people who had her took care of her to make sure she could be—" He stopped. Continued with "adopted."

But as seamlessly as he'd transitioned, Carmen knew what he'd meant to say. *So she could be sold.*

The utter outrage of the unspoken word burned through her. That her precious baby daughter could have been *sold*. Had nearly been sold.

And even though Lila had been saved, other mothers' daughters *were* sold. Every day. All over the world. Including right here in Manaus.

Somewhere in Carmen's brain, the thought registered that she wanted to think about that, harder than ever before. Work harder than ever before to stop these tragedies. But right at that moment, she couldn't think past having Lila in her arms.

Santos said, "I was about to start the interrogation when I learned that you arrived. I better get back."

The detective left and pulled the door shut behind him.

Phil sank into the nearest chair and pulled Carmen onto his lap, just hugged them and hugged them.

"We got you, baby," he repeated over and over.

And Carmen kept saying, "We love you so much."

She didn't know how much time passed before Detective Santos returned with a handful of printouts. "The ambulance is here. If you fill out the paperwork now, you won't have to come back to the station again today. I'll stop by See-Love-Aid tomorrow, and we'll talk. Today, just enjoy your baby."

Carmen kept holding Lila. Phil filled out the paperwork. She only signed her name on the bottom of a few sheets and didn't even put the baby down for that.

Ian and Daniela waited in the hallway, walked out with them. Carmen thanked both of them, and so did Phil.

When the medic said only one of the parents could go in the back of the ambulance with Lila to the hospital, Ian immediately offered a ride. Apparently, Pierre had gone back to See-Love-Aid a short while ago, but he'd left them the truck.

Since Phil hadn't even held Lila yet, Carmen gave her daughter a million kisses, then handed her over to her father. "You take her. I'll go with Ian and Daniela."

Phil kissed her hard, teary-eyed, and got in the back of the ambulance with Lila.

Carmen could barely sit still in the truck as they followed behind them. "It really happened, right? She's back?"

While Ian drove, Daniela hugged Carmen tightly. "She's back."

Lila is back. Thank God, Lila is back.

She caught her reflection in the rearview mirror, all the makeup the girls had put on her. Flinched. She looked like a clown. Not that she cared. But still, she tried to rub some off with the back of her hand.

"Check the glove compartment," Daniela said.

And when Carmen found an old, wrinkled napkin, Daniela took it from her and wiped off the makeup as the pickup rattled toward the hospital.

"How did you find her?" Carmen asked finally.

At first, all that had mattered was that Lila was alive and safe, but now Carmen wanted to know everything.

"Carol took her." Ian's voice was clipped, his expression tight with anger.

His words made no sense. "Why?" Carmen blinked at him. "Carol is about to have her own baby."

Daniela gave Carmen a squeeze. "Her baby is sick."

"Sick how?"

"A problem with her heart. Inoperable. She's not expected to live a day or two beyond delivery. Carol has known for a while now. She actually had a date for inducement in Rio."

A somber silence fell over the truck's cab.

"Lila wasn't stolen to be sold into adoption. Carol was going to have her baby in Rio," Ian said. "Take the birth certificate, then pretend that Lila was that baby. The difference is big now, but in a year..."

Carmen shook her head, wiped her tears, horrified, relieved, confused, trying to get a grip. "And Lila is such a little thing anyway. Carol could have gotten away with it."

Thank God, Carol had been stopped, was all she could think.

And good luck to Lila, because she was going to be thirty before her parents ever let her out of their sight again.

* * *

Ian

Midnight passed by the time Lila Heyerdahl was finally released from the hospital to the custody of her incredibly grateful mother and father.

Daniela and Ian stayed with the Heyerdahls until the end and drove them back to See-Love-Aid through a city shrouded in darkness. Since there wasn't enough room in the pickup's cab, Phil volunteered to ride in the back.

Of course, at See-Love-Aid, nobody slept. They'd all waited up, and everyone came running, everyone talking and laughing at the same time, everyone wanting to at least pat the baby's head. Lila ate up her sudden celebrity status and blew bubbles. At the end, they all piled into the cafeteria, the only place large enough to hold the crowd.

"Why?"

"How?"

"Carol?"

"How could she?"

Carmen ended up answering the questions, holding her finally sleeping baby, shaking her head every time anyone asked if she wanted someone to give her a break. She looked as if she might never put that kid down again.

Phil sat glued to her side, his arms around his wife and child.

"Carol's baby is sick." Carmen's eyes filled with tears. "I think, maybe she couldn't handle the thought of losing her baby, on top of losing her husband."

Ian wasn't sure if she was crying for Carol or herself. Probably both.

He stood in the back by the door, Daniela in front of him. She'd done well today. Carol had messed with his head, but Daniela's head had remained clear. She really was something. She was going to be an excellent investigator. He was damned proud of her.

While Carmen answered more questions, Daniela leaned back against Ian's chest.

He should have pushed her away. He didn't. They'd both had an emotionally exhausting day.

As everyone crowded around Carmen and Phil, Ian pulled toward the door. The people in the cafeteria were a family. He wanted to give them their private family moment.

He headed up to the volunteer dorms.

Daniela followed him, bouncing on the steps, still wired, high on adrenaline. She'd just solved her first case.

"You got that baby back for those parents," he told her.

She grinned. "So you think I'll be good at this job?"

"Better than good. You can partner with me anytime."

She grinned wider. Her eyes lit up. Her dark hair framed her face, loosened from the tight bun she'd had it in all day. She looked like a true river goddess.

He could have looked at her all night.

He turned his attention to the chipped tile of the hallway, then to their room as they walked in.

It was the middle of the night, but they were both sticky, so they headed to the showers. Girls on the left, boys on the right.

Ian returned to their room first. He stretched out on the bed.

Maybe forcing himself to *act* relaxed would make him *feel* relaxed.

Since Daniela had come into his life, he'd stopped sleeping naked. He always wore at least boxer briefs, and sometimes a T-shirt too. And now that they were sharing a room, he made sure the sheet was pulled at least to his waist.

Bad enough that she kept wearing that flimsy nightgown. All right, so not that flimsy. The white material covered everything down to her knees. Still, as far as he was concerned, she would tempt a saint who was a thousand years dead.

Thank God, tomorrow they'd be out of here, back to separate bedrooms at home, then off on separate missions. Sure, he'd be worried about her every day. But he knew she could handle whatever came her way.

As he waited for her, he braced himself for the sight of her, ready to turn out the light as soon as she reached her bed.

But when Daniela came in, she wasn't wearing her nightgown. She returned from the bathroom in a bath towel. And then she locked the door behind her and dropped the towel. Drops of water glistened on her naked skin as if she'd been painted with diamonds.

"Christ," he breathed.

* * *

Daniela

Daniela's heart beat in her throat. Her skin was on fire just from Ian looking at her, his gaze pure molten lava, as if he was never going to take his eyes off her ever again.

Walking over to him took every ounce of courage she had.

She put her pride on the line. She laid her body and heart bare for him. This was it.

Lila Heyerdahl was safe.

Tonight was the night. Tonight, Daniela would finally be Ian's, and then forever after. After all these years, coming together here in Brazil, where they'd first met, felt right. *Fate.*

She'd prepared a long, convincing speech in the shower. She couldn't remember a word.

"I love you," she said simply.

He watched her as if he'd been lost in the jungle for a month and suddenly came across a waiter carrying a steak dinner on a tray.

Or maybe that was just a trick of the light, because he said, his voice past strangled, "Please put on your clothes."

"I love you," she said again.

He closed his eyes. "Stop this."

And then he was off his bed. And then he was shrugging into his jeans, grabbing his sneakers, and then he was out the door. Running away once again.

She stared after him as the door swung shut, her heart pounding. She sat on her bed, light-headed. *He will come back.* She'd just startled him. *He will come back.*

She'd given him her heart. All these years, she hadn't even been sure if she had a heart to give. But she did. And she was glad. And as soon as Ian thought about it, he'd be glad too.

He loved her. His love had been there in the way he looked at her, in the million things he did for her, in the tone of his voice when he talked to her. In that single, spectacular kiss they'd shared. *He will come back.*

But when she woke in the morning, his bed was still empty.

And Daniela felt her newfound heart crack right to its core.

She was stunned. She was cold, which was physically impossible in this heat, but there she was, shivering. She was angry.

She wanted Ian to come back, but now she wanted it so she could yell at him. *I love you. And if you could let go of your stupid hang-ups about us, you'd love me too. I can't believe you're such a coward!*

That anger got her going at last.

She dressed. Packed. Stood in the middle of the room.

And then she cried like the stupid, infatuated girl she still was. Ian was right. She hadn't grown up. He'd said no a dozen times, and she kept throwing herself at him.

Maybe he didn't love her.

Maybe he had never loved her romantically, only as a friend, exactly as he'd said. Maybe he was never going to love her the way she craved. Maybe she'd made all that great love up in her head.

He'd offered friendship, and she'd gone crazy with it.

Bobby at GWU thought she was into him.

Maybe she was to Ian what Bobby was to her. An unrequited love she didn't want to hurt because they were *friends*. She thought about how uncomfortable Bobby had made her feel at times.

Then she thought about how Ian tried to get away from her every time she pushed the relationship issue.

God, I've been stupid.

She was mortified.

But this was it now. She squared her shoulders and squared her jaw. This was the end. She *had* grown up finally. She *was* a woman. *A strong woman.* And she was going to build herself a good life, a life that didn't revolve around hopelessly pining for Ian Slaney.

He'd saved her four years ago. She would forever be grateful to him. But she was going to stop ruining both of their lives with her stupid unrequited love, right this second.

Should have known, a little voice, the voice of young Daniela, beaten-down Daniela in Rosa's house, said in her head. Her mother had died and left her alone. Then Pedro had passed her on and abandoned her at Rosa's. Rosa passed her on too. Then Finch had died and left her too. Why had she thought that Ian would want her forever? Of course he wouldn't.

Daniela squeezed her eyes shut and tried not to scream.

She hated that timid voice of insecurity. Hated it every time it came back. She was no longer the helpless little Daniela, at the mercy of others.

She pulled out her phone and reserved a seat on the next plane from Manaus to the US. She didn't care if Ian could get on the same flight or not. In fact, she preferred going home on separate planes.

CHAPTER
EIGHTEEN

Ian

Daniela had left him in Brazil. *What the hell?*

As Ian sat on the plane, going home alone, his feelings must have shown on his face, because the flight attendants gave him a wide berth.

He'd meant to stay in Brazil for a few more days, go back to Rio, find Marcos Morais, and have a heart-to-heart, better yet, a fist-to-face, with the man. But Ian didn't like the way Daniela had left.

He'd upset her. More than that—he'd hurt her. He had to make it right.

Since he hadn't slept all night, he'd had time to think. He was trying to do right by Daniela, but she saw that as a rejection.

He had been a pretty big part of her life in the last couple of years. She had no family in the US and few friends, no wide network of support.

So, right now, Ian needed to go after her, spend a few days with her, iron things out between them, make sure she was okay. Make sure that she knew she was important to him, that he wanted her in his life, wanted to be in her life for as long as she'd let him. Romance…could not happen. But he was desperate to go back to the way things had been between them for the past four years.

While he convinced her, he'd file his reports at work, *then* take a leave of absence and return to Brazil, finally bring Finch's murderers to justice.

He wanted to track down Goat Man through Marcos Morais. He might even do some tracking from the US first, from the CPRU office where he had access to all kinds of international law databases. For the first time, he had a name, a place to start.

He would run searches, go back to Rio, take out Marcus Morais and Goat Man.

And if he followed this plan, Daniela and he could have a breather from each other too. Maybe she'd use the time apart to meet some nice young man.

Maybe it was for the best that she'd left him in Manaus. The solo flight gave Ian time to try to figure out what the hell to say to her.

Christ, when she'd dropped that towel.

Yes, she was a woman, dammit. Of course, he knew that. Of course, he responded to her. He wasn't dead.

He wasn't a conscienceless bastard either. He was too old for her, too jaded.

He planned on having that talk as soon as he got home, but when he finally walked through the door to their apartment, he found her packing. Not unpacking from the Brazil trip, but packing up everything.

She wore faded old jeans and a baggy T-shirt that covered nearly all of her, but he was still seeing her naked. What was wrong with him?

She had a steaming cup of coffee in one hand and was laying out clothes with the other.

He half expected her to throw the cup at him.

"You're right," she said instead, no high emotions in her tone, professionally cool. "I need to make my own life." She put shoes in a bag. "I'm going to spend the night with Crystal. I just talked to her. There's an empty studio apartment in her building. I'm going to rent it tomorrow."

Ian dropped his backpack by the door, then walked into the living room, folded his tired body into his recliner, and just watched her, a mix of emotions flooding through him.

She paused the packing long enough to look at him. "You saved me from a terrible life. Then you brought me to the US and you gave me a wonderful new life here. But somehow, it's all connected to you. You ended up *being* my life. I need to make a life for myself."

He nodded numbly. *Exactly.* Hadn't he been trying to tell her the same thing forever?

Every word she said was true. Every word also hurt like hell.

He hadn't thought about her moving out completely. But, okay, she was right. He couldn't expect her to be independent of him and be unwilling to let her go at the same time. Of course, she had to make a life of her own. Of course, she couldn't do it from his apartment. And yet...

No *and yet*. He filled his lungs. "Let me know if I can help with anything."

She flashed a half smile. "The whole point of independence is that I need to learn to do things without your help."

Well, he hated the sound of that.

"You don't have to run out of here like this," he said. "I'm going to take some time off from work and go back to Brazil. I want to find something that'll link Marcos Morais and Goat Man to Finch's murder and put them behind bars."

She stopped moving. Was that worry crossing her face? But then, after a long moment, she simply nodded and went back to folding shirts. "I'm almost packed. Crystal is expecting me."

As he watched her roll up socks from the laundry basket, disjointed thoughts floated through his brain: the day he'd found her, Finch, Marcos Morais and his diamonds. Then some of those thoughts solidified and made Ian sit up straight.

"When Finch told you to leave for a few days, just before he was killed… Did you pack? Did you take anything with you?"

She turned away. She didn't like talking about her life before DC. But after a few of seconds of silence, she finally said, over her shoulder, "I packed up a few dresses, my hairbrush, sandals. Probably more than I should have. I kind of worried that he didn't mean it when he said I could come back. I thought maybe he was sending me away for good."

His stomach clenched. He could picture her, scared, rejected, being sent back to a life of abuse she'd barely escaped. He'd thought a lot about Finch and how he'd come by her. Had Finch thought he'd simply hired a housemaid?

Maybe he had. Finch had always been too optimistic for his own good. He looked at the sunny side of life. Danger? What danger? What darkness?

"Could he have sewn some diamonds into the hem of your clothes?" Ian asked Daniela. "Do you still have those clothes?"

She put her coffee on the kitchen counter. "I've gained weight since. I threw things out when they got tight."

He tried not to look at her body. She'd filled out, yes, but only what was needed. She'd been too thin when he'd found her. Years of not having enough to eat had left its mark on her back then. Now she glowed with health, her skin and hair shining, and…And he wasn't going to think about how striking she looked.

"How about shoes?" He came out of the recliner. "Do you have the sandals? He could have put diamonds into the heels."

"They fell apart." She flashed an apologetic look. "They were old rubber sandals. I tossed them last year."

He ran his fingers through his hair, pacing now. A bitter laugh bubbled up his throat. "Can you imagine? If Finch hid the diamonds in your clothes, then sent you off for a few days. And then he's killed, and you never knew, and tossed it all in the garbage?"

She started pacing too and looked as frustrated as he felt. "Why didn't Finch tell me?" Then she whirled around. Her face lit up. "Wait! I have the bag."

She flew to the hallway closet, dropped to her knees, and began chucking things out over her shoulders.

He was right there. "What bag?"

"Finch's bag that I took with me that night. I used it when you brought me to the US. The handle was broken, but I fixed it. I know I have it somewhere."

He dropped to his knees next to her and edged her aside a little so he could dig in too.

The closet was a mess, the catch-all for all things they rarely used: old shoes, bags, a rain slicker from when he'd taken her to see Niagara Falls, umbrellas, flashlight, first aid kit, a toolbox, shoeshine kit.

Then she grabbed a chunk of dirty canvas way in the back and pulled out a bag, all bent out of shape, with mismatched handles, presenting it to him with the aplomb of a magician who'd just produced a rabbit from a hat.

And he stared at her with just as much amazement as if she had. "If Finch hid the diamonds in the bag…"

They sat on the floor, facing each other, the bag between them.

"Then we have them," she said with undisguised triumph.

The bag stood open, empty. Ian reached in and felt around anyway. No inside pockets. No outside pockets either. The bag was pretty simple, about the size of carry-on luggage. Finch had probably used it exactly for that purpose.

"Did he specifically give you this bag?" Ian asked as he raised his gaze to Daniela.

She shook her head. "He kept cassava in it under the sink. That's why I took it. I thought he wouldn't miss it. It was broken anyway."

Disappointment washed through Ian. If Finch hadn't given it to her…

He lifted the bag, turned it all around, upside down, shook it. Nothing. Except…"It does feel heavy."

"Heavy-duty canvas. And it's big."

But he was already tapping the bottom—structured and rectangular, with something stiff sewn in between two layers of fabric to give the bag shape. A thick piece of plastic maybe. He ran his fingers all around it. A *very* thick piece of plastic. *Too thick.*

He grabbed for his pocketknife but came up empty, bit back a curse as he remembered. He'd forgotten to take the knife out of his pocket when they'd left for Brazil, and security had taken it away at the airport. Can't take stuff like that on a plane.

He scooted over to the hall table and opened the drawer, retrieved Finch's knife he'd brought to the US when he'd brought Daniela all those years ago. He freed the blade, then carefully cut into the canvas bag.

He'd been right about the piece of plastic. There were two sheets. And sandwiched between them…"A bag of rock salt?"

"No." Daniela helped him work the thing out—a pound bag of sugar, with Lavras Raw Natural Sugar in blue font stamped on the bag.

The contents had the brownish white color of raw sugar, large grained. Sugar crystals as big as the ones in rock candy. Probably made for those fancy upscale artisan coffee places.

But why would Finch hide a bag of sugar. Unless…

Ian cut the bag open and poured some into his palm. Licked the granules. "Sweet."

Daniela raised an unimpressed eyebrow at this method of investigation. "It's sugar."

"Yes, but do you know what these crystals remind me of?" He held out his palm for her inspection.

She stared at him. "Sugar?"

"Raw diamonds. This is almost exactly what small diamonds look like before they're cut."

"How do you know what raw diamonds look like?"

"Murfreesboro, Arkansas." He grinned, feeling more optimistic by the second. "Crater of Diamonds State Park. Went there as a kid with my mother. She had family nearby. Tourists can look for diamonds out in the field. Before you go out, some guy shows you what to look for."

"Does anyone ever find anything?"

"Every single day. Biggest one ever found was over sixteen carats."

"I want to go there," she said immediately, with a smile of pure enthusiasm.

He nearly said he would take her but bit back the words before they could slip out. Instead, as she leaned closer, he lifted his palm for her inspection.

She flashed him a dubious look. Took a granule. Put it on her tongue. "Definitely sugar."

Ian hummed. "We'll see."

He took the handful of granules to the counter and tossed them into Daniela's steaming cup of coffee. He stirred with his finger and ignored the heat, his blood rushing faster in his veins as he waited. "Grab one of the blue bath towels."

Daniela ran to the bathroom and was back in two seconds. She lay the folded towel on the kitchen counter. Ian poured the coffee onto it.

The coffee soaked into the towel. The sugar had melted. Except for two granules. He picked them up and rinsed them very carefully in the sink.

"I'll be damned." He held them out on his palm. "Raw diamonds."

They turned at the same time to stare at the bag of sugar they'd left on the floor.

"There could be a bunch more in there." Excitement bubbled in Daniela's voice.

"I'm betting there are. Diamonds are not like drugs," he thought out loud. "Airport dogs can't sniff them out. And mixed in with the sugar, nobody can spot them with the naked eye." He looked at her. "It's a pretty damn good disguise. Any minute now, I'm going to be forced to think that Marcos Morais is smarter than he looks. I'm not going to like it."

She rolled her eyes, but she was smiling. "Can you use this to get him?"

"You bet."

Her smile widened, and she jumped forward to hug him, but just for a second, just an expression of sheer joy, completely lacking romantic overtones. Then she stepped back.

Little by little, her face turned serious. Her eyes were clear green pools. "Could I ask one thing? The last thing. I swear."

Like there was anything he wouldn't give her. He nodded.

"Please don't go back to Brazil. I don't want you killed or to end up in a Brazilian jail if you kill Marcos. There has to be a way to put him away now that we have proof."

That she worried about him made his heart ache. "Finch was my friend. I didn't rush right down there when he first called that he was in trouble. If I had, he wouldn't be dead now. I want the bastards who killed him."

He wanted the bastards *dead*. Anything else felt like the betrayal of a friendship, a betrayal of Finch.

Daniela's gaze softened. "You couldn't save Linda, so you wanted to save Finch, but you got there too late. He's the one who stole the diamonds. Finch was responsible for his actions and the consequences. Just like Linda was responsible for what she did. Not you. You're not responsible for what other people do."

"Who told you that?"

"You did. And that hippy shrink you forced me to see when you brought me to DC."

"I'm definitely regretting that. I sent you there so you could deal with what happened to you, not so you can psychoanalyze me."

Her lips twisted into a half smile. "Unintended consequences."

He grumbled.

She turned somber. "You need to let go of revenge."

"I want it."

"You deserve better. You deserve more. You don't need to punish yourself by getting into dangerous situations."

"I'm seriously regretting that shrink. You should have talked me out of it."

"*Nossa Senhora Aparecida!* How much did I beg? I despised her! She was so damn cheerful about everything, I wanted to drown her." An outraged peal of laughter escaped her.

The laughter was good. At least she didn't hate his guts.

He knew he'd messed up. Big-time. But wasn't sure where. He'd never had anything but good intentions where Daniela was concerned.

This wasn't that bad, was it? It was good that she was starting her own separate life.

But all he could think of was how much he didn't want her to finish packing and leave him.

"You don't really want revenge," she said as she walked to her suitcase and zipped it up.

"I don't?"

"You want your family back. And you want your friend back. The thing is, if you'd been brave enough to accept what I offered you in Manaus, you could have had both in me," she said with a heartbreaking smile as she grabbed the suitcase, passed by him, and walked out of his life.

* * *

Ian

Ian woke to an empty apartment in the morning. The place was depressing. Maybe he'd start looking for something smaller. An apartment where he wouldn't have to look at Daniela's bedroom door and expect her to walk out any second. A kitchen she hadn't cooked in. A living room she hadn't decorated.

She'd been wrong yesterday about him wanting a family again.

He had to let Daniela go. He was determined to see this through. He wanted only the best for her, and he wasn't it.

He turned on the TV just so the place wouldn't be so quiet. Some announcer was overhyping a solar storm and its effects on satellites, what would happen if all the satellites were knocked out all at once. Ian clicked the TV off. He missed the days when news was news. When journalists reported on the things that happened, instead of endlessly hyping things that "might" happen and what celebrities wore to the gym.

His mother popped in as he was having breakfast. She'd colored her hair back to blond. And, apparently, she'd developed some serious skills with the eyeliner that would make a drag queen proud.

"Where is Daniela?" was her first question.

"Good to know who comes first with you," Ian grumbled into his coffee. Then sighed. "She moved out."

Iris came to sit at the table with him. "What are you talking about?"

Might as well get it over with. "We kind of had a fight."

"She's right."

He rolled his eyes. "Thanks for the vote of confidence."

For a cheerful, softhearted woman, his mother faked a pretty good "mean look." "Don't make me choose between the two of you."

He chewed eggs that tasted like garden dirt. Everything felt off this morning. He could swear someone stole the caffeine out of his coffee. He couldn't perk up for anything.

"Why?" his mother demanded, either oblivious or uncaring of his misery.

"She wanted things I couldn't give."

"You mean she wanted a real relationship. How is it that I'm the only person who's seen this coming?"

He stared at her, appalled, giving up on the eggs. "You always treated her like she was my little sister. Like she was your daughter!"

"My daughter-in-law. Really. I've been hoping quietly like a good mother and not being pushy about it. But an idiot could see that you two were made for each other."

Acid bubbled up in his stomach. "I don't want to talk about it. I'm not going to ruin her life."

"Good. I love that girl. You mess with her, and you answer to me."

He stared at her. Didn't know what to say. Had all the women in his life gone crazy? Was it a worldwide hormone wave? Maybe solar storms drew female hormones like the moon drew the oceans?

He might have been dumb about Daniela, but he wasn't dumb enough to ask that question out loud.

His mother sighed. "I was okay without your father, you know."

"What does that have to do with anything?"

"I fear that you think we would have had it easier if he hadn't left. I know you wanted to be the exact opposite, a good provider for Linda and the boys. I know you blame yourself for not staying home when she asked. But you couldn't have stayed. That's not how the army works."

He closed his eyes trying to block out the words, rubbed the pads of his fingers over his eyelids.

"You're scared."

"I'm not scared." He opened his eyes so he could glare at her. "I'm trying to do the right thing here."

"For whom?" She flashed the you-can't-fool-your-own-mother look. "You still feel guilty about Linda and Connor and Colin. For years, you punished yourself with senseless fights, and the drinking, and those floozies. Don't think I don't know. All that punishment and you still don't think you deserve better." She paused. "I partially agree."

He blinked. "You do?"

"I don't think you deserve Daniela, not if you keep acting the coward. I raised you better than that." She rose, kissed him on the top of his head. "I love you."

And then she left.

Ian went into work, trying not to think about what his mother said, because then he might have to admit that she was right, and he wasn't ready for that.

He filed his reports, ran a search on Marcos Morais, and found out which diamond mine he had provided security for last. Then he packed up the diamond-sugar mix, put in a letter explaining Marcos Morais's theft and connection to Goat Man and Goat Man's description, and sent it via courier with door-to-door delivery to the guy who owned the mine.

The mine owner would have all the resources in Brazil and wouldn't rest while Marcos and his accomplice were still in one piece. Not as satisfying as Ian taking Marcos out, but not as dangerous either.

When he was done, he walked into Karin Kovacs's office. "Any new cases coming in?"

The boss looked up from her computer. She had a sunburn on her nose. Maybe she'd been on a vacation. "I'm deciding on assignments right now."

Ian thought about his empty apartment. "I'd like something far away. Something that'll take a while."

She watched him. "Do you want to talk about what's going on?"

About as much as he wanted to sit in a tub filled with piranhas. "I just want to work."

She considered him for a couple of seconds. "An American businessman disappeared in Russia. Could be mob related. The Russians don't really want us there but agreed as part of some kind of diplomatic exchange. The bureaucracy over there will be enough to make you tear out your hair. They'll do whatever they can to stonewall you. Are you ready for months of diplomatic maneuvering?"

Just the thing he needed to keep his mind off Daniela. "I'll take it."

He turned to leave, but then stopped and stuck his head back in the door again. "What are you assigning Daniela?"

Karin raised an eyebrow. "She came in first thing this morning and quit. You're friends, aren't you? I thought you'd know all about it."

She quit.

Good.

Ian didn't want her anywhere near danger. He wondered what she was going to do next. He wanted to offer his help. As he left Karin, his hand was in his pocket, on his phone, ready to call Daniela.

But by the time he walked out of the CPRU office into the hallway, he realized he shouldn't. He wished he could be the man she needed, but he wasn't. Hanging on to her would be unforgivably selfish. No matter what anybody said, he had to let her go.

Rocket booster, say good-bye to rocket and prepare to plummet.

PART
THREE

CHAPTER
NINETEEN

6 months later

Eduardo

Rio de Janeiro, Brazil

Eduardo sat on the ornate cast-iron bench in front of his brother's grave as rain drizzled from the gray, unforgiving sky. Darker clouds gathered on the horizon, but he should have some time before the storm hit.

He touched the gravestone he'd bought for his brother—the black granite bigger and fancier than he could afford, but he didn't care. If only he could talk to Marcos one last time. If only they could have one last drink together.

But time turned back for no man. Time flowed only forward, like the Amazon, and took whatever it damn well pleased.

Eduardo had lost Marcos, a fact he needed to accept, the same way he needed to accept that he'd also lost his father.

Marcos's brutal murder six months ago had shaken Raul Morais so much, the old man had spent a fortune on investigating why his eldest had been killed. He'd found out about the stolen diamonds. And then he'd exploded with rage. He could not forgive Marcos turning criminal. He refused to even attend the funeral.

He hated Eduardo too now. He'd found out that Eduardo and Marcos had plotted together from the beginning. The old man changed his will, disinheriting Eduardo completely. And then he'd divorced wife number three, married a new one, barely twenty, and gotten her pregnant on the wedding night.

Eduardo had only seen the bitch in the papers. Joaquim the butler-body-guard had Eduardo escorted off the premises when he'd tried to visit. The mansion where the future president of Brazil was going to be raised did not admit criminals.

Eduardo wanted to murder all of them. He'd spent months fantasizing how he would do it, even though he knew that security would never let him anywhere near the family mansion again. He'd been banished.

His fury had no outlet.

Until this morning. The American private investigator Marcos had hired before he'd been killed called while Eduardo was drinking his first cup of coffee. He'd found Ian Slaney, Finch's thieving buddy.

Eduardo patted the black granite, then let it go, pulled the plane ticket to Washington DC from his pocket, and showed it to Marcos's headstone. "I'm going today. I'm going to avenge you, brother."

Leaving Brazil might be the best course of action, in any case. He'd done a good job of hiding so far, always on the move. But he couldn't for a moment forget that he too had a price on his head.

* * *

Daniela

Daniela pushed her hair behind her ear as she looked in the mirror. She liked her new hairstyle, short, sassy, easy. With the hours she was putting in at work and school, she didn't have time to care for hair that reached below her waist.

She'd grown tired of wearing it in a bun at her nape. She no longer wanted the old-fashioned, matronly bun so she could look older for Ian. The pixie cut made her look the young, hip professional she was.

"You could try going blond," Iris said on speaker. "I think it'd look good on you. Of course, everything looks good on the young and beautiful." Her words had an undertone.

"Having seconds thoughts about emerald?" Daniela asked as she spritzed a tiny bit of perfume on her neck.

"You should have talked me out of it. I look like Kermit."

As much as Daniela loved her, she did secretly think that, with the new glasses, Iris had a slightly froggish appearance. "I could pop in tomorrow. I'll help you dye it back to black."

"Would you? Thank you." She paused. "Ian called earlier."

Daniela's pulse sped up. "Everything okay?"

"He seems to be in no imminent danger. Other than frustration slowly killing him." Another pause. "He asked about you."

"Any idea when he'll be coming home?"

"Not yet. I'll go and check on his place tomorrow."

"Don't worry about it. I can swing by after we do your hair."

"Are you sure?"

"I wanted to pick up a few things anyway." And Iris's knees were giving her more and more trouble lately. She was beginning to find stairs challenging. Whenever she could, Daniela was more than happy to help.

"You're a sweetheart." Iris smacked a kiss. "Wait. I have to go. Barry is here. Have fun tonight. Find true love."

"You too."

Iris laughed. "Honestly? I'm just looking to get laid. Don't tell Ian. But I'm not going to say no if Barry asks. You never know when it's going to be the last time, at my age."

"Not for a long while. You're a beautiful, vivacious woman."

"Damn right. And I want to go out with a bang." She giggled like a teenager. "Pun intended."

"I fully support the effort. But let me just say this ahead of time, I'm not going to want any details."

"You and Ian could be twins. It's scary." Iris tried for a disgruntled grumble, then closed with "Have fun. I love you."

"I love you too, Iris."

She truly did. She felt as if she'd found another mother in the older woman. And Crystal was like the sister Daniela had never had.

Daniela had accused Ian of wanting his family back, but maybe she wanted the same thing, because somehow she'd managed to gather a small family around herself. And Bobby…

Maybe Bobby was another puzzle piece that would help her create that wholeness she craved.

She clicked off the phone and turned around slowly, doing one last mirror check. Her teal dress was fun and flirty, a light silk, flaring at the knees. Perfect for her date.

She'd learned to appreciate Bobby for never giving up, for always coming back, for wanting her without wavering. For knowing what he wanted and being brave enough to stick with it. She no longer wanted a man larger than life, the legendary hero, the completely unattainable.

She'd had a pretty good talk with her shrink about that. How she'd always felt guilty about her past, so maybe she thought she didn't deserve true happiness and chose Ian, a man she subconsciously knew she could never have.

If she wanted a better future, she needed to learn to make better choices.

The intercom chimed. She pressed it and said, "I'm on my way down," at the same time as Bobby said, "I'm here."

Purse. Keys. Shoes. And then she was running down the stairs.

Crystal texted her:

> *Want to go out?*

Daniela texted her back:

> *Going out with Bobby. Want to come?*

Crystal wrote:

> *Too fabulous to be 3rd wheel. Will magnanimously give him privacy to pop the question.*

Daniela typed:

> *He's not going to propose!*

To which Crystal said:

> *Get back to me on that later.*

And she signed off with an icon of a madly waving penguin.

"Hey, beautiful." Bobby took Daniela's hand as soon as she stepped through the apartment building's front door. He twirled her around. Gave a wolf whistle. Then he pulled her in and kissed her.

He had a firm body—from golf and tennis, both of which he was teaching her. He was lighthearted and fun, and he unabashedly, unapologetically wanted her. Which he proved by deepening the kiss, pulling her tighter into his embrace, and then whispering into her ear, "We don't have to go out for dinner. We could order in, hang out on your couch, and watch Netflix."

She knew what that meant. And part of her even wanted it. But every time the opportunity came up, she felt she wasn't ready.

She kissed him back.

I'll have to be ready soon.

They'd been dating for three months. He was a great guy, but he wasn't going to wait forever.

She tugged him toward his blue Prius parked by the curb. "Come on. You promised me the roast duck. Don't think you'll weasel out of it."

He grinned back, his hair in golden spikes, his blue eyes sparkling with happiness. "I wouldn't dream."

As he drove to the restaurant, he reached over and took her hand. "I'll have to go to the Montreal office."

They both worked for the same law firm, Bobby as a junior attorney, Daniela as an assistant. She'd entered law school after all. She liked the law. Especially human rights law. The cases were international, interesting, required plenty of investigation. She was challenged and got to use her skills.

She'd already assisted on a case in India that resulted in a dozen child brides being given back to their families so they could finish growing up and going to school. And she'd assisted on a case of sex trafficking from Mexico to the US, to make sure that the victims' rights were protected.

She was happy. She was becoming a person who helped others.

She could have been happy at CPRU too, but it'd been a job she'd applied for to prove a point to Ian. No more of that. Law school and the new job had given her the new start she'd needed. She felt content. She felt that she was in the right place for this point in her life.

Maybe even with the right man. She smiled at Bobby. "How long will you have to be in Montreal?"

He groaned. "A full month. I'm going to miss you like crazy."

"When are you leaving?"

"Next week. Want to cook me a good-bye dinner?"

She kept her smile. "One good-bye dinner, coming up. And then when you get back, I'll cook you a welcome-home dinner."

"I love you, you know that?"

She could almost, *almost*, say it back. The words were on the tip of her tongue, but by the time she was about to release them, Bobby was pulling into a parking spot. They were at the restaurant.

During dinner, they talked about cases, people at work, plans for the summer, the possibility of Bobby trading his car in for a newer model, if he could get promoted from junior attorney.

"Either a newer car," he said, holding her gaze, "or I could switch to a larger apartment."

He took her hand on the table. She let him play with her fingers. Was he getting ready to ask her to move in with him?

Was she ready to say yes?

"Or maybe just an apartment closer to work," she said. Rush-hour traffic was the bane of both of their existences.

The duck tasted great. They had a fun time together. Bobby was gentle, attentive, and he loved her. When, postdate, he asked to come up to her place, she said yes.

She made two decaf cappuccinos.

He flipped through the TV channels and settled on a basketball game. As she brought over the cups and set them on the coffee table, he reached for her and pulled her onto his lap.

"I want you crazy much." He kissed her.

He was a good kisser.

He was also extremely good at manipulating her out of her dress. She barely even realized what was happening before she was in her panties and bra, on her back on the couch, Bobbie over her.

He kissed her neck. "God, you're beautiful."

He caressed her breasts through the lace of her bra. He pressed his erection between her legs. Then he eased back a little and put his hand inside her panties.

She unbuckled his belt and slipped her hands in, between the pants and his underwear, cupped him, rubbed her palm against him. He groaned into her ear.

While his fingers played with her, she slid hers inside his silk briefs. He pressed his hot length into her palm.

"I know you're not ready for more—"—he gasped the words in a ragged whisper—"but..." He groaned. "You're driving me crazy."

She wrapped her fingers around his hard length and worked him as he pumped into her hand. Then he bowed his back and came, and collapsed on top of her, breathing hard, laughing weakly.

He gathered her against him and kissed her. "I love you. And I can't wait to be able to do that inside you. I know you don't jump into bed with people easily, and I respect you for that. I love you for that. I'm not going to push."

He kissed her again, this time without heat, with mellow love and affection.

She kissed him back. And decided that next week, after the good-bye dinner, she was going to let him inside her bedroom, in her bed, inside her.

But first, she was going to tell him about her past. She didn't want to have secrets from the first man who'd ever told her he loved her, someone who was working up to asking her to move in with him, and maybe more. Letting him believe that her reluctance stemmed from old-fashioned morals and shyness was the same as lying.

Here was a man who loved her, someone she could grow to love back. They couldn't build their future on lies. She'd built an entire relationship with Ian out of nothing but fantasies. She'd learned from that mistake.

This time, she wanted something solid and real.

* * *

Eduardo

Eduardo had a name, Ian Slaney, and he had an address. Trouble was, he'd been in DC for two weeks and nobody had showed up at the address yet.

He'd picked the lock—no security system, piece of cake—but he found nothing to help him to track down his target. At least he wasn't at a complete dead end. The apartment hadn't been cleaned out: cans in the kitchen cabinets, clothes in the closet, books on the shelf. Maybe Ian Slaney was on a trip and would be back soon.

So Eduardo rented a place across the courtyard, in the same apartment complex, on the same floor. From his bedroom, he could monitor Slaney's windows. Any sign of movement, and he could be over there in two minutes.

***

Daniela

Daniela was swamped between school and work. Ian had called, his usual once-a-week check-in. He'd asked about Bobby. He was okay with the relationship, even encouraged it.

Daniela was glad that they'd found their way back to friendship.

Bobby called every night. Tonight, he was in high spirits. The case he was working on finally moved forward. Daniela suspected he'd had a few drinks out of his hotel room's mini fridge.

"What are you wearing?" he asked.

"Judge's robes and nothing under." A fantasy of his that he'd told her about.

"God, you're torturing me."

She grinned. "What are you wearing?"

"Legal briefs." He snickered.

She rolled her eyes. But she had a smile on her face.

"I miss you," he said next.

"I miss you too."

She had chickened out of telling him about her past before he'd left. But she was determined to do it right away when he returned. She'd cook for him. They'd have a good talk. Then they would go to bed and see where they could take their relationship.

"So, a cop, a lawyer, and a judge walk into a bar," Bobby began.

She settled in and let him tell her silly jokes for almost an hour, and enjoyed the company.

After they said their good-byes and hung up, she felt restless. She wasn't ready to go to sleep.

She thought about the legal dictionaries and college notes she'd left behind at Ian's apartment and decided to drive over and get them. She wanted to check on his apartment for him anyway. He'd been away for over six months. She had a key. She went over every couple of weeks to make sure he didn't have a leaky pipe or an ant infestation, or…okay, because she missed the place.

She glanced at the clock on the microwave as she headed out. Past nine p.m. Good. At least, she wouldn't have to fight traffic.

She was there in thirty minutes, let herself in, walked around, checked out every corner. Everything looked fine. She cracked a window open to let some fresh air in, since the apartment smelled stale.

Then she went back to her old room—everything still as she'd left it—and browsed through her bookshelf, pulling out the books she wanted.

She ended up with a bigger pile on her bed than she'd anticipated. She went to look for a cardboard box. She didn't find any.

She did find Ian's gym bag. He wouldn't mind if she borrowed that. She'd bring it back. They'd probably meet up anyway when he finally returned.

She packed the bag full of books and set it by the door. Then she grabbed a bottle of water from the fridge. Of course, since the fridge was unplugged, the water was warm. She didn't care.

She walked into Ian's bedroom and regarded his empty bed.

Old emotions, needs, dreams bubbled up. She fought them back, but she did walk over and sit on the rumpled cover. She put the water bottle on the nightstand. Lay down. She turned her head and inhaled. Even after months, his pillow still smelled like Ian.

Longing washed over her, so strongly that it stole her breath. *Stupid, stupid, stupid.* She shouldn't have come here.

But she didn't leave. She curled up in Ian's bed and fell asleep.

CHAPTER
TWENTY

Ian

"Case is rolled up. I'm heading home," Ian told Daniela over the phone. Man, he was ready. Russia was great, actually a lot better than he'd expected, but he couldn't wait to sleep in his own bed again.

"When?"

"Tuesday."

"That's the day Bobby is coming back from Montreal."

She sounded happy. He found himself carefully listening to her voice every time they talked.

"How is that going?" he asked.

"He's been hinting that he wants us to move in together. Crystal says he's going to propose."

A crack formed inside Ian's chest, rapidly growing into a sinkhole. "You should follow your heart."

"I will."

"Congratulations." He winced. He should have said that first. He wanted nothing but the best for her.

She laughed on the other end. "Let's wait with that until the engagement actually happens."

He tried to imagine her with Bobby. Wasn't hard. She had pictures of the two of them posted to her social media pages. Bobby wasn't an ugly kid. They looked good together.

Kid had had good grades in law school. Good job now, with good prospects. No red flags. Ian had run a background check on him and his family. Upper-middle class, decent people.

Ian was going to support the relationship if it killed him.

***

Eduardo

Eduardo watched the apartment across the courtyard. No lights on tonight.

There'd been lights a week ago. Not Ian Slaney. A young woman. The cleaning girl? A girlfriend?

He didn't go over. He didn't want to show himself to her. She might tell Slaney that a stranger was snooping around, and then Ian might never come home. Or he'd come prepared. Eduardo wanted to catch the bastard unaware.

Like Marcos had been caught unaware. Never knowing death would pounce, until they'd brought out the machetes.

***

Daniela

"Dinner was perfection." Bobby leaned back in his chair. "Thank you. Are you ready for your presentation Friday?"

See-Love-Aid was having a big conference at the convention center on human trafficking. The goal was to solicit funds for dissemination of information so people would recognize signs of trafficking and report it. See-Love-Aid was making flyers for truckers and managers of large farms who regularly came in contact with migrant workers. When, months ago, See-Love-Aid was looking for corporate sponsors, Daniela brought the issue up at the law firm where she and Bobby worked.

The firm agreed to a very generous sponsorship. As a result, they were invited to give the introductory speech. But since the lawyers billed about a gazillion dollars a second and didn't have the time to hang out at the conference, they were sending Daniela.

"I'm ready." She put the dirty plates in the sink. "It's just a ten-minute little thing."

Bobby stood to help with the dishes.

Daniela tried to wave him away. The kitchen in her apartment was tiny. "It's your welcome-home dinner. You're not allowed to work."

He snuck his hands around her waist from behind and dipped his head to kiss her neck. "Am I allowed to do this?"

She could feel him harden against her backside as he kept kissing her.

She filled her lungs. Either she was doing this or not.

Doing it. Definitely doing it.

She turned off the water, dried her hands. Dishes could wait.

She turned around and gave him access to her mouth. "Everything is allowed on the day of your return."

His blue eyes filled with hope and desire. "Everything?"

She smiled. "I'm prepared to be fully welcoming."

"Naked and welcoming?"

"If that's how you like it."

"That's how I like it," he said so fast, it sounded like one word.

And then he was kissing her, lifting her, her legs around his waist as he carried her to her bedroom.

Somehow, he got them on the bed without ever letting go of her. And she smiled at him because, maybe, just maybe, this could work.

He was yanking up his shirt when she could finally break their lips apart for long enough to say, "I need to tell you something first."

He pulled back. Searched her face. "You're not a virgin, are you? I mean, I don't care. I don't mind. I already knew that you're kind of old-fashioned about sex. I like it. I love you."

And she still couldn't say *I love you* back. Maybe after she came clean.

She sat up against the headboard, tucked her feet under herself, and clasped her hands together on her lap. Drew a deep breath. They needed to get this out of the way. She met his patient gaze.

"I'm hardly a virgin." And then she told him everything, starting with her mother.

He stared at her openmouthed, a horrified look settling over his face.

Horrified *for* her? Because she'd been through a lot growing up? She couldn't tell. She went on with her story, barely paused long enough to draw breath. She wanted it all out. No more secrets. She wanted this relationship to have a chance.

When she finished, she wrapped her arms around herself. "So that's it. That's me."

"Are you kidding me?" His eyes narrowed, his voice harsher than she'd ever heard it. He sounded angry and, at the same time, ready to cry. "Why would you make up something like this?"

She shook her head.

"Seriously? Dani? You used to be a prostitute?" He drew farther away from her, as far as he could get without falling off the end of the bed.

Her heart sank. "Yes."

He gave a shaky, incredulous laugh. "Man, I respected you enough to wait. I mean...I thought this was it, like I was going to propose." He reached back to scratch his neck. Dropped his hand. "Shit. I've been looking at rings online."

He jumped up, then he backed away from her as if she was contagious. "So you, like, fucked dozens of guys." Hurt and revulsion mixed in his eyes. "For money."

"Probably hundreds."

She shut off all emotion. If she allowed herself to feel now, she would shatter. Her skin felt incredibly tight, her heart cold and hard, as if made of glass.

She'd been prepared for a long talk, lots of questions and explanations. She'd thought the night might go badly, but not this badly. Not with this much loathing on Bobby's face, loathing that was quickly turning into hate.

"You almost fooled me." The words snapped with hard clicks, like armor snapping into place.

"I'm sorry. I wanted to tell you, but it never seemed like the right time. But I'm right here, right now, telling you the truth."

He half turned from her. He had a faraway look in his eyes, as if he was no longer listening. "I can't do this," he said at last. "It's too much for me. I'm sorry. I can't imagine having sex with someone who..."

He didn't finish.

And then he was walking out, without saying good-bye, without saying anything else.

Daniela curled up into as tiny a ball as she could manage. The old numbness came back. She felt as violated as when that first logger had come up to the bamboo hut and pushed her on her back.

She hadn't expected Bobby to be happy about her past, but she hadn't expected pure revulsion, not this much hate.

Ian had always accepted her, never made her feel dirty, never made her feel worthless or that she should hide anything about herself.

Of course, Ian didn't want her either.

Bobby's leaving didn't make her cry, but that thought did. Because all this time, she'd been only pretending she didn't care that Ian didn't want her. And she wished she could keep on pretending, because once she began crying, she couldn't stop.

In the morning, she had to spend an extra hour on her makeup to hide the redness and swelling around her eyes.

When she walked into the office, hoping against hope that she could avoid Bobby, the first thing she saw was a note on her desk. "Please see Lucy in HR."

So Daniela went, a sick feeling spreading in her stomach.

Lucy was waiting for her. The grandmotherly Korean-American woman ushered her to a chair. "I'm afraid I have bad news for you. You know you were here on a probationary period, and I'm sorry, but decisions have been made, and this position will not be made permanent. Nothing that you did. They're just not going to need as many people as they thought."

Daniela nodded numbly. She didn't fight for the job. It hadn't been Lucy's decision. Lucy didn't even have to explain it, really. With at-will employment, any company could fire any employee without giving a reason.

Daniela went home, went to bed. Since she hadn't slept all night, she passed out eventually. When she woke, the sky was dark outside.

She washed her face, went out, drove to the nearest bar, and ordered whiskey. Ian had told her once that oblivion lived in a bottle. Tonight, Daniela needed oblivion.

Men came up to her; she ignored them. When the bartender cut her off, she stumbled outside. She knew she shouldn't drive, so she walked toward home, still remembering the horror and revulsion on Bobby's face. When she saw a drunk a block over with a bottle in a paper bag, she bought the bottle off him for twenty bucks. To hell with the bartender.

The booze tasted pretty bad compared to the bar's top-shelf whiskey. She thought it might be gin. She drank as she walked, barely feeling the chill in the air.

A car passed her. Backed up. Two guys who'd hit on her in the bar earlier grinned at her as the one on the passenger side rolled down his window. Blond, scrawny twenty-something. The other one could have been his twin, only bulkier in the chest and belly. In dress shirts with ties, they were office types, possibly even other lawyers.

"Hey, pretty thing, want a ride?"

"I don't want anything." But that wasn't true. She wanted one thing, one man, had wanted him for years, but she couldn't have him. She was still in love with Ian Slaney.

She was just drunk enough to admit it finally. Maybe she should have gotten wasted sooner. The whole fiasco with Bobby could have been avoided.

She looked at the men.

"A thousand dollars," she said.

They glanced at each other. Laughed. The one on the passenger side said, "Okay, babe."

She could have said five thousand. The amount wouldn't have mattered. They would have agreed. They had no intention of paying, just taking her, using her, and dumping her on another dark corner.

But she wasn't that Daniela anymore.

She might be drunk and heartbroken, but she was nobody's victim, not ever again.

"A thousand dollars and I won't kick your ass," she said.

The men weren't happy with *that*.

They got out of the car, looked up and down the abandoned sidewalk, then tried to drag her into the backseat.

Ian had trained her years ago for moments like this. She tossed the empty bottle and beat the men off, hurt them enough that they left, cursing her out and calling her a crazy bitch.

She swore after them in Portuguese. Ian had been right not to let her forget the language. The way the fiery words rolled off her tongue was immensely satisfying.

Then she fell over her own feet and scraped her hands on the pavement, banged her cheek. She pushed up, stayed on her ass, watched the blood run down her wrists. Her skin stung and burned.

A cab rolled down the street. She held up a bloody hand. The cabbie ignored her and kept on going.

She was completely drunk for the first time in her life, but she was still smart enough to know that sitting here, alone, in the middle of the night, was stupid.

Crystal was in Boston, visiting her parents. Iris would have a heart attack. And she didn't like to drive in the dark, at night. Her eyes were getting finicky. So Daniela swallowed her pride, pulled out her cell phone, and called Ian.

He answered on the second ring with "What's wrong?"

"Why do you always assume that I can't handle myself and need your help?" she mumbled.

"You're calling me at past two in the morning."

The blood trickled onto the phone from her hand. She stared at it with the rapt attention of a drunk. "I'm bleeding."

"Where are you?" His voice turned sharp, full of tension.

"I'm on the street." Right. That wasn't helpful. She looked up, read the street signs, and gave him the intersection.

"I'll be right there. Don't move."

"I don't think I can." A dull ache spread through her body.

She ended the call and slipped the phone into her back pocket...on the third try. It rang almost immediately, Ian calling her back. She ignored him. She was afraid if she picked up, she might tell him that she still loved him.

***

Ian

I'm bleeding. I'm on the street.

Ian had never been so scared in his life. Every muscle in his body was so tight, he thought he'd break. He could barely breathe.

He'd just gotten back from Moscow. He'd ended up having to stay an extra couple of days to tie up loose ends. He was loopy with jet lag. Then the call. What the hell happened?

I'm bleeding.

Had she been mugged? Shot? Raped?

I'm on the street.

He hadn't seen her in six months, but she'd always sounded fine on the phone. Until just now. Now was the opposite of fine.

He drove twice the speed limit, through red lights. Thank God the streets were empty. For the first time in a long time, he was praying. He couldn't imagine his life without Daniela in it.

Truth was, she'd saved him...

Before he could think more about that stun grenade, he was at the intersection, and he could see her. She was sitting on the sidewalk.

She raised her head and looked at him as he parked by the curb, then ran to her. She looked so lost, it shattered not just his heart but every organ he had. He felt liquefied inside.

He noted the blood and that she wasn't too terribly hurt, nothing life threatening. He picked her up, carried her to the car, and put her in the passenger seat.

He didn't go around. He knelt on the curb in front of her. "Who did this to you?"

The bastard was so fucking dead.

She flashed a goofy smile. "Hard liquor."

He could definitely smell *that* on her. "Your little call knocked ten years off my life, you know that?" He could almost breathe normally. "What happened?"

"I'll tell you later." Her beautiful eyes hung on his face. "Could you please take me home?"

"Sure."

"To your place," she added.

He leaned in, fastened her seat belt, then closed the door on her.

All the way home, she didn't say anything. She just closed her eyes and sank into the seat, her bloody hands on her lap.

When he got to the condo, he lifted her again and carried her up.

She lay her head on his shoulder. "I can walk."

"I don't care." He carried her straight to his bathroom and sat her on the closed toilet lid, rummaged around for peroxide in the mirrored cabinet.

He cleaned her hands, disinfected the scrapes, put on waterproof bandages. He brought her one of his T-shirts. "Take a shower."

Then he left her.

Then he paced his bedroom, a million thoughts exploding through his brain.

She came out fifteen minutes later, the T-shirt hanging off her shoulders, the hem coming to her knees. She looked halfway between a sex symbol and a waif.

He stepped to his bed and pulled down the covers. "You're sleeping here tonight. I don't think I can stand letting you out of my sight."

She climbed into bed.

He kicked off his shoes and got in next to her. He left the light on.

He tried to take her into his arms, but he was on top of the covers, so it didn't work. So, with a muffled curse, he got under the covers with her. Then he did take her into his arms, and she turned into his chest, and his world began to reassemble itself.

"Now tell me what happened."

She did. And then she made him promise that he wouldn't kill Bobby. "You can't kill him for not wanting to sleep with an ex-whore."

He took her chin and forced her to look at him. "There's nothing wrong with you."

She rolled her eyes and parroted back the words he must have told her a thousand times after he'd first brought her to the US. "There's not one thing wrong with me or bad about me."

"Damn right."

She lowered her head. "You don't want to sleep with me either."

Christ. He gently took her chin, brought her face back up again, and then he kissed her.

And kissed her, and kissed her, until they had their legs wrapped around each other, and he had his hand under her T-shirt, on her perfect breast, and he was so hard, he thought the top of his head would blow off from all the pressure building inside him.

He pulled back, catching his breath. "We can't do this tonight."

Immediately, the hurt of rejection was back in her eyes.

"Don't get me wrong, I want to." He caressed her cheek. "More than anything."

"Then why?"

"You're drunk."

"Not that drunk." The beginnings of a smile knocked the hurt off her face. "As long as we do it lying down."

She was killing him.

"If we are to take this step, I'd prefer both of us completely sober."

"When?"

"In the morning."

Her smile grew, leaving room for nothing else in his field of vision or in his heart.

He watched her, hopelessly sunk. "If you still feel the same in the morning."

"I will." She kept the goofy grin for another moment, then her gaze grew more serious, more curious. "Why now? What made you change your mind?"

"I don't have the energy to keep denying that I'm hopelessly in love with you. Worrying about you all these years wore me down. I didn't realize how much you took out of me."

She poked him with her elbow, but she was grinning.

"I came to a realization tonight," he said, turning serious.

"I'm the best, and you don't want the rest?"

She was a cute drunk, he had to give her that. "I've known that for years."

She looked indescribably pleased.

"I used to think," he said, "that because I saved you, if you gave yourself to me, it'd be like a payment, which wouldn't be right. You don't owe me anything."

She opened her mouth, but he put a finger over her soft lips.

"But tonight," he told her, "I realized that it's the other way around. You saved me. If you hadn't come into my life, I'd be dead by now. I would have picked the wrong fight, or I would have dissolved my liver in whiskey. I'm here today because of you. No doubt about it."

She looked thoughtful, in a tipsy, hazy kind of way, but when she moved his finger and spoke, the words came out sure and clear. "If I saved your life, and, as you say, you owe me…I'm taking it. I'm taking everything."

"I'm yours to take. In the morning."

She looked grumbly.

"Morning will come faster than you'll be ready for, believe me. Hangovers are my area of expertise."

"Hmpf."

"Okay." He turned the light off. Then he tucked her against him. "Now go to sleep."

For about half a minute, she was still. Then she said, "I feel like an anaconda is squirming inside my stomach."

"And that's why you're never going to get drunk like this again."

"Merda," she said with feeling.

"Monte de merda," he agreed.

CHAPTER
TWENTY-ONE

Daniela

Daniela was so happy and excited, if she hadn't had all that alcohol in her system, she never would have been able to fall asleep.

Something, maybe a car horn outside, woke her hours later. Sunlight fell in a golden swath across the bed, across Ian. He had a rugged face. A soldier's face. To her, it was the most handsome face in the world.

She put a hand over his chest, over his steadily beating heart, and watched him, feeling completely contented and happy.

His hand came up and covered hers. He opened his eyes and looked at her. "How are you feeling?"

She burrowed into his embrace. "Like I am exactly where I am supposed to be."

He brushed his lips over her forehead and tightened his arms around her.

But before she could float off into the bliss of waking up with him like this, her gaze fell on the bedside clock and she shot out of bed—pain slicing into her head from the sudden movement. *Oh, not now.*

She could *not* have a hangover!

"I have a presentation at the convention center in an hour." She ran for the bathroom to brush her teeth.

"I thought you said they let you go."

"I'm not doing this for the firm," she said around her toothbrush before pulling it out of her mouth so she could say the rest more clearly. "I'm doing this for See-Love-Aid. The firm won't send a replacement. They'll just blow it off. No lawyer is going to take a billable hour and give it away for free."

"You got clothes?" Ian stuck his head in the door.

"I left a couple of dresses here when I moved. One of those will work."

"Take an aspirin. Here. I'll drive you." He padded away, called back, "I'll make coffee."

They made it to the convention center in the nick of time, and she showed up at the back entrance of the stage just when the conference organizer was about to have a nervous meltdown, judging by her wide-eyed, frazzled expression.

The sixty-something woman in an impeccable red suit stepped forward, grabbed Daniela's hand, and squeezed a little too hard. "I thought you weren't going to make it."

"Sorry to worry you. Presentation cued up?"

"Yes. Here is the remote for the slide projector." The woman dropped the small plastic controller into Daniela's hand, then gently shoved her out onto the stage.

And then the spotlight hit her.

Wow. Okay.

The walk to the microphone at the podium at the front of the stage wasn't bad. But then her eyes adjusted to the bright light, and she could make out the audience.

The enormous room seated at least a thousand people. More people than lived in her village on the Içana. Most were on their cell phones, tapping away.

As she looked around, she understood that many of them had come only because their bosses sent them. Like the law firm had sent Daniela. Their job was to show up and maybe bring back some flyers. Or they'd come for the continuing education credit they would receive for attending the conference.

How was she going to reach them?

She gripped the remote, knowing her slideshow wasn't going to cut it. She had planned on talking statistics and showing pictures of exploited children. But everyone there had seen pictures of scruffy children before.

Her knees trembled, and she grabbed the podium for support. Then Ian's tall form appeared at the edge of the first row, and ducking down—*Excuse me. Excuse me.*—he went all the way to the middle and sat down right in front of her, a smile on his face.

Daniela filled her lungs and locked her knees.

"Hi," she began. "I'm Daniela Wintermann."

People looked up but then went back to quickly finish the texts they'd been typing.

"Until very recently, I worked for Hooper, Hinze & Quarles, one of the sponsors of this conference. I'm a law school student."

People nodded absently. She spoke in unaccented English, she was dressed in a sharp black dress, she was a professional—she was just like them. They'd seen presenters like her before. They'd been to conferences like this before. They'd heard hundreds of interchangeable speeches.

"I was trafficked at age fifteen. I am a former child prostitute." She announced her deepest, darkest secret, on stage, to a thousand strangers.

The phones went down, and the heads came up. The audience stared.

She told her story—the logger, her mother, Pedro, Rosa—and the phones stayed in laps.

She did click on the slide projector then. A group of young women huddled in the corner of a cornfield was the first image, the aftermath of a rescue op on the Mexican border.

"We are not just formerly trafficked persons." She showed a handful of similar pictures of abused bodies with hopeful faces. "We are women with endless potential. We have endured. And now we are going to thrive. The past does not define us. We define our future."

She received a standing ovation. Ian was the first on his feet, applauding madly. And as the conference organizer waiting at the back of the stage hugged her, the woman said, with a sheen in her blue eyes, "That speech just paid our budget for a year. What would it take to have you come and work for us permanently? You are the most amazing teacher I've ever met. There are things I've been trying to explain for a decade, and I think this is the first time an audience finally understands."

"Thank you. Can I call you about that?" Daniela said, because Ian was hurrying down the back hallway.

He hugged her and lifted her off her feet. "I'm so proud of you."

She was proud of herself.

When they were in the car on the way home, he asked, "How do you feel?"

"I feel as free as fish in water." She grinned. "I know who I am, and I'm okay with my past. I don't need to hide anymore. I'm fine the way I am."

He reached over for her hand and held it all the way home, then all the way up to their apartment. Then they were inside—no more words for a while. He picked her up and carried her to his bedroom, laid her on the bed.

He kissed her.

Her whole body felt tingly everywhere they touched, something she'd never felt with any man. She loved his solid bulk, the strength of his arms that made her feel safe and as if she belonged in them.

She kissed him back, letting him explore her mouth, then exploring his. She could have gone for hours just kissing him. And she knew he would let her. He was letting her call the shots. She was in charge.

She liked that thought, but it also made her nervous.

"What is it?" he whispered against the curve of her jaw, his hands soothing her back.

She pulled up and braced herself on her hands so she could look at him. "I want this to work. I want to be able to enjoy this. With you. And I want it to be good for you so you'll agree to do it again."

He smiled. "You can pretty much take worrying about me wanting this again off the table. I haven't even had it yet and I want it again already." His eyes turned serious. "Why do you think you won't enjoy it?"

"I didn't. Before." She looked at his shoulder. She couldn't look at him.

Oh God. How stupid could she be? Never, *never,* bring up *before,* especially when they were in bed and they'd almost…Now he'd start to think about her with other men and change his mind and—

"Hey. This is not going to be like before. This time, you're making love with a man who loves you to pieces. Totally crazy about you. I mean, major nut cakes."

A smile took over her face. No ghosts of the past here, nobody and nothing but Ian and her, and they loved each other.

She kissed him again.

His hands slipped to the bottom of her dress. "I'd like to take this off."

She sat up to straddle him and lifted her arms. The material caught on her elbow. "Merda."

"Don't swear."

"You swear."

"I'm an ex-alcoholic ex-soldier with anger management issues. You are a brilliant woman, a lady with class."

Her heart swelled. He'd been saying things like that to her since they'd met, treating her as if she was someone good and precious.

And then he was all surprised that she'd fallen in love with him. *Men.*

He helped the dress off her. She let her arms drop, didn't try to hide herself from him.

Others had told her before that she was pretty or beautiful. He didn't.

He gave a strangled laugh. "I'm so hard, I'm going to embarrass myself any second now, and I'm still thinking you're too innocent to touch the way I want, that I have no right to put my hands on you—"

She slipped out of her bra, then took his hands and put them on her breasts.

He ran his thumbs lightly over her nipples. The sudden pleasure was so overwhelming, she let her head drop back and arched her spine, her breasts pressing into his touch.

He gave another strangled laugh. "Maybe we should put your top back on. I don't know how long I'm going to last like this."

She rocked against him.

"We should take this slow," he rasped.

She looked at him. "Could we take your clothes off?"

He was watching her as if she was some kind of miracle. "Yeah. Sure."

He let her go, moved out from under her long enough to strip. She lay down on the bed and watched him, her body clamoring for him to return to her.

He lay down next to her on top of the covers.

She kissed his collarbone and let her hands explore the wide expanse of his chest. She was enjoying this, just playing, so much more than she'd expected.

But soon an urgency overtook her, and both of them grew more serious, needing, wanting, then finally, joining. And then the pleasure built inside her into a giant wave, like rainwater rushing down from the jungle, and the water broke over her like a river, floated her into bliss.

Afterward, she lay soaked in happiness, tucked into his arms.

He kissed the top of her head. "Are you crying?"

She reached up to touch her cheek, felt moisture on her skin.

Ian came up on his elbow to look at her, worry in his gaze. "Did I hurt you?"

She shook her head. "It was amazing. Beautiful, and a lot more than I imagined. I want to do it every day."

He gave a quick bark of a laugh. "I might grow old eventually."

"I want us to grow old together," she said.

He kissed the corner of her mouth, then whispered against her lips, "We will."

Several minutes later, as she lay with her head on his shoulder again, she said, "You're right. I'm a new woman. But you're a new man too. You're not the angry, drinking Ian that you were after Linda."

She expected him to shut down the conversation, but he said, "I'm still angry over Linda and the boys. I shouldn't have left her. I didn't understand that she was feeling so bad. I don't know if I'll ever forgive myself for not grasping that. And I don't know if I'll ever forgive her."

His chest rose as he drew a deep breath. "You know, the VA sent me to a rehab place once. Hope Hill. It's in a small town in Pennsylvania. First day there, my counselor looked me in the eye and said that I was an alcoholic with anger management issues and self-destructive tendencies."

Daniela pressed tighter against him, holding on to him.

Ian said, "So the guy asks me, 'What do you think about that, Slaney?'"

Ian snorted. "I told him I was thinking about how much trouble I'd get into for punching him in the face." He paused. "So then the guy says, 'Oh wonderful.' I swear, he looked happy. 'You consider the consequences of your actions. You didn't act on your impulse. You just considered it. Very well done.'" Ian paused again. "I couldn't tell if he was really smart or too stupid to live. I checked myself out and came back to DC."

"I've always known you to be a good man," Daniela told him.

"You probably have some mosquito-borne disease that makes you completely biased and blind to my faults. There's no end to the weird shit a person can catch in the Amazon." He rubbed her shoulder with the pad of his thumb.

She smiled against his warm skin. "I don't think I've ever felt this safe, or this happy."

She wiggled up, reversed their positions, maneuvered him so that his head was on her shoulder as she held him. "I want you to feel the same way." She kissed the top of his head. "Do I make you feel safe?"

"Safe…other things…" His voice grew distracted, his lips brushing against the side of her breast as they moved with the words. "It's all good. Believe me."

***

Eduardo

Eduardo watched Ian drive the woman to a different apartment, kiss her before he dropped her off.

Not the maid but his lover.

Eduardo smiled. So much better this way. This way, before Ian was killed, he could experience the grief of losing someone he loved.

As Ian pulled away, into traffic, Eduardo parked by the curb in the freed-up space and watched the woman float to the apartment building's front door. She radiated happiness. Ian Slaney must have done something right this morning.

She looked Brazilian, might even have some Baniwa blood in her—a little familiar, but Eduardo couldn't think when or where he might have met her.

He was prepared to wait all day, but she came out two hours later.

She'd changed her clothes, carried nothing but a small purse. She paused for a moment in the open door, and an old memory clicked into place in Eduardo's brain. *Finch's whore.*

She looked a little older and a lot more sophisticated, a lot more sure of herself, but she was definitely the girl Eduardo had talked to when he'd first gone to Santana to find Finch. He remembered her now.

Eduardo scrambled to process the implications. Would she recognize him? He was older too. He'd gone gray after Marcos's death. He didn't have his goatee anymore. Age had weakened his eyes, so he was now wearing glasses. He'd put on a few pounds, which had changed his face, added the infernal jowls he hated.

The woman was on the move. Eduardo had no time to hesitate. He would just have to risk it.

She walked with a smile and a bounce, looked like a woman in love. All was well in her world. Eduardo counted on that cloud of happiness to dim her instincts.

He started the car and drove ahead, turned into the alleyway between two apartment buildings. He parked the car about three meters in, got out and went around, opened the trunk. When from the corner of his eye he saw the woman pass behind him, he made a production of leaning into the trunk, pulling back, swearing in Portuguese.

She stopped on the sidewalk.

He turned. Flashed her a self-depreciating smile. "Almost pitched head-first into the trunk. I can't put weight on this leg. Just had…*como se diz*…knee replacement."

She stepped closer. "Let me help," she said in Portuguese. "Are you from Brazil?"

"São Paulo." He nodded toward the suitcase in the back and switched to Portuguese too. "Came up to see my brother. Something's still wrong with this knee." He tapped his left leg. "My brother knows a surgeon here who's willing to give it a look."

She leaned in for his suitcase, looked back over her shoulder with a smile, maybe to tell him that she too was Brazilian. Her mouth froze half-open. Her eyes narrowed for a second, then flashed with recognition. And then she moved, fast, but not as fast as the Taser.

Zwak!

She toppled into the trunk, twitching for just a second or two before she went limp.

He scooped in her legs, then slammed down the lid. The next second, he was behind the wheel. The second after that, they were gone.

"For you, Marcos," Eduardo said as he drove down the boulevard. "I will avenge you. I am a good brother."

He had the bait. Now he just had to set the trap.

CHAPTER
TWENTY-TWO

Ian

Ian whistled as he walked to his car. Okay, maybe he swaggered more than he walked. His phone pinged with a text message from Daniela.

And the next instant, the bubble of happiness popped. The goofy-ass grin he'd been wearing all morning slid off his face as he read the screen.

The first text was an address, followed by, *Come alone or the girl dies.*

He dialed her immediately. The call rang and rang, but she didn't pick up. This was not something she would joke with. Not her. She'd been in plenty of danger; she wouldn't make a game of it. She didn't think danger was fun, like someone who'd had a safe life and played with danger for adrenaline. She didn't even like roller coasters.

Worry gutted him in an instant, cutting him to shreds. Hot fury built him back up. *Nobody* was going to touch Daniela. *Nobody.*

He slammed into his car, put the address into the GPS, and peeled out of the gas station.

Who would take her?

She hadn't been taken for money. Ian didn't have any. He'd spent his saved-up combat pay on Daniela's college tuition. He'd donated Linda's life insurance to an organization that helped young mothers with postpartum depression.

She'd been taken by someone who wanted to hurt Ian. Maybe even by someone who wanted to hurt her too.

His mind raced.

The only case they'd worked together had been Lila Heyerdahl's in Brazil. Another kidnapping. But Ian shook his head even as he thought of Carol and Essie—both in prison.

Marcos Morais was dead.

Because his father was so high profile, Marcos's death had made the Brazilian news. Ian had kept track.

But Goat Man? Since Ian never knew his name, he couldn't be certain what happened to him, couldn't follow up.

Ian had a feeling he was about to meet the bastard. Acid bubbled in his stomach at the thought that Daniela had met him already.

In twenty minutes, he was in one of the worst neighborhoods of the city: graffiti, broken windows, cracked sidewalks overgrown with weeds, abandoned houses.

The GPS led him to a boarded-up store.

Padlocked front. He went around and checked the back, found a window that had been busted.

He cursed himself for not having his gun, but he'd only run out to pick up flowers for Daniela, stopped to put gas in his car on the way.

At least he had Finch's pocketknife. At a minimum, Ian always carried a knife and a lighter, basic emergency preparedness he'd kept up from his army days. He pulled the knife, opened it, had the blade ready, but hidden by his side.

The sun blinded him, reflecting off the whitewashed bricks. The inside of the building gaped dark. He peered in through the broken window, keeping his body to the side, in cover. Looming shadows waited in there, a bunch of dusty shelving.

Whoever hid inside would be able to easily see Ian's head outlined against the light. Could shoot him if he wanted. He had to be standing ready, had to have heard Ian pull up in the front. No element of surprise.

So Ian called in, "Whatever you want from me, I'll give it to you. Just let her go right now."

And a heavily accented voice called out, "Come in."

The voice came maybe a few feet from the window, to Ian's left, from behind tall shelving draped with plastic.

Ian stepped in but didn't stop. He ducked and rolled in the opposite direction, and as he heard something crackle and buzz by him, he pushed to his feet the next second in a fight-ready stance.

He smelled mold and dust and rats.

He could see the guy now, around five-eight, thick waist. The Taser in his hand would take time to recharge.

Ian took the opportunity and lunged forward.

The little bastard was fast. He skittered back and knocked a shelf over, right on top of Ian. By the time Ian fought through that obstacle, the man had disappeared.

Too much tall shelving and other furniture cluttered the room, too dark to see.

"Daniela!" Ian shouted.

But instead of Daniela, the little bastard responded, "I have her gagged. But I'm going to take the gag out now, so when I cut her, you can hear her scream."

Ian eased toward the voice as quickly and quietly as he could. "Why?"

His eyes were adjusting to the lack of light at last, so he avoided tripping over a wooden crate.

"For Marcos Morais, my brother."

Somewhere ahead and to the right, Daniela gave a muffled, pained groan, as if she'd been hurt but was refusing to scream.

"If you hurt her," Ian called out, "so help me God, what I'll do to you will make your brother's death look like a picnic."

"Such love, and for a puta like her," the man mocked. "Love her enough to take her place?"

"Yes." Ian stepped out of the cover of the last shelf, and then he could see Daniela at last. He kept his breathing controlled. Kept his fury cold. *No mistakes.*

The man had her tied to an old furnace. He had a knife at her throat. A line of blood stretched from her ear to her collarbone, nearly black in the dark. A thin line. Not a deep cut. The Goat Man was playing. For now.

"Drop your knife," he said.

Ian did.

"Go over there." Morais nodded toward radiator pipes against the wall about twenty feet from him.

Ian followed his instruction.

A handful of plastic ties waited for him on the ground. Looked like the bastard had come prepared.

"Tie yourself to the pipes."

"You cut her loose, I tie myself up. That's the deal."

The man pressed his knife against Daniela's throat. "You tie yourself first."

She didn't whimper. Her eyes showed no fear, only resolution. She was ready. And Ian trusted her. So he tied one hand to the pipe.

"You let her go, I'll tie the other hand." Not that he could, one-handed.

But the guy didn't seem to be thinking that far ahead—maybe he'd always had others to do his dirty business for him before. He cut Daniela loose. Or almost loose. He grabbed her by the wrist, shooting a triumphant look at Ian.

Ian just shook his head.

Even as he did, Daniela lunged into action.

With a kick to the chest, she knocked Morais back. He tried to grab for her again. She twisted like an eel. He caught nothing but air.

Rage reddened his face as he wielded the sharp blade. "Puta!"

He'd vastly underestimated her. Ian almost felt sorry for the bastard.

Daniela kicked up toward the guy's neck, hooking her foot around his nape and yanking down, putting the man on his knees. She mixed the military techniques Ian had taught her with capoeira. She certainly was a pleasure to watch in action.

The guy struggled up, but only barely. Only because Daniela was playing with him.

Ian pulled the lighter from his pocket with his free hand and melted the plastic tie that still restrained the other one. Four seconds, and he was free. But he wasn't needed.

Daniela kicked the guy's ass with beautiful efficiency, her moves as choreographed as a dance. If this was an action movie, the shot would have been slowed down so the audience could fully enjoy it.

Goat Man moaned as his nose broke with a crunch. But he didn't give up fighting. He still had the knife. And Daniela faltered, as if her knee went out. Goat Man charged her.

Ian stepped between them. Four years ago, he would have let himself get nicked just to feel something. Now he shifted to the side and, elbow to the back of the guy's neck, sent Morais sprawling.

The man was on his stomach on the ground, his nose bleeding. Then he rolled and came up again, spitting blood as he did.

Ian had to give him credit, he did know how to fight. But Ian had no patience for this. He wanted to make sure Daniela was okay. He stepped in, deflected the knife, and his uppercut sent Goat Man flying across the room, sending up a cloud of dust when he landed.

Daniela headed over, flipped him on his stomach, twisted his right arm behind his back, and took control of the knife at last. "He only got me tied up," she told Ian with an apologetic look over her shoulder, "because I was out of it. He tasered me."

"I figured something like that." Probably her knee had buckled for the same reason. Muscles got twitchy after a shot of that kind of electricity. "I didn't step in because I thought you couldn't handle him. I just didn't want to waste any time here. We have better things to do."

He pulled his phone and called the police. The sooner they got here, the better. Before he gave in to the temptation to do something regrettable. Not that he'd regret stepping on the guy's neck, but he didn't want his time with Daniela to be restricted to prison visits.

Thank God she was safe.

He burned to get in a few more punches, but Daniela had already broken the guy's nose. Too much more damage, and they'd spend the rest of the day at the police precinct answering questions.

Ian tied the man's hands behind his back with a plastic tie while the guy swore steadily in Portuguese.

"Thank God we're not partners anymore at CPRU," Ian grumbled at Daniela. "I'd never see any action. When you kick ass like that, I feel superfluous."

"Next time I get kidnapped, when you arrive to rescue me, I'll fall into a dead faint."

"I'd appreciate it." Ian glanced at Morais, who was shooting them looks that burned with hate, breathing noisily through his mouth. Ian gave the man a speculative look. "He could escape his restraints, and then we'd have to catch him again."

Morais folded to the ground with a groan and stayed there. Police sirens wailed in the distance.

Ian grunted. "And there goes the universe, conspiring to suck every drop of fun out of my day."

* * *

Daniela

Daniela was looking at the cut on her neck in the bathroom mirror when Ian walked in.

"Naked. In the shower."

She cast him a quick glance over her shoulder but began stripping.

They were back in Ian's apartment after having spent the last two hours at the police station.

Eduardo had been so incensed by his capture, he was screaming threats, admitting to the kidnapping, even bragging about killing Finch. The police had it all on tape. Eduardo wasn't going to see the outside of a prison again.

Daniela shed the last piece of her clothing and stepped into the shower. Ian was right behind her. She barely had time to turn on the water before she was pushed against the wall, her back to the tile, and Ian was lifting her legs, wrapping them around his waist.

Her body immediately flooded with desire, her voice breathless as she said, "What happened to going slow and barely daring to touch me? What happened to me being a fragile flower?"

"You're not fragile."

"Thanks for noticing."

He covered himself with protection and pressed against her. His eyes filled with raw emotion. "I need you now."

"I need you too." She tilted her hips, and then he pushed inside. She was ready for him, wanting him so much, her eyes were rolling back in her head.

"Marry me."

Now he asked her? She couldn't speak. He awoke her body like no other man could. And he did it by touching her heart before he touched anything else.

Their bodies melded together, every move needed and perfect.

She hadn't known that making love would be like this, could be like this. The way he worshipped her body erased the dark memories of her past. And when she saw herself reflected in his loving eyes, she *could* see herself as some-one good, as good as everyone else.

He held her effortlessly. Took her higher and higher.

The deep, primal connection stole her breath. She kissed him with all her heart, all her soul, and wanted the moment to never end.

They marked each other, claimed each other. And her heart soared.

More. She wanted more. Closer.

She moved against him.

He groaned, the sound rumbling up from deep inside his chest. And he gave her everything she needed, drove into her until she couldn't breathe.

Then they were spiraling into bliss.

Much later, when they lay on the bed in each other's arms, the phone rang in the living room, the landline. No way could she walk. She was spent. And Ian didn't look like he was getting up either.

The answering machine picked up.

"Hi, Ian," a familiar voice said. "This is Carmen Heyerdahl. Phil and I wanted to invite you and Daniela to Lila's christening. It'll be at my parents' church in Philadelphia on Easter Sunday. I don't have your address, just your phone, so I couldn't send an invite. I'm calling because we're hoping you could save the date for us. We'd love for you to be here." She left a number for them to call back, then the message ended.

Ian grinned. "Let's go up to Philly and see Lila. I bet she's grown like you wouldn't believe."

Daniela grinned back. "I bet she's talking." She held Ian's gaze. "Let's go, and while we're up there, we can invite Carmen and Phil to the wedding."

He turned serious. "Are you saying yes?"

"I'm saying, let's be partners forever."

He made a contented jaguar sound—a deep rumbling purr—and was rolling her under him before she had a chance to tease him about it.

"Let's celebrate." Ian kissed her, the kiss deep and searching. Cherishing. Mind melting. Then he whispered against her lips, "We're going to be together forever, and there's not one thing wrong with that. Everything about this is right."

Oh, finally! Daniela kissed him back, floating on the great river of *happy*. Maybe there were rapids up ahead, maybe they'd get battered and bruised yet, but they were in the water together, and they were never going to let go of each other.

"Tell me how much you love me," she whispered against his lips.

He nibbled his way down to her collarbone. Then lower. "I love you more than piranhas love chicken wings."

A quick note from the author...

Thank you so much for going on this adventure with me into Daniela and Ian's world! I cannot tell you how much I love these characters. I hope you enjoyed getting to know them.

CUT SCENE: Originally, I had one more scene at the end of the book, but I cut it because after dealing with some difficult issues, I wanted to leave the story on a funny, light-hearted note and I loved Ian's piranha line. However, if you'd like to read the cut scene, I'd be happy to send it to you completely FREE. Just please let me know at www.danamarton.com/girl-in-the-water-cut

If you haven't read the other two books in the series, FORCED DISAP-PEARANCE and FLASH FIRE, please check them out. And if you're curious how the Civilian Personnel Recovery Unit (where Ian works) was formed, you can read about it in AGENTS UNDER FIRE.

Thank you so much for reading my stories!!! Thank you for being friends online and for all the wonderful emails you send. And thank you for the reviews! Online reviews make a HUGE difference for authors.

Some advertising venues won't accept a book now until it has a certain number of reviews. So if you have a moment, could I ask for a review on this book? Even if you have time only for a sentence or two, it'd make such a big difference to me. Pretty please? THANK YOU!!!

Wishing you all the best,
Dana

CPSIA information can be obtained
at www.ICGtesting.com
Printed in the USA
LVOW12s2311260317
528556LV00002B/129/P